Mandy Magro lives in Cairns, Far North Queensland, with her daughter, Chloe Rose. With pristine aqua-blue coastline in one direction and sweeping rural landscapes in the other, she describes her home as heaven on earth. A passionate woman and a romantic at heart, she loves writing about soul-deep love, the Australian rural way of life and all the wonderful characters who live there.

www.facebook.com/mandymagroauthor
www.mandymagro.com

MANDY MAGRO

Jacaranda

mira

This edition published by Mira 2019
First published by Penguin Group (Australia) 2012
ISBN 9781489263582

JACARANDA
© 2012 by Mandy Magro
Australian Copyright 2012
New Zealand Copyright 2012

This is a work of fiction. Names, characters, places, and incidents are either the product of the author's imagination or are used fictitiously, and any resemblance to actual persons, living or dead, business establishments, events, or locales is entirely coincidental.

Published by
Mira
An imprint of Harlequin Enterprises (Australia) Pty Limited (ABN 47 001 180 918), a subsidiary of HarperCollins Publishers Australia Pty Limited (ABN 36 009 913 517)
Level 13, 201 Elizabeth St
SYDNEY NSW 2000
AUSTRALIA

® and TM (apart from those relating to FSC®) are trademarks of Harlequin Enterprises Limited or its corporate affiliates. Trademarks indicated with ® are registered in Australia, New Zealand and in other countries.

A catalogue record for this book is available from the National Library of Australia
www.librariesaustralia.nla.gov.au

Printed and bound in Australia by McPherson's Printing Group

MIX
Paper from
responsible sources
FSC® C001695

For my stepdad, Trevor
My sisters, Karla, Talia, Mia and Rochelle
You all mean the world to me

And in memory of my
beloved dog, Mack

PROLOGUE

Six-year-old Molly Jones nervously gripped her grandfather's weathered hand as she looked into the skies above her. It looked so serene and peaceful up there, like it was part of a totally different world; a world in which she hoped heaven existed. White fluffy clouds drifted in an infinite sea of blue, and for a moment she felt like she was back in a magical place full of safety and happiness. Standing under her favourite jacaranda tree, she stared up at the canopy of beautiful purple flowers and remembered picnics with her mum and dad on the lush grass beneath the tree. They would eat the treats her grandma baked for them and then she would snuggle into her dad as her mum read out loud from her favourite books. But those days were gone forever now, all because the bad man had driven his car drunk.

When Molly climbed into her grandfather's lap she could feel his body shaking. She had never seen her granddad cry before. Tears poured down her own cheeks and dripped onto the pretty dress her mum had made her only a week ago for her birthday. She buried her face into his chest as he wrapped his arms around her and kissed her tenderly on the cheek, the faint scent of tobacco on his shirt a familiar comfort.

'We'll make it through this, little one,' he whispered in her ear.

Her grandma reached out and stroked her hair and Molly tried to imagine it was all going to be okay. She squeezed her eyes shut, hoping that when she opened them she'd find this was just a terrifying nightmare and her mum would be there to soothe her back to sleep as she always was. But her ears could not block out the priest's solemn voice as he read the words no six-year-old girl should hear.

'Why did you have to die?' Molly whispered as she began sobbing uncontrollably, the thought of never seeing her parents again making her tremble with fear. How would she ever live without them?

CHAPTER

1

The blistering sun shone unrelentingly on Molly Jones. The sheer heat of it felt like it had the power to burn right through her long-sleeved button-up shirt and sear her already olive skin to a crisp. She took a swig from her water bottle and tied her long, wavy, jet-black hair back into a ponytail, pulling the broad brim of her hat down to shade her petite features from the unforgiving rays. It was a typical summer's day in Dimbulah, Tropical North Queensland – hot enough to fry an egg on the bonnet of her Land Cruiser.

Molly stepped into the second round yard, the one that was home to her newest horsy recruit, and double-checked that the gate was securely shut behind her. She knew there was no hope of ever getting the wild horse back if he made a sudden break for it. Outside the confines of the round yard there was nothing but farmland for miles, Jacaranda Farm making up a thousand hectares of it. Beyond that was untamed countryside in which a wayward horse would easily be concealed if it wanted to be. And Buck most certainly would want to. He was the most challenging horse Molly had ever worked with but she wasn't going to give up on him. How could she? Her daughter had her heart set on the gelding being her very own one day.

It was only a few months ago that they'd had to put down Rose's beloved old bombproof horse, Jimmy, due to cancer. It had broken Rose's heart, and Molly's. That was why Buck was here, to be Rose's new horse, and Molly was going to make sure he was the best horse he could be before Rose sat in the saddle. Safety was her number-one priority, especially for her precious little girl.

Molly smiled as she remembered Rose, her six-year-old, begging her to bring Buck home with them from Silverspur Station. The station owner had been about to send the horse to the meatworks because it had kicked him viciously in the back, leaving a purple bruise the size of a football. Mind you, the station owner wasn't the nicest of blokes either – he'd probably done something to deserve it. Molly found herself unable to deny Rose her wish, admiring her little daughter's passion for horses – a passion that matched her own. And she felt there was something special about the horse too, underneath its rebellious bravado. Molly truly believed that the horse had just been mistreated, misunderstood, and harshly trained by the hard hand of the station owner's son. Rose had aptly named the horse Buck, as that was all he seemed to want to do. That is, when he wasn't trying to bite you.

Ignoring the beads of sweat rolling down her cheeks, Molly kept her gaze soft but steady, being careful not to look directly into Buck's big brown eyes as he stood warily in front of her. She knew direct eye contact was very unsettling to a nervous horse, arousing its powerful fight-or-flight instincts. Not the ideal way to make a horse feel at ease.

Molly kept her distance and squatted so Buck could see she was nothing to be afraid of, stealing a few moments to admire his striking features. Buck was a beautiful boy, his chestnut coat closer to red than brown, with four white socks and an adorable white star on his forehead that was slightly hidden by his unruly forelock. She was looking forward to being able to get close enough to groom him. His mane and tail were in need of a decent brush.

Continuing on with the training and keeping her voice soft and low, she talked to him soothingly. She could see the tension in his body gradually easing. He moved his mouth and his ears flickered more slowly.

Molly stood carefully and took a few steps towards Buck, a little off to one side, to make sure she didn't walk into the blind spot in his vision and startle him. Buck gently raised his muzzle twice. That, together with a light stamp of his front hoof, indicated his pleasure at Molly's kind approach to him.

Molly was overjoyed. In the two gruelling months she had been working with Buck, a few hours almost every day, this was the closest he had allowed her to get. She reminded herself to remain calm. Horses could feel your emotions, and she needed to stay relaxed. 'Baby steps, take it slow,' she whispered to herself, a mantra she repeated over and over in her mind as she weighed up what to do next.

She moved even closer to Buck, slowly easing her way into his space. She could now reach out and rub her hand over his neck. Should she? Or would that be pushing the boundaries too far, too soon? She hesitated, her hand raised softly at her side, seconds ticking by like minutes. Buck stepped back from her, uneasy again. She shook her head gently. Not today, but maybe next time. She might even be able to get a bridle on him by the end of the month. Or was that just wishful thinking? Only time and hard work would tell.

Like her father and her grandfather before her, Molly was known around the small Dimbulah community as a 'horse whisperer'.

She didn't like the name much. Her work wasn't some black magic she performed on the horses that came to her for their last chance before the meatworks. Molly just knew how to watch a horse and read its body language. She was patient when trying to gain a horse's trust, letting it approach her in its own time. Too many people went at it like a bull at a gate when they tried to befriend a horse, and that baffled Molly. How would they like it if some stranger came storming up to them, trying to wrap a rope around their throat, demanding they do what they were told for no good reason? Humans confused Molly at times, but horses were another matter entirely. Understanding horses was second nature to her, as natural as breathing.

Molly began to run out of daylight and decided to head back to the homestead. She was starving, and dying for a nice long shower. A quick glance around the shelter in the round yard confirmed Buck had sufficient food and water for the night. Tomorrow she would give him a treat of molasses, if he behaved. But only a small one – she didn't want him too full of beans. She whistled up her dog, Skip, and he raced to her side, his tail wagging madly as he barked his hello. She gave him a loving scratch on the chops, giggling as he licked her hand enthusiastically.

Skip had been resting in the shade of a massive wattle tree for most of the day, watching his mistress at work with her clientele of horses, in between doggy naps and chasing the chooks. Molly knew he'd never intentionally hurt the chooks, the chasing was just a bit of excitement for him, to release any pent-up energy. He had been born and bred to round up the cattle on Molly's property, and he saw the chickens as something that needed rounding up too. The poor buggers would run off in a flurry of feathers, clucking like mad, with Skip in tow. The dog was a purebred border collie and a purebred pain in the butt when he wanted to be, but Molly loved him to bits. He had been her companion for nine years, and she could not ask for a better mate.

On her way back to the homestead, a flock of red-tail black cockatoos soared noisily overhead. Molly turned to watch them, admiring their beauty as they flew towards the setting sun through a sky turning beautiful shades of orange and pink. The last of the sun's rays sent speckles of golden light skipping over the shimmering water of the dam. Molly had spent so many happy hours at the dam while she was growing up. It was a wonderful place to laze away a hot summer's day with a good group of mates.

Skip barked insistently as a rabbit bounded across the grass. Molly quickly grabbed him by the collar – it was too close to nightfall, when the dingoes made themselves known. Skip would never stand a chance against a pack of them.

Molly gazed out at the endless views of fruit trees that lay in front of her. She could just make out the boundaries of Jacaranda Farm and could hear her neighbour, Fred, out in his tractor, spraying his crops. Up here in the tropics it was a constant battle to keep the crop from being covered in scale, attacked by insects or stung by bugs.

As she passed the workers' cottage Molly waved cheerfully to three men who were sitting around the rickety old timber table on the front patio, playing a game of cards. The jackaroos were swigging on icy-cold beers and swatting at the constant stream of flies with their soiled hats.

'Hey, Molly, want to play a round?' Heath called, smiling in a way that momentarily stopped Molly in her tracks as she admired the intensity of his deep-blue eyes. She instantly reprimanded herself for doing so. How could she even look at him in that way? Jenny wouldn't be too impressed with her perving on her man *and* she wouldn't blame her, Molly thought kindly. Friends weren't meant to cross that boundary. It was an unspoken vow between women, and one Molly believed in very strongly. It had been just over a year now, but Molly's heart still ached each and every time she recalled the horrific day she lost Jenny – her workmate and dear friend – when one of the horses tragically kicked her in the head. Molly had seen the entire thing. Jenny had died in her arms, her unborn baby dying along with her. Telling Heath he had lost his childhood sweetheart, *and* his unborn child, was the second hardest thing Molly had ever had to do. Coping with the loss of her parents was the first.

'Yeah, come on, Molly!' Kenny added, his cheeky grin shining out from his dust-covered face.

'Nah, not tonight, guys. I'm buggered. But thanks anyway. I'll catch you all in the morning,' said Molly. 'You even get to sleep in, seeing it's Christmas Day! Oh, and don't forget to leave some milk and biscuits out for Santa!'

'Bugger! I don't have any milk *or* biscuits so he'll have to be happy with a glass of beer and a vegemite sanga!' Trev replied.

Molly chuckled. 'I'm sure Santa will love your Aussie hospitality, Trev. After all, we know he wears stubbies and a pair of pluggers, and delivers the presents out the back of his dusty old ute.'

Trev grinned. 'Sounds like my kind of Santa!'

Molly shook her head, smiling. The three jackaroos were a permanent fixture of Jacaranda Farm, assisting with the mustering and animal husbandry and also tending to the maintenance and picking of the fruit. There was always plenty to do and the three prided themselves on working hard. As well as breeding top-quality Santa Gertrudis cattle and Australian stock horses, Molly's family grew two different varieties of mangoes on the farm, mainly for the markets down in Brisbane, Sydney and Melbourne. Even though the men's specialty was stock work, Heath, Kenny and Trev were more than happy to pick the mangoes when needed. This meant Molly didn't have to get in many casual workers for the mango harvest and the men had work all year round on the property rather than just in the mustering season.

The blokes always gave her a laugh and she had become good mates with them over the years they had worked together. Heath, Kenny and Trev were totally different characters, but they all shared the qualities she loved: honesty, loyalty and a down-to-earth way of looking at life. She knew they would all support her in a flash if she ever needed it. Especially Heath, who had been working on Jacaranda Farm since Rose was only a couple of months old. He had arrived along with his long-time girlfriend, Jenny, and Molly had become very good friends with both of them almost instantly, feeling like she had known them forever. Jenny quickly became the sister she'd never had.

Molly was so grateful to have Heath around; he had seen her through her worst, as she had with him, and he'd always been there for her and Rose. He was the perfect example of what a real mate was.

Molly kicked her boots free at the bottom of the steps to the homestead, grimacing as she peeled off her sweaty socks. Delicious cooking smells wafted out to the verandah and Molly hoped dessert would be her grandma's famous apple pie. She could hear Rose laughing inside the house and felt a sudden urge to pick her little girl up and kiss her a hundred times over.

She knelt down and gave Skip a friendly scratch behind the ears. 'I'll bring the leftovers out for you, buddy.'

Skip let out a quick, short bark and wagged his tail in anticipation. Molly loved the fact he always answered her.

'Now go and lay down on your bed and I'll catch you after dinner.'

Skip promptly followed her orders, walking around in circles on his rug before lying down and resting his head on his paws, his big, brown eyes watching Molly as she disappeared into the house in search of her precious daughter.

*

As Molly sat down at the kitchen table Rose jumped into her lap to give her a cuddle. Rose had been out feeding the cattle with her GG, Great Granddad David. Molly smiled as her daughter explained how she had seen a bull climbing over the back of a cow and that GG had said it was trying to play leapfrog. It was so cool that the cows played games like she did at school.

Molly laughed. For all the challenges of being a single mother, she could not begin to imagine her life without Rose.

At nineteen Molly had thought she knew everything, but boy, had she been wrong. She had fallen for a cowboy one drunken night at the Mount Garnett rodeo, and nine months later Rose had entered her world. Molly's life had changed forever, but she had never laid eyes on the cowboy again. The morning after their night together she had woken alone in her swag. She never even knew the cowboy's name. It was almost like he'd been a figment of her imagination and Rose an immaculate conception. If only it had been that simple.

'Dinner's ready!' called Elizabeth, Molly's grandmother. 'It's time to go and wash your hands, Rose.'

Rose screwed up her face but obeyed all the same.

'Wow, Granddad, that was a ripper of a story to tell Rose. I'd never have come up with that one myself,' Molly said admiringly.

'Well, I had to think of something quick smart when she asked me what the bull was doing. I don't think she's old enough for the birds and bees chat just yet!' David scratched his bald head with stubby fingers and grinned. 'How'd you go with Buck today, sweetheart? Rose keeps going on about riding him one day. It's hard to see that happening for a long time yet though.'

'He finally let me get closer to him today. And he didn't even try to bite me, which is a change from last week!' Molly rubbed her sore thigh muscles, wincing. 'I reckon with enough time and patience he'll turn into a fine horse for Rose, as far away as that seems at the moment.'

'That's great to hear you're making progress, love. It takes a certain kind of person to understand horses and you really do have the gift. I'll die a happy man knowing you'll be taking over from where I've left off. And if your dad could see you now, well, I know he'd be so very proud of you.'

Molly watched the familiar twitch beneath David's eye at the mention of her father. That twitch was testament to the pain of his son's loss, a pain he and Elizabeth had always done their best to hide for Molly's sake. 'I'd hope he would be, Granddad, *and* I don't want to hear any talk of you kicking the bucket! You've got a lot of life left in you. Anyways, you and Grandma have to be here the day I tie the knot with my knight in shining armour – that's if he ever rides in on his white horse.'

'Well, love, you aren't getting any younger. At the rate you're going, you'll end up with some clown riding in on a donkey.'

Molly laughed. At twenty-six she was still young – she knew David was only teasing. But she also knew he yearned for her to meet a guy who would love her and Rose as he felt they deserved to be loved. She could understand his concerns; she felt the same. She just hadn't been lucky enough to meet the right bloke yet, the one she would marry and live happily ever after with. The only place he seemed to exist was in her dreams.

Molly had grown up in this old timber Queenslander, warmed by the love of her grandparents. The house had been built on the highest point of the property, with verandahs on all sides and huge casement windows, so the views over the paddocks were incredible. Molly often stood and gazed out the windows, captivated by the beauty she was surrounded by. Watching the horses and cattle grounded her and made her feel as though she was in touch with the earth she farmed on.

Everywhere you looked there were horses – in photos and paintings and sculptures that capture the essence and beauty of the magnificent creatures – and you'd find akubras, whips, spurs and saddles throughout the homestead. Cowhide rugs dressed the worn timber floors. To Molly, the whole house felt alive with stories of the past and hopes for the future.

The family had lived for four generations on Jacaranda Farm and Molly was very proud of the fact. There had been tough years with not much money coming in, but the family had stuck it out. Now they were one of the wealthiest families in Dimbulah. It was thanks to her granddad, who had figured out a way to make the fruit flower out of season, making Jacaranda the only farm in Australia with mangoes twice a year. Many other farmers around the area had tried to discover their secret – everything from buying Molly's granddad too many beers down the pub to offering him large amounts of money – but David kept the information close to his heart. Only Molly knew what the secret was, and she was not about to tell another living soul. It was their key to success, and helped them through the bad times with the livestock market – which was a lot of the time these days.

Molly knew some men would love to get their hands on such a profitable farm, so she was wary of potential suitors. She was determined not to fall for someone who only saw Jacaranda in terms of financial gain, or even worse, could not understand her connection to the place. Her mother and father were buried here, under the beautiful jacaranda tree outside. Living here made her feel close to them in a way that perhaps only her grandparents could truly understand.

'Do you need a hand with anything else for tomorrow?' Molly asked Elizabeth.

'Should be right, thanks, love. I've just got to finish the mango chutney and we're all set.'

It was the Joneses' turn to hold the community's Christmas bash this year, and Elizabeth and Molly had been preparing for weeks, making everything from rum balls to Christmas pudding and their famous mango chutney for the baked ham. They had enough food to feed an army, so no one would go home hungry. Rose was beside herself with excitement. Tonight Molly would help her leave the traditional biscuits and milk on the dining table for Santa. She smiled as she recalled Rose saying with concern that Santa would be so busy tomorrow, he probably wouldn't have time to eat, so it was very important to remember to leave out his treats. Rose was always so very thoughtful. Molly sighed contentedly. Tomorrow was going to be a wonderful day.

CHAPTER

2

The overhead fluorescent light flickered to life as Heath dropped his towel to the floor and began rummaging through his drawers in search of jocks, jeans and a T-shirt. Droplets of water ran down his broad, hairless chest, meeting with the carved muscles of his abs as they continued on a downward path. He hadn't bothered to dry off completely after his shower, the rivulets of water on his body keeping him cool in the stifling tropical heat. Garp, Jenny's pet cat, meowed his hello from the comfort of Heath's bed as he gracefully stretched his rested limbs. Heath glanced over at him as he pulled on his jeans, smiling at the way Garp was lying on his back with all four legs casually splayed out around him – a very compromising position but a favourite of Garp's. Modesty was not one of the cat's virtues.

'Ah, mate, you have the life. Lazing about all day, no need to worry about much other than when you're going to eat next. And even then I prepare it for you. I think I'll come back as a cat in my next life. I like the sound of having nine lives.' Heath gave him a scratch and Garp's purring became louder. 'Jenny picked a

winner when she spotted you at the RSPCA. You're a wonderful
daily reminder of her, buddy.'

Heath made his way out to the lounge room, chuckling to himself
as he passed Kenny and Trev on the couch, their attention glued
to *Who Wants to be a Millionaire*, both blokes shouting out the
answers as if the competitor could hear them through the television.
Heath pulled his leather jacket from the back of the dining chair
and shrugged it on, keen to get on his Harley and feel the breeze
whipping around him; it was stifling in a jacket in this bloody heat.

'Righto, you two party animals. I'm off to finish my Christmas
shopping. There are two hours of late-night shopping left and in
typical blokey fashion I've left the most important present until the
very last minute. Catch you both later on.'

Heath vanished out the front door to half-hearted goodbyes.
Not that it bothered him. Trev and Kenny were impossible to talk
to when they were watching the telly, especially when it involved
some kind of game show. The pair were constantly trying to outdo
each other in a healthy banter type of way. Heath found it hilarious
to watch.

The shovel-head Harley Davidson rumbled to life, its deep grunt
echoing around the massive shed to make it sound more like five
bikes instead of one. Heath loved the powerful roar of the engine;
it always pumped him up, making him feel close to invincible.
It was similar to riding a horse for him, but brought him closer
to euphoria. The only other sensation that could top riding his
Harley was making love to a beautiful woman. Not that he had
experienced that for a very long time. He had to be madly in love
before he could do that. One-night stands were not on his agenda.
Why bother? It was meaningless. Life was full of meaningless shit,
so why should making love just be another meaningless act? No,
love was everything to him, and more. And making love was an

extension of this, nothing less. Jenny was the first woman he had ever loved in this way but life had dealt him a low blow and taken her from him in the most painful of ways. He just needed to let her go, to get on with his life, and for the first time in the past year he really felt like he could. He finally believed he could breathe again, that he could love again. And it felt wonderful. Like he'd been given a second chance.

*

Heath held the bracelet in his hand, turning it over in the light to examine the finer details of it. It was beautiful, just like her. God, he hoped she liked it. Would she? Was he doing the right thing buying it? Or should he just stick to what he normally bought her? Like an RM Williams shirt or a pair of Wrangler jeans? That would be the safest bet, he thought. But why play safe in the game of love? What was wrong with throwing all your cards on the table? The fact he was delusional for even thinking he had a chance with her, that's what was wrong with it. Oh, bugger it, he thought. Take the plunge, regret it later.

'I'll take it,' he pronounced excitedly.

The Mareeba cemetery sat cloaked in darkness, the eeriness of the place not worrying Heath one bit as he pulled in on his Harley. He had been here a hundred times over, especially on nights when he found himself incapable of sleeping. He turned the motor off, the instant silence creating a slight ringing in his ears as he adjusted to the stillness. Pulling his torch and a bunch of brightly coloured flowers from the leather saddle bags on his Harley, he turned in the direction of the grave he had come to visit. A familiar heaviness sat on his heart as he began the short walk down the perfectly manicured lawn.

It didn't take him long to find the place Jenny had been laid to rest. Even without a torch he would have known how to find it. He knelt down in front of the enormous headstone, the enchanting photo of Jenny bringing a faint smile to his lips. She had the most addictive of smiles, with a knack for cheering up even the saddest of souls. Placing the flowers in the permanent vase, Heath began rubbing the dust from the headstone with his hand while reading the inscription out softly to himself, as he had done many times before.

In loving memory of Jenny Marie Coleman.
5 December 1986 – 12 November 2010
If tears could build a stairway and memories a lane, we'd
walk right up to heaven and bring you home again.
You will be in our hearts forever.

'Merry Christmas, Jenny,' Heath whispered as he got comfortable on the grass, letting the peacefulness wash over him for a few minutes as he gathered his thoughts. He had come to talk with Jenny, tell her what was on his mind and in his heart. He thought it was time he acknowledged how he felt, and stopped trying to ignore the deep feelings he had.

Heath picked at the grass, twirling it between his fingers as he began to speak. 'Well, Jenny, it's been over a year now and I still miss you every day, but I've come to accept that you are gone and never coming back. I feel bad saying this, but I have to move on with my life. I really want a family of my own. And knowing you as I do, I reckon you would encourage that.'

Heath exhaled slowly, his emotions fighting to get the better of him. But he wouldn't let them. He had cried for long enough now. He wanted to find happiness in his life again. 'I'm falling in love,

Jenny, with a woman you know very well. I'm not too sure if it's the right thing to be doing, seeing she was like a sister to you, but as they say, you can't control love. It just happens. I don't know if anything's going to come out of it. I mean, I don't even know if she feels the same way. But I have to find out; I have to explore the possibility. I'll regret it forever if I don't. I can't risk her falling for another man just because I was too afraid to tell her how I feel. I hope you can understand all this, Jenny, and that you give me your blessing.' Heath stopped, chuckling as he added, 'And I wish you could give me some advice. You know how clueless I can be sometimes when it comes to women.'

*

Heath dropped back on the throttle, reducing the loud growl of the Harley to a gentle purr as he idled past the Jacaranda homestead, his eyes drawn to Molly's bedroom window. Soft light filtered through the parted curtains as they ruffled in the tropical evening breeze, Molly's silhouette moving beyond them. He looked away, not wanting her to catch him staring; the last thing he needed right now was for her to think he was invading her privacy. His intuition told him to take things very slowly, otherwise he chanced scaring her away. He knew she was going to be hesitant – shocked, even – when he eventually admitted how he felt.

Parking the Harley back in the shed, Heath sighed and pulled his helmet free. He could feel the destiny of love dragging him down a road he was wary of, but a road that also led to so many wonderful possibilities. He wasn't sure what his future held, but he was going to give this all that he had. Molly Jones was worth it, and so was her darling little Rose.

CHAPTER
3

The birds chorused loudly outside Molly's bedroom window, forcing her to pull the thin cotton sheet over her head to try to drown out their celebrations. It was her first morning off for months, but sleeping in was proving impossible, thanks to her body clock. After tossing and turning like a category-four cyclone under her sheet until she resembled a cocooned moth, she finally conceded she might as well get up.

The house was silent as she tiptoed down the long hallway, pausing for a moment to run her fingertip over a fading black-and-white photo of her dad riding saddle bronc – a trained bucking horse – in the seventies. She whispered, 'Merry Christmas, Dad,' before sneaking past Rose's bedroom, avoiding those boards in the old timber floor that she knew creaked.

Molly knew her grandparents would already be out on the verandah, sitting in their favourite cane chairs with steaming cups of tea. Molly loved this time of the day, too. As her best mate, Jade, always said, with the rising of the sun came a brand new day to forget the trials of yesterday, and the chance to create experiences you could reminisce about tomorrow. It was a nice way to view the world, Molly thought.

'Merry Christmas, guys!' Molly said as she joined her grandparents, kissing them both on the cheek. 'What a brilliant day for it.'

'Merry Christmas, darling,' Elizabeth replied warmly.

'Merry Christmas, love. Where's the little princess then? I thought she'd be up by now with ants in her pants.' David drained the last of his tea then inspected the cup as though it had a hole in it.

'Still sleeping, but not for much longer, I bet. I can't wait until she sees what we've got her. What time's Uncle Rob arriving?'

'He said he'll be here at eight so I better get in and start breakfast.' Elizabeth slowly pushed herself out of the chair, trying to stretch her arthritic legs back to life. 'I think I just heard Rose's door open – watch out, you two, she's going to be a livewire this morning.' Elizabeth chuckled as she stepped into the house, the flyscreen door shutting softly behind her.

Molly and David listened to Rose's footsteps gathering momentum on the hard wooden floors until she finally erupted through the screen door, beaming from ear to ear and clapping her hands with joy. 'Merry Christmas, Mum and GG!'

Molly scooped Rose up as her daughter wrapped her small arms and legs around her, squeezing so tightly that Molly felt as though she had a boa constrictor attached to her. They shared an Eskimo kiss, a morning ritual between them.

'Merry Christmas, sweetheart. I wonder what Santa's brought you, seeing you've been such a good girl this year! And I know he's been because the bickies and milk are all gone and the bugger left crumbs all over the table.' Molly chuckled, winking at David. 'Now, you better jump down and give GG a kiss and cuddle, too, before we have breakfast and open presents.'

Molly watched as Rose cuddled her granddad, a part of her feeling guilty that Rose had never had a father to share Christmas with. She wondered if she was ever going to meet the man who would sweep her off her feet and fulfill her dream of creating a new family for Rose.

*

Smack on eight o'clock Uncle Rob came tearing along the dirt drive, a thick cloud of red dust rolling out behind him as far as the eye could see. Molly jumped with fright when he pulled in and his rusty old Toyota backfired loudly.

'When are you going to bury the old beast, Uncle Rob? I think she's truly fulfilled her duties for you for this lifetime,' Molly called out from where she was perched on the front steps with a cuppa.

Rob grinned as he and the two spare tyres around his waist rolled out of the driver's side door. Molly giggled, watching him try to pull his faded blue stubbies up under his belly. They kept sliding down again far enough for everyone to see his bum poking out of the top. It wasn't a pretty sight. Still, she loved her uncle with all her heart. He was a typical Aussie larrikin – always willing to lend a helping hand to anyone – and made you smile whenever he was around. He always wore the same thing: a Bonds singlet, stubbies, a pair of thongs that he updated from Kmart twice a year, and his beloved akubra, which had seen better days. The only time he changed was when he was driving his cattle truck, and then he wore his RM Williams boots instead of his pluggers.

Molly's aunt, Cheryl, enthusiastically motioned for Molly to come over to the Toyota, pointing at the two beautiful border collie puppies in the back with a huge grin on her round, freckled face. Cheryl was a top cook who loved her food, and it showed in her size-eighteen figure. She was well known for the cake stand she held at the various local markets, and her orange and almond cake was to die for. She and Rob had never had any children. After years of trying, Cheryl had resigned herself to the fact she and Rob just couldn't, instead doting on the many children in the extended family, especially Rose.

Molly, Rob and Cheryl crept into the house, trying to hide the puppies in their arms, a giant task in itself. Rose spotted the wriggling bundles as soon as Molly walked into the kitchen. 'Oh wow! Puppies! Oh, Mum, they're beautiful! Where did you find them? Did Santa bring them? Can I keep them?'

Rose's smile melted Molly's heart. 'Of course you can keep them, honey. They're your Christmas presents. I couldn't pick just one so I got you both of them. A boy and a girl. It'll be nice for the puppies to have each other to grow up with, even though they're going to drive Skip mad.'

'I'm going to call the boy Mack after Uncle Rob's truck, and I'll call the girl Sasha just because I really like the name Sasha,' Rose announced proudly as she sat on the floor to play with her new friends, giggling as they licked her toes.

'Aw, kids, hey. You gotta love their innocent little hearts. Bless them,' Cheryl chortled while popping a whole rum ball in her mouth, leaving traces of coconut stuck to her bright-pink lipstick.

'They're border collies, Rose, like Skip, so they'll need training. Otherwise, they'll get bored and get up to all sorts of trouble,' Rob said as he knelt to give Rose a quick kiss on the cheek.

Rose looked up at Rob very seriously. 'I'll make them the best cattle-mustering dogs in town. You just wait and see. GG will help me, won't you, GG?'

David stroked her hair. 'Of course I will, sweetheart. It'll be my pleasure.'

Rob's belly growled loudly. 'Right, you mob. I think that's our cue to start the day's festivities. Breakfast looks and smells great, Mum, as always. I'd better eat or I'll fade away to a shadow.'

*

After breakfast they went into the lounge room where gifts were heaped under the Christmas tree. The puppies tumbled around in the growing mounds of paper as Rose unwrapped present after present.

'Knock, knock! Merry Christmas!' Heath called from the front door, his hands trembling slightly as he envisioned giving Molly her gift.

'Come in, Heath!' Molly called back.

'I would, but I kinda need a hand to get in.'

Molly jumped up and went to meet him at the door. She could barely see Heath's face over the enormous gift he was holding. He peeked around the present, smiling charmingly, his eyes bluer then she'd ever seen them before. He looked so happy.

'Santa forgot to drop this one off last night for Rose so I thought I'd deliver it myself. Apparently it's a castle.'

Molly pulled open the screen door. 'Oh, Heath, you spoil her.' She reached up on her tiptoes and kissed him on the cheek, his six-foot well-built frame towering over her five foot, three inches. 'Merry Christmas, buddy.'

Heath put Rose's present on the side table and pulled the small gift from his jeans pocket, at the same time praying he was doing the right thing. There was no turning back now, he thought. 'And this is for you.' He gently took Molly's hand and placed the present in her palm, closing her fingers around it, enjoying the feeling of her hand resting in his.

Molly felt a rush of warmth. Heath always gave her and Rose something for Christmas and birthdays. He never forgot. He really was the most thoughtful man she had ever met. She stared at the gift, not wanting to ruin the beautiful wrapping paper.

'Go on then. Open it!' he said, his cheeky smile lighting up his sun-kissed, handsome face, his blue eyes holding Molly's gaze just long enough for her to feel like she could fall into them. A zap of something unfamiliar coursed through her, a sensation that made her toes curl. What was going on? Just recently she had found herself wondering what was going through his mind when he looked at her that way – a way he had never looked at her before. But these moments were so fleeting that she found herself second-guessing whether she'd really seen it, *or* felt it. Was she just overreacting? Was she reading something into it that wasn't even there? She knew she had a tendency to do so. She shrugged it off, choosing instead to focus on the kindness of Heath's gift-giving.

Molly felt her breath catch in her throat as she pulled the Montana Silversmiths bracelet from the box. The centre of it sparkled with a stunning horseshoe design encrusted with Swarovski crystals.

'Oh, Heath. This is just gorgeous. I love it!' She reached out and threw her arms around his broad shoulders. He hugged Molly's back, the strength in his muscular body making her feel safe and secure. He gave her a quick peck on the cheek, relieved that she had responded in the way he had hoped.

'I'm so stoked that you like it. I was worried that you wouldn't.'

Molly beamed at him as she slid the bracelet onto her slender wrist. 'Oh, Heath! Why wouldn't I? It's beautiful. I've never been bought jewellery before.'

'Great. Brilliant. I'm glad it's made you happy. Well, must run, the lads are waiting for me to make Christmas brekky. Eggs, ham and beans on toast.'

'Not so fast. I have gifts for you and the guys too.' Molly grabbed him by the arm. 'Come into the lounge.' Molly had bought Heath a new pair of spurs for his bull riding and she couldn't wait to see his face when he opened them. For Kenny she had ordered a year's subscription to a pig-hunting magazine, and for Trev she had decided on a bottle of Johnny Walker Black, his favourite.

'As long as I'm not intruding, I don't want to interrupt your family get-together.'

'Of course not! You *are* family to us, you know that. Why don't you give Rose her present now?'

Heath's face lit up. 'I'd love to!'

Molly motioned for him to walk in front of her down the hall. 'Age before beauty!'

'Oh geez, thanks, mate. Rub it in that I'm three years older than you,' Heath replied, chuckling, flattered that Molly had invited him to stay.

Molly glanced at his butt – she couldn't help it. It looked perfect in his Wrangler jeans. With his sandy-brown hair, cropped close to his head, golden-tanned skin, and tattoos adorning all the right places, Molly had to admit that Heath Miller oozed sex appeal from every single powerful inch of him. Especially when he was riding his pride and joy, his Harley Davidson motorbike; it made his bad-boy image even badder. Her thoughts began to wander in a direction she wasn't at all comfortable with. 'Stop it,' she mumbled to herself, 'he's like a brother to you, and Jenny was like your sister.'

'Pardon?' Heath said over his shoulder.

Molly felt her face flush red, like she had just been caught snogging someone behind the tuckshop. 'Oh, nothing.'

Goodness, girl, get a grip on yourself, she thought.

*

By eleven o'clock the sun was glowing brilliantly in the azure skies and the temperature had soared above forty degrees. Christmas Day in north Queensland was always a scorcher.

Dusty old utes, family four-wheel drives, restored classic Holdens and shiny new Land Cruisers with all the country bells and whistles were parked around the front of the homestead, under the big shady gum trees. Men were beginning to huddle in large groups, beer in hand, firmly shaking hands and wishing their fellow farmers a Merry Christmas whilst the women gave loving hugs and kisses in between ordering their children to behave themselves. There was close to one hundred people with still a few more to come, and it was organised chaos, but it was fantastic. Molly loved it. Big Christmas gatherings were part and parcel of a small country community.

An hour later, the kids had resorted to playing under the sprinklers. Some of the adults who'd already enjoyed a few beers had let their guard down, deciding to join in the fun. The Sunny Cowgirls' song, 'Aussie Jingle Bells', was blaring from the stereo Rob had set up on the back verandah and Molly bopped away happily to the music as she helped prepare the food in the massive kitchen. Molly had inherited Elizabeth's love of cooking and had spent so much time in the kitchen with her grandma when she was growing up. Molly was so proud of her. Elizabeth was the strongest woman she had ever known. Born and bred on a remote cattle station, it was in her grandma's blood to have guts of steel and yet she was so compassionate and loving, with magic hugs that mended everything from grazed knees to broken hearts.

Molly could see Kenny, Trev and Heath out of the big bay window, setting up the makeshift cricket pitch for the traditional afternoon game. Glancing at the bracelet on her arm she smiled reflectively, feeling blessed to have Heath in her life. He was the perfect example of what she wanted from a man: kind, thoughtful, loyal and loving *and* so wonderful with Rose. Under different circumstances, in another lifetime, she would have gone for him in a flash, but the past had made it impossible. She *had* to be happy with the close mateship they shared. Didn't she?

The older men were crowded around the smoking barbecue, good-naturedly slapping each other on the back, no doubt talking about fruit prices, cattle, horses, and the impact of climate change on their farms and what the government should be doing about it. It was a conversation Molly heard regularly at the local pub when she joined her grandfather there for a beer with his mates, a weekly occurence seeing as the pub was only half an hour down the road from Jacaranda Farm. David was in charge of the barbecue, as he had been for as long as Molly could remember. He proudly wore a bright red Santa hat on his bald head and an apron that read 'Laughing stock ... Cattle with a sense of humour'. Molly had given it to him that morning and he had loved it so much he had been wearing it ever since, pointing it out to all his mates when they had arrived. He looked so happy and *that* made Molly happy too. She watched as he worked the barbecue like a pro, expertly flipping sausages, hamburger patties, steak, prawns and Moreton Bay bugs. Molly's mouth watered at the thought of tucking into a few bugs. They were glorious, her favourite seafood in the world.

The women bustled around the large kitchen preparing trays of delicious food whilst brutally swatting at the blowflies with their tea towels. Molly was impressed with their strike rate. She wouldn't like to be a blowfly in the kitchen today; there was no chance of survival.

Her next-door neighbour, Kathy, was stirring a pot of potent brandy custard that would lavishly garnish her scrumptious Christmas pudding. Molly always made sure she left enough room for Kathy's decadent pudding. Although you had to watch out for the sixpence that Kathy put into it every year. If you chomped down too hard on it, you'd probably break a tooth. It was traditional to make a wish if you were lucky enough to get the sixpence and then hand it back to Kathy for her to use again next year – after thoroughly washing it.

Cheryl was adding sprigs of parsley from Elizabeth's herb garden to the salads as she danced and wiggled to the country music floating in from the verandah. Molly shimmied beside her and the two grabbed hands, spinning each other around the kitchen.

The ladies talked nonstop, filling each other in on the happenings of the week, month or year, depending on when they had last seen each other. Molly revelled in being one of the group. These women all carried an aura of strength after the years of trials and tribulations they had experienced. Living on the land was a beautiful way of life, but also one of hardship because you were so reliant on Mother Nature. Be it drought, or maybe a cyclone, you could never tell what she was going to throw at you next.

'Hi, ladies! It smells fantastic in here!' came a voice from the doorway. Molly squealed as she turned around to see her best mate, Jade. The two girls hugged for a moment then pulled back, grinning.

'Jade! It feels like forever since I've seen you! I didn't know you were coming home. Merry Christmas, matey!'

'Merry Christmas, Molly! I didn't think I was going to make it back from Byron Bay in time for Christmas, but looking at the smile on your face I'm so glad I did. God, I've missed you, buddy!'

'I've missed you too, Jade! How was the massage course?'

'Brilliant! I have loads to tell you,' Jade said with a wink.

The two girls grabbed a couple of beers and headed outside to the shade of the jacaranda tree. Molly straightened up the sunflowers she and Rose had put there earlier that morning for her parents before sitting down on the ground beside Jade. For a moment they sipped their beers in comfortable silence, watching the children and a few of the adults playing under the sprinklers, laughing at Kenny as he chased Heath with a bucket filled with ice. Heath made a mad dash for safety but within seconds he slipped and hit the ground with a thump, giving Kenny the perfect opportunity to empty the bucket's icy contents all over him. The look on Heath's face was priceless and Kenny buckled over in laughter. The kids saw that it was on for young and old and joined in the fun by tackling both Heath and Kenny on the ground. Molly smiled. The guys were so great with all the kids, but especially Rose. They protected her fiercely, and Molly thought it was touching the way the men took it on themselves to 'father' Rose.

'So, what have I missed in the few months I've been away? Anyone, say, fall in love?' Jade asked, raising her eyebrows.

Molly laughed. 'You mean have *I* met anyone?'

Jade took a swig of beer. 'Well, have you?'

Molly looked down and picked at the grass, wishing she could say yes. 'Nope. Zip. Nada. I just don't seem to have much luck in that department.'

Jade sighed. 'The right one will come along. You just wait. Everyone has a soul mate out there.'

'Forever the optimist, you are! Yeah, maybe one day. We'll see. But enough about me,' Molly answered, wanting to change the subject. 'Tell me all about your trip away, mate. I'm sure you got up to loads of exciting stuff, knowing you. Did you meet any sexy lovers while you were doing your massage course? I want all the juicy details!'

Jade grinned cheekily. 'You know me too well, Molly Jones! There *was* one girl ... We hit it off big time, but it was just good fun. We both knew after the course was over she'd be heading back to Tassie and I was coming back here. We promised to keep in touch, but I doubt I'll hear from her again. That's fine, though. There are plenty of fish in the lesbian sea these days!'

Molly laughed and shook her head. 'You always amaze me, Jade. I can't even find myself one man and you find women everywhere! You have to tell me your secret.'

'Well, my dear friend, I reckon you've got to open up that heart of yours – then the men will flood to you like a river after a torrential downpour. I know first-hand that you have a big heart, Molly Jones. You just have to learn to trust it *and* listen to it, stop being so afraid to fall in love,' Jade said, tapping Molly gently on the heart.

Molly rolled her eyes. Jade was always one for a spiritual speech. 'Yeah, well, most of the men I meet expect more than just your heart to be open, mate, and as they say, good cowgirls keep their calves together.'

'Hey, what are you saying?' Jade squealed, pushing Molly's arm playfully.

Molly knew Jade couldn't help herself when it came to love. She wasn't one for monogamy – at least not yet. And it had been quite a while. She had told Molly while they were still at high school that she wasn't attracted to guys and that she'd rather the luscious curves of a woman's body any day. Jade had copped a lot of bullying at school for it, but Molly had stuck by her mate, proud of Jade for being true to herself and sticking to her guns. When Jade had first come out of the closet the town of Dimbulah – population 1400, according to the welcome sign – had been gossip central, but eventually the whispers subsided and people had gotten on with their lives, accepting Jade for who she was. It was only the occasional newcomer who had something nasty to say about her and the locals had no time for anyone so narrow-minded. The proof of the pudding was Jade's successful beauty salon and massage business.

Jade was a free-spirited soul, and brought a different way of looking at the world to Molly's attention. She had even taught Molly how to meditate a few years back, with a heck of a lot of patience, and now Molly didn't let a day go by without at least five minutes of meditating, even if it was while she was sat in one of the paddocks with the horses.

'Hey, there's a new barmaid in town, and guess what? She's gay,' Molly said in mock horror, covering her mouth with her hand.

'How the hell do you know that?' Jade said with a snort of a giggle.

'Apparently Kenny tried hitting on her last weekend and she kindly told him that if she liked blokes she'd have gone for him in a flash, but she was more interested in women. She even asked him if he knew of any likely single ladies in town!' Molly said with a grin. '*And* he told her about you!'

'Oh, poor Kenny, he never has any luck on the love front. But, it sounds like good news for me,' Jade said, smirking.

'Well, next time you're at the pub you should introduce yourself.'

'I sure will! Speaking of the pub, are you going there for New Year's Eve? There's a new band coming to town and apparently they're brilliant.'

'Wouldn't be anywhere else,' said Molly.

Jade grinned. 'Woohoo! Make sure you wear comfy shoes. We're going to dance the night away. We haven't had a chance to go out in ages. The whole town will be at the Bull Bar. It'll be a hoot!'

'I know. Granddad and Grandma are going to look after Rose for me so I can go out and party. You know I don't do that so much any more! It takes too long for me to get over it the next day and I'd prefer to be spending time with Rose or out working with the horses than dealing with a bloody hangover. The days of being young, wild and reckless are long gone, thankfully. I wouldn't change my life now for anything, or anyone.'

Jade gave Molly a sly nudge in the ribs. 'Who knows, my friend? You just might meet your knight in shining armour ... You'd better dress to impress.'

'Yeah, well, Granddad reckons if I don't hurry up and meet him soon I'll be marrying some clown on a donkey!'

Jade cracked up and Molly laughed along with her.

*

Once Elizabeth rang the old cow bell to announce that lunch was ready, everybody lined up to fill their plates to the brim and sat down at the tables Rose had decorated with tinsel and glitter. Afterwards, some chose to stay sitting at the tables under the golden wattle trees, talking idly, while others lay in the shade on the grass, covering their faces with their hats for a cat nap before the celebrations began again. That was the way at Jacaranda Farm. Here, you got to be yourself and completely relax.

At about four o'clock, when it had cooled down a little, the annual Christmas cricket match began. This tradition had been handed down through generations. The ones sitting on the side-lines, choosing to watch instead of play, were many years ago the ones out there giving the ball a fair old whack. Now it was the next generation's turn to run about as the older generation watched on from the comfort of their fold-out chairs. It was the natural flow of life, beautiful and comforting. Molly and Heath's team won, as they did almost every year, and the trophy – a toilet seat decorated with corks and tin cans – was handed out in a mock-solemn ceremony. Molly and Heath triumphantly held it up in the air to loud cheers.

By six o'clock people were starting to head home to the comfort of their lounge chairs, televisions and beds. Molly looked on, amused, as sober friends and family, those that had been given the responsibility of driving home, loaded inebriated loved ones and testy, overtired children into their cars. Many women had insisted on helping to clean up while the men had packed away all the chairs and tables. You wouldn't have known there'd been over a hundred people enjoying Christmas together in Molly's backyard. All that remained was the tinsel some larrikin had wrapped around Molly's Land Cruiser, making it look like a car fit for the Mardi Gras, not for the red, dusty roads she drove daily.

Molly watched from the front verandah as Rose played with Skip and the puppies on the front lawn, giggling and squealing as they ran after her playfully. Rose had not let the puppies out of her sight since the morning. Ominous black clouds filled the sky, the impending downpour marking the end of a glorious Christmas day, as it did almost every year. Today had been so lovely, Molly thought, surrounded by close friends and family. She just wished she had been able to share it with her parents too. It still hurt on special days like Christmas and birthdays that they weren't there with her. It made her long for a big family of her own to help fill the void her parents had left in her heart. Rose deserved a father, and the gift of a brother or sister, perhaps both. Molly didn't want her growing up without siblings; she knew from experience that it could be very lonely.

'Merry Christmas, Mum and Dad,' she whispered, as two beautiful Ulysses butterflies suddenly flew into view and darted around in the garden together. She instantly felt goosebumps all over. Ulysses butterflies had been her parents' favourite. Molly knew then it was a sign from her parents that they were with her, and her eyes filled with tears.

CHAPTER

4

'Get up! Get up! Move along, you lot! We haven't got all day!'
Molly yelled as she pushed the meandering cattle towards the
yards, admiring the deep cherry-red of their coats in the morning
sunlight. Her grandfather had chosen the Santa Gertrudis for their
renowned resistance to ticks, pinkeye and grass tetany, which was
vital in the harsh conditions of Dimbulah. Santa Gertrudis had the
perseverance to walk long distances for food and water, making
them perfect for the hot and dry environment. The cows were also
exceptionally maternal, known to 'babysit' up to twenty calves
when the rest of the herd was busy grazing. Molly found that fact
very endearing.

Licking her cracked lips, Molly lifted her hat and wiped the
beading sweat from her forehead with her sleeve. She felt as if she
had sweated out a few litres of water and her shirt clung to her like
clingwrap. Even though it was Boxing Day, everyone on Jacaranda
Farm was straight back to work. The only days they got off every
year were Christmas Day and New Year's Day. Other than that,

when the fruit was ready to pick or the cattle needed tending to they all had to work rain, hail, shine *or* public holiday. No rest for the wicked, Molly thought, pulling her water bottle from the saddle bag and taking a few long gulps from it. She and Kenny had spent most of the morning rounding up the small mob ahead of her for drenching. It wasn't one of her favourite jobs but it had to be done to stop the cattle getting intestinal worms. It would have been a heck of a lot easier if Heath and Trev had been there to help, but they were busy picking mangoes. David couldn't help either – he managed the packing shed, ensuring the fruit left the shed in top condition. Even Rose was working today, helping Elizabeth with all the baking for a cancer fundraiser, in between playing with her new puppies and her castle. Molly smiled as she remembered the look of glee on Rose's face when she had opened Heath's present. He had seemed equally thrilled by her response. Molly gently touched the bracelet Heath had given her, still in awe of how stunning it was. Why had he bought her something so expensive? In the past he had bought her gift vouchers for the local western shop, clothes, or books on training horses. This bracelet, it was different. Wasn't jewellery a bit, well, personal, something a boyfriend would buy? Jenny wouldn't approve, she was sure of it, and the very thought made her feel guilty for even accepting such a gift from Heath. Why did she? But, perhaps there was nothing to concern herself with; maybe she was just over-thinking things like she usually did. She jumped as Kenny cracked his whip, snapping her back to the here and now.

'Are you right to shut the gates, Kenny?' she bellowed, heading towards a shady spot under a few ironbark trees.

'No wucken furries!' he called back, his tall, lanky frame sitting casually in the saddle. He was so skinny Molly swore she could just about blow him right off his horse with one big breath. Not that he should be thin – he certainly ate like there was no tomorrow. Molly wished she could eat half as much as him without worrying about putting on weight. She wasn't too concerned, though; with the amount of hard work she put in on the farm she could afford to indulge in the odd treat.

Molly was about to dismount when she felt her mount Leroy coil like a spring beneath her. She smoothly tightened the reins and pulled him back, talking calmly to him as she scanned her surroundings for danger, trusting in Leroy's capability to sense it long before she could. He gave a shrill whinny and suddenly he was rearing up, nearly unseating her. Molly tensed all her muscles and held on for dear life as she spotted a giant king brown snake slither across the earth beneath them. Leroy's hoofs hit the ground and the snake struck out, barely missing the horse's front leg before it disappeared into a patch of scrub. Leroy's flanks twitched fiercely as Molly tried to calm him down, stroking his neck from where she sat in the saddle.

'Good boy, good boy. It's gone now. You're okay. It's gone, mate.'

Kenny trotted up beside her. 'What was that all about? Are you all right, Molly?'

Molly gave Leroy a proud rub. 'I'm all good, Kenny. Leroy here just spotted a king brown, that's all. Didn't you, buddy?'

'What? Shit, has it gone?' Kenny scanned the ground frantically. 'I bloody hate snakes. They make my skin crawl.'

'Yes, Kenny, you big girl, it's gone!' Molly laughed. Kenny was most certainly the larrikin of the bunch, and if you factored in alcohol, he was the town nudist, finding himself in the lock-up on a handful of occasions because of his X-rated displays, but never seeming to learn his lesson. Molly appreciated his light-hearted approach to life. So many people chose to take life too seriously, and she wasn't immune to doing that herself. Kenny taught her how to lighten up, enjoy the simple things in life. It was an admirable trait.

Kenny smiled bashfully as he hopped down off his horse. 'Well, that's good. Time for smoko then, I reckon, before I starve to death.'

After a few minutes Leroy relaxed and Molly slid out of the saddle. She gave him a quick scratch around the lips, which he loved. He let her know how much he enjoyed it by smiling back at her in a horsy kind of way.

'Thank goodness I have you to take care of me, mate. I would've trodden right on top of that snake if you hadn't warned me. Cheers, buddy. I owe you one.'

In the shade of the ironbarks Molly and Kenny demolished half a fruitcake and a few litres of water in less than ten minutes before settling back against a tree trunk.

'Okay, I've got a joke for you, Molly. Why did the chicken cross the road?'

Molly rolled her eyes. 'Um, to get to the other side?'

'Because there was a sexy-looking rooster on the other side of the road!'

Molly couldn't help but laugh at the ridiculousness of it. 'Oh, Kenny. That's a shocker.'

'I know, but it made you laugh, didn't it?' he replied smugly as he stretched his arms high in the air and yawned broadly. Just then, a massive grasshopper flew straight into Kenny's mouth like a 747 coming in for landing. Kenny leapt up with his mouth hanging open, the grasshopper going crazy, desperate to escape. Kenny's body jerked around like a dancer in a club. He was trying to talk, but with his mouth so full of the panicked green insect Molly couldn't make out a word. She was just about to help him, tears of laughter streaming down her face, when the grasshopper discovered its escape route. It sped out of Kenny's cavernous mouth like it was jet-propelled, hitting Molly in the side of the head with a soft noise before darting away into the safety of the branches above them. Kenny just stood and stared at Molly, wide-eyed, shaking his head slowly from side to side.

'Holy crap, Kenny! Now *that* was funny! Was that part of the joke?' Molly hollered as she collapsed to the ground in fits of laughter.

'How freaking insane was that?' he said, trying to catch his breath. 'I thought my life had been full of crazy shit, but that, that takes the cake! Imagine if the bugger had gone the wrong way and flown down my throat! I could have choked to death. I can just see the headlines now: "Dimbulah man cheats death after being attacked by a grasshopper!" '

That set Molly off again and her whole body shook in uncontrollable laughter.

Getting back to work, they pushed the cattle one by one through the crush, applying the drench meticulously. Molly carefully assessed the physical condition of each animal, happy at the end of the afternoon that they had a healthy herd. All she had to do now was fatten them up, ready for the saleyards in six months' time. Soon she would take a truckload over to Rob's; he had an endless supply of fodder thanks to the friendly, wet climate in Malanda. It was extremely dry this time of the year on Jacaranda Farm and that meant costly feeding bills. She made a mental note to ring her uncle tonight and sort it out as she shut the last of the paddock gates and bolted it securely.

Molly and Kenny mounted their horses and headed back in the direction of the stables, their pace casual. They enjoyed the peacefulness of the late afternoon, the earth gradually beginning to shadow as the sun began its descent over the distant mountains.

'Well, I'm beat, Kenny. How 'bout you?' Molly asked while taking off Leroy's saddle and placing it over the hitching rail nearby.

'Yeah, me too, mate. I've had a pretty traumatic day after nearly choking on that grasshopper.'

'Oh, don't start me laughing again, Kenny! My cheeks still hurt!'

*

Molly pushed open the shed door and shivered delightfully as the cool air-conditioning caressed her skin. She was hoping to find Rose there, but the shed was empty except for David.

'Hi, Granddad. Need a hand finishing up before dinner?'

David looked up from his bookwork; his thick glasses perched on the end of his nose. 'Oh, hi, love. That's good of you, but I'm almost finished here. How did you and Kenny go with the drenching?'

'Yeah, really good. The cattle look in tip-top condition. They just need a good bit of fodder to fatten them up for the saleyards. I thought I'd take them over to Rob and Cheryl's sometime next week.'

'That'd be such a help, love, thanks. I'd be lost without you.'

Molly wrapped her arm around David's shoulder. 'And I'd be lost without you.'

She whistled to Skip, who was napping on the old lounge in the corner of the air-conditioned shed. 'Come on, boy, time to head home. Looks like you've had a hard day cooped up in here with the aircon. I don't know how you cope.'

David chuckled. 'I want to come back as a dog in my next life, I reckon, Molly.'

Dusk was upon them when she stepped back through the shed door and out into the world. Molly looked above as the skies filled with thousands of screeching bats and a horrible stench filled the air. She swiftly grabbed her nose to squash her nostrils shut.

Molly's family was one of the lucky ones that could afford to put up huge nets to prevent the catastrophic damage the bats could wreak in one night of ravenous feeding. Other farmers simply had to hedge their bets, which could be devastating to the bank balance. Bats were a protected species, much to Molly's fury. She thought they were wretched creatures, full of awful diseases. She knew of several horses having to be put down because of the horrific hendra virus, which was carried in bat faeces. It made her blood boil with anger. But there was nothing anyone could do to cull them, and the bats were beginning to reproduce in plague proportions. She shook her head at the unfairness of it before turning her attention back to Skip, who was dancing like billy-o around her feet, waiting for some attention. She leant down and gave him a cuddle around the neck, chortling at his antics.

CHAPTER
5

Molly, Jade, Heath, Kenny and Trev sang along to Alan Jackson's 'Good Time' at the top of their lungs as they bounced along the rough dirt road towards the pub. The stereo in Trev's old Toyota Land Cruiser sent vibrations through the seat, pumping the group up for tonight's New Year's Eve bash. Trev swerved a few times to miss the kangaroos that jumped without warning from the sides of the road. Panicked by the headlights, they hopped this way and that as if drunk, not deciding until the last death-defying second which side of the road they wanted to get off.

Molly wasn't surprised by all the cars out the front of the Bull Bar. It was as though every man and his dog had decided it was the place to celebrate tonight. The more the merrier, she thought, as she slid out of the back seat.

Jade smiled as she pointed to a group of guys standing outside the pub. They were dressed to the nines in women's clothing, heels and all. 'Come on, Molly. Let's go and find out why they're dressed like a bunch of sheilas!'

'Hey! Molly Jones,' one of them slurred, seeing her heading in their direction. He held his beer up in the air like a trophy before losing his footing in the tremendously high heels and wearing half the beer on his head in his attempt to save himself.

'Kurt! Hi! Gee whiz, you lot look pretty tonight. What's the occasion?' Molly asked as she took in the state of them all.

Kurt looked to the others for an answer, but they all just burst out laughing. After regaining a bit of composure, Kurt cleared his throat to answer. 'Okay, let me explain, Molly. It all started when Jimbo here decided to put on some of his missus' red lipstick for a laugh. What happened after that is a bit of a blur, but I know it involved tequila shots ... Then we were so drunk we couldn't be arsed getting changed back into our jeans and stuff, so we thought, what the hell, we'll just come as we are for a bit of a hoot!'

'Hmm, I don't think any of you will be getting lucky tonight dressed like that. And trust me, in the morning your feet are going to ache like buggery. I'm looking forward to seeing you lot trying to dance in those shoes. Anyways, let's get in there and have ourselves some shots too!' Molly exclaimed.

Jade smiled cheekily. 'You're on, my friend. Let's get smashed and dance like a group of headless chooks!'

Molly giggled. 'I like your simile, Jade. You come out with some beauties sometimes. But I don't think I'm too keen on getting smashed – just happily tipsy will be sufficient for me.'

'Sounds like a plan to me, ladies,' Heath answered, thrilled to be out with Molly. She looked so darn sexy in her going-out garb. He was used to seeing her in her work jeans and a singlet, which was a nice sight, but this was even better. Tonight Molly had on her going-out jeans, black leather boots and a tight blue top that revealed just a hint of her voluptuous cleavage. He wished he had the guts to just grab her and kiss her right then and there, but his sense of reason warned him not to. Now wasn't the time.

*

Molly screwed up her face as she sucked the chunk of lemon she was given along with her tequila shot. Jade slammed her shot glass down on the bar, licking her lips, quickly ordering another round for the five of them from the new barmaid, Melinda. Molly smiled as she watched Jade and Melinda share a moment across the bar, chuffed that Kenny had introduced the pair a few days ago at the weekly dart competition at the pub. It looked to her as if there was a definite spark between the two women.

Molly checked out the crowd in the Bull Bar, trying to see how many faces she recognised. It seemed like a lifetime ago that she and Jade had hung out here every weekend, drinking with the boys and playing pool. They had been pretty wild back then. Looking back on it, Molly was surprised neither of them had ended up in the lock-up for the night.

She remembered one time when she was eighteen. After she and Jade had downed too many shooters, they'd decided it would be a great idea to catch as many cane toads as they could and tie rocks to their back legs with string. They had then tossed the toads on the roofs of unsuspecting Dimbulah residents, who'd been rudely woken at three in the morning by toads jumping around on their tin roofs and making one heck of a racket. Thank God nobody had figured out who it was. The town had been in an uproar for weeks, with concerned members of the community even holding a meeting in the town hall. Molly had run off the rails a bit back then, drinking and partying, which had broken her grandparents' hearts. Now she realised how much they must have worried about her and how hard they had tried to make up for her parents not being there. But everything had changed when Rose came along. Molly was truly sorry for the pain she had caused her grandparents, and she had done her best to make up for it over the past few years.

The mechanical bull took pride of place in the centre of the Bull Bar and both men and women were lining up to give it a shot. Melinda leant over the bar and yelled over the music.

'You ladies should give it a go. The deal is, if you can ride it for eight seconds you get a hundred-dollar bar tab.'

Jade raised her eyebrows at Molly. 'I'm game if you are, buddy!'

Molly nodded and grinned. A mechanical bull was nothing compared to a bucking horse. She and Jade looked at the guys to see if they wanted to give it a go. Trev shook his head firmly, yelling over the music.

'Nah, I'm getting too old for that stuff. I'm going to go for a wander around, catch up with a few people I haven't seen for a while. If you want me later, I'll probably be at the pool table kicking some butt.'

Molly turned to Heath. He grinned like a naughty schoolboy. 'Bloody oath! Count me in, ladies.'

Kenny was always up for anything, so Molly didn't even bother to ask him. The four of them stood in the line for the bull, cracking up as they watched people trying to ride drunk and coming spectacularly unstuck. Some of the girls had skirts on and were so busy trying to keep their knickers from showing they had no chance of lasting the eight seconds. Other women tried too hard to look sexy, hoping the eligible young cowboys watching from the sidelines imagined they were riding them instead of the bull.

'Buckle bunnies,' Molly whispered into Jade's ear and they both laughed hysterically.

Finally it was Molly's turn and she felt herself blushing as all eyes fell upon her. She shook the embarrassment off and climbed on top of the man-made beast. At the sound of a bell, the bull suddenly began to move, and Molly was lurched through the air, doing her best to hold on. The crowd wolf-whistled and hollered as they watched her move like a pro with every buck, their cheers getting louder and louder as she got closer to the eight-second bell. There was a massive roar when the bell rang out and Molly grinned victoriously as she headed back to her mates. She noticed some of the men looking at her, clearly impressed by the fact that a woman had lasted the eight seconds. She couldn't help being quietly proud of her effort, proving that women could ride the mechanical bull just as well as the men.

Heath was next up. A bunch of women screamed like lovesick teenagers when he walked into the spotlight – it was as though he was Tim McGraw. Molly rolled her eyes at Jade and they both laughed. Heath tipped his hat to Molly, smirking sexily beneath it, sending a quiver through her entire body. She was taken aback. What was *that* all about? If this was flirting, it had to stop, even if it was harmless. Although she had to admit that he looked hot up there. She bit her bottom lip, her mind in a spin. God, what was she getting herself into? She refused to allow herself to think like this. It was immoral! The bell rung out, pronouncing Heath had made the eight seconds. He threw his hat up in the air, grinning broadly as he jumped off, winking at Molly.

Within seconds, women were swarming over Heath like moths to a flame. Molly smiled ruefully to herself. She couldn't deny that she could see the attraction. But it made her uncomfortable even to be thinking that way about Heath. After all, he'd been her good mate since forever – and not to mention one of her dearest mate's boyfriends. She glanced again at the women fawning over

Heath – Heath seemed uncomfortable with the attention – then quickly looked away, telling herself she didn't mind at all. It would be nice to see him move on in life, meet a woman he could love again. Wouldn't it?

At that moment, Molly saw Trev across the room, playing pool with a big group of guys he used to muster with. She knew some of their faces from when she had done some mustering up north. She caught Trev's eye and he grinned and gave her a big thumbs up, congratulating her on her eight-second ride. She smiled back warmly, feeling blessed to have a father figure like Trev in her life. She pulled out a bar stool and sat down, enjoying watching the happy crowd while reflecting on her deep bond with Trev. He had gone to school with her dad, so he was practically part of the family. When Molly's father Peter died, Trev had offered to help Molly's grandfather out with the everyday running of the farm – and ended up helping to raise Molly as well. He had never been married or had children and he was happy with that, always saying that the land was his missus and his dogs were his kids. As long as Trev had his three Johns – his John Wayne movies, his Johnny Cash music and the family's John Deere tractor – he was content. His weather-beaten face showed the years he had worked out in the sun, and he looked ten years older than his forty-eight years. He smoked rollies like a chimney and drank beer like it was water, but he was the hardest worker Molly had ever met. They were lucky to have him on Jacaranda Farm.

The crowd cheered as the band was introduced and took centre stage. They belted out their first tune of the night, the all-time classic Garth Brooks' song 'Ain't Going Down (Til the Sun Comes Up)', sending the throng of partiers into a massive bootscooting frenzy. The whole place shook as people boogied on the dance floor, the tables and even the bar. Molly thought it was just like a scene out of the movie *Coyote Ugly*.

She closed her eyes and danced with Jade until her legs ached and her throat was hoarse from singing. When she signalled to Jade that she was going back to the bar for a drink, Jade nodded and followed her off the dance floor.

The girls collapsed on bar stools, happy to have a rest. Molly leant back on her elbows and squinted through all the smoke and colourful flashing lights, trying to see the band. She'd been so busy dancing she hadn't even checked them out properly. A sharp pang hit her when she finally caught a glimpse of the lead singer. He looked strangely familiar. Could it be? But his hair was different and he was a bigger build than she remembered. Then again, it had been seven years ... And she'd been so drunk that night ... Oh my God, Molly thought, almost panicking. It *couldn't* be him, could it? She turned to Jade, but found Jade and Melinda were deep in conversation. As she watched, Melinda leaned in to whisper in Jade's ear, and Jade responded with her sexiest smile. Molly smiled and looked away. No way was she going to interrupt her friend at this point.

Molly's mind began to race, a thousand questions coming to the surface, begging to be answered. What if it *really* is him? Should I just go right up to him and start talking to him or will he think I'm just some chick trying to hit on him? Will he be the type of father for Rose that I've been dreaming of all these years? Is he a man I could fall for? Love? Create a life with? Shit! Slow down, she thought, I'm not even sure it's him yet and if it *is* him I don't even know him from a bar of soap ...

The loud cheers as the band finished a song brought Molly back to the present. She stared again at the lead singer, more and more convinced she *did* know him. She noticed her hands were shaking. She began to wonder if she'd just had too much to drink. She couldn't even ask Jade what she thought because Jade had never met him in the first place. Heart pounding crazily, Molly knew she had to get a closer look. She slipped off her stool and headed inconspicuously in the direction of the stage.

She weaved her way through the dance floor, squeezing past the people packed in like canned sardines, and taking cover behind one of the massive speakers so she could see the singer without him seeing her – or so she thought. But their eyes met briefly and Molly hit the deck like she was an actress in some Hollywood shoot-em-out movie. She kept her gaze fixed on the floor as she caught her breath, calling herself all the names under the sun for reacting in such a crazed manner. It *was* him. Now she had seen him up close she was one hundred and ten per cent sure. She knew he had recognised her too. His eyes had stayed locked onto hers for that second too long and he had smiled at her like he knew her. What in the hell was she going to do now?

Molly had dreamt about this day for the last seven years and in her dreams she was always so strong and confident. She'd imagined if she met him again she would just walk right on up and proudly tell him that he had a beautiful daughter. But now it was really happening, here she was hiding behind a giant speaker and cowering on the floor! She wondered if he had ever thought about her after that night. She had never forgotten him. How could she? She had spent the first years of Rose's life desperately wishing she could see him again. But so much had changed since that time. She wasn't the wild, carefree girl who had slept with a stranger in the back of her Land Cruiser. That girl had disappeared when Rose was born. Molly reasoned with herself that she had to eventually get up off the floor so she jumped up and raced back to the bar, apologising as she bumped into people in her haste to get away. She sat down beside Jade, her head in a spin.

'Molly? What's up, mate?' Jade asked in concern. 'You look like you've just seen a ghost.'

Molly took a minute to catch her breath before trying to explain, talking a hundred miles a minute.

Heath had just come up but moved a little away from the girls, enough to give them some privacy. He could tell from the deliberate way Molly was leaning in and whispering in Jade's ear that they needed to talk about something serious and he wasn't one for eavesdropping, especially on women's conversations. He just hoped that Molly was okay, because if it had been a bloke in the crowd that had bothered her, he would knock his bloody lights out.

Jade covered her mouth, her eyes wide. 'The singer is Rose's dad? Oh my God. Are you sure?'

Jade listened, still in shock, as Molly told the story, this time slowly enough for Jade to understand. Jade sat with her mouth hanging open like a fish just waiting for the hook to fall in.

Molly clicked her fingers in Jade's face to snap her out of it. 'What am I going to do, Jade? Holy shit! I know he saw me and I do *really* feel like he should know he has a daughter. I mean, I've waited years for this day! But we only knew each other for one night ... I reckon he's going to freak out!'

Jade nodded. 'You have to give him the benefit of the doubt, Molly, for Rose's sake. She'd love to get to know her dad – if that's what he wants, of course. If he doesn't, well, to hell with him. At least you'll know in your heart that you did the right thing. But this isn't the time or place to be telling him something as serious as this. And you need time to think about it rationally before you go doing or saying anything you might regret, okay?'

Molly took a deep breath, exhaling slowly. 'Yep, I know you're right. I'll take my time and have a think. I don't even know the guy, really. This is so crazy!'

Jade gave Molly a hug. 'You'll be right. You're a strong woman and a brilliant mum. You'll do what's best for Rose. Just remember I have your back if you need it, okay?'

Molly squeezed Jade tightly, brushing away a tear. 'Thanks, mate. I'm so lucky to have you.'

Noticing the girls had finished chatting, Heath moved back over near them, placing his hand protectively on Molly's back.

'Is everything okay? You look a bit shaken up.'

Molly nodded. She wanted Heath to enjoy his night, not be worrying about her, so she put on her biggest smile. 'Yeah, mate, nothing to worry about. Just a bit of girly stuff, that's all.'

'Good. I thought I was going to have to knock some bugger out!' Heath smiled, relieved Molly *appeared* to be okay. But was she? His senses told him otherwise. But she clearly didn't want to tell him, and he couldn't force her.

'Thanks, Heath. I can always count on you, but don't worry, I'm fine. Now let's grab a beer, shall we?'

*

Molly watched nervously, shuffling from foot to foot, as the band took a break and the DJ took over on stage. She watched as the singer moved through the crowd, making his way towards her. Holy crap! She felt as though it was all happening in slow motion. As he moved closer and closer her heart was pounding, faster and faster. Then he was leaning into her space, his hand outstretched to shake hers. Gee whiz, she thought, this is a little formal after we've seen each other naked. She shook his hand, smiling timidly, her face going a brighter shade of red by the second. He eventually pulled his hand free from her firm grip.

'Hi, I'm Mark. We've met before, haven't we? I'm sure I know your face from somewhere.'

Molly's heart skipped a beat. He didn't remember! Then again, how could she blame him? They'd both been so drunk.

'Um, yeah, I'm Molly Jones. We, ah, met many years ago, at the Mount Garnett rodeo, actually.'

Mark looked up at the ceiling for a few seconds as if searching his brain for a foggy memory, then looked back at Molly with a flash of recognition. 'Oh, yes. *Now* I remember. God, you must think I'm such a shit! I'm sorry I took off without saying goodbye, but as I remember it you just wouldn't bloody wake up. No matter how much I shook you. You mumbled something about how I should bugger off and let you sleep ... So I did.' He ran his fingers through his hair. 'Wow, how amazing to meet you again like this. I couldn't help noticing this gorgeous woman hiding behind the speaker and checking me out. Have to say I liked the death roll you performed for me too,' he added with a cheeky grin.

Molly felt every litre of blood in her body rush to her face and she thanked God it was so dark in the pub. 'Oh, no, that was ... I just had a leg cramp from all the dancing, that's all. No worries. Um, sorry about telling you to bugger off, I was feeling pretty dusty that morning. *Way* too many Bundys the night before, I'm afraid.'

'So my wicked plan to get you drunk and have my way with you worked like a dream, did it?' Mark joked.

Molly wasn't sure how to respond. Mark pulled a stool close to Molly's, turning his back to Heath, who was standing nearby. Molly didn't know if Mark's move had been deliberate or not, but she could see Heath was not impressed. In fact, if looks could kill, Mark would have been dead on the spot. She briefly wondered what was up with Heath tonight. He seemed to be very protective of her. She hoped nothing was bothering him.

'So, Molly Jones, what's been happening since I saw you last? You must be married by now, a beautiful woman like yourself?'

Molly shook her head, uncomfortable with the question. 'Nope, not married.'

Mark looked pleased. 'Fair enough. So what do you do for a living?' he asked.

Molly found this an easier question to answer. 'Oh, I work with horses. Teaching them that they can trust us humans, and also training them up to be good at whatever it is their owners want them to do. I'm still amazed I get paid to do something I'm so passionate about. Horses are my life. I love them.'

Mark looked impressed. 'Wow! You do have a great job. Funny that you should mention it – I have a mare that needs some training. She's a bit green, was broken in by some guy down south but she's been turned out for a few years. I reckon with some training she'll make a fine horse, but I haven't ridden her yet because I know she'd throw me straight off if I tried. Maybe I could hire you to help me out with her. What do you reckon?'

'Sure, I'd love to. But since you don't live around here, how would that actually work?'

Mark raised his eyebrows. 'Well, Miss Jones, it just so happens that I'm house-sitting a property out on Wolfram Camp Road for the next year. A mate of my brother's has had to go to New Guinea to manage one of the mines over there and I owed my brother a huge favour. The guy was desperate – he was in a tight spot with wanting to take on the job, but had no one to look after his place. So, ta-da, here I am! It'll be nice to stop in one place for a while. I'm just about always on the road with the band.'

Molly tried to take in everything Mark was saying. It sounded like Rose would have the chance to finally meet her father, and to make things even better, he would be living near them for a while. What a stroke of luck!

'Well, it's always good to have new faces around here, especially ones that can sing like you do. I loved the way you belted the songs out up there. Your voice reminds me a little of Jimmy Barnes,' Molly replied happily, finding herself relaxing in his company. From first impressions – well, second ones, really, if she factored in the Mount Garnett rodeo – Mark seemed like a really nice guy.

'Geez, thanks, Molly. I've had a few people tell me I sound like Jimmy, and to me that's a huge compliment. I admire the bloke's musical talents.'

Molly smiled genuinely. 'You're more than welcome, it's well deserved. Anyway, tell me how you got into music. I had no idea you were even in a band when I met you in Garnett.'

'I wasn't really in a band then. Just dipping my feet in the water, so to speak, by writing songs and practising them at home, where no one could hear me. Let's just say that music saved me. That's why I'm so passionate about it.' Mark glanced at his watch. 'Anyhoo, been nice meeting you, again, Miss Jones. My break's over so I better get back to work. Before I run off, what do you reckon about my horse?'

'I'd love to work with her. Bring her over during the week if you like.'

'It's a deal,' Mark answered. 'So, to get in touch with you I'd have to get your number?'

'Oh, of course! I didn't think of that.'

Molly asked Melinda for a pen, writing her number down on a cardboard coaster and passing it to Mark, who shoved it firmly in his pocket, giving her an adorable smile as he did so.

'Right, then, I'll give you a call next week, Molly.'

*

'Ten, nine, eight, seven, six, five, four, three, two, one ... Happy New Year!' The passion and joy of the crowd singing out made Molly break out in goosebumps all over her. She adored this town and she loved the people in it.

Jade wrapped her arms around her, jumping up and down like a yo-yo. 'Happy New Year, babe! This year is going to be a great one. I can feel it in my bones!'

Molly laughed. 'Same to you, buddy! I think the feeling you have in your bones is alcohol, though!'

Molly tapped Heath on the shoulder, aware he had been quiet since she had spoken to Mark. Not knowing what to do about it she pretended she hadn't noticed. 'Hey, you. Got a new year's hug for me?'

Heath turned, smiling. How could he not? He could never stay angry at her for too long, even though she had completely ignored him at the bar when that jerk had turned up. Who did the dickhead think he was anyway? Molly wasn't the type for one-night stands, so Heath found a little solace in the fact that the bloke wouldn't have a chance in hell with her. He leant in and picked Molly up off the floor, spinning her around in circles.

Molly laughed out loud, throwing her head back, watching the ceiling revolve. When Heath stopped to put her back on the ground their eyes caught for a moment too long. Molly felt her heart lunge out of her chest, her legs barely able to hold her up.

Heath grinned at her. And then, with no warning, he placed his tattooed hands around her face and kissed her gently on the lips, lingering long enough for her to want more of him. She was filled with the desire to run her tongue over his, to taste his sweetness. It was so intense. She very nearly gave into it.

'Happy New Year, Molly,' he whispered in her ear, his warm breath filling her with a passionate quiver.

Molly felt her legs go weak; her mind trying to catch up with what had just happened. No! She couldn't go there with Heath. Or could she? She didn't want to ruin a friendship. He was way too important to her *and* Rose. And it would be as bad as cheating behind Jenny's back. She swiftly took stock of the situation, gathering her emotions up and packing them into her imaginary suitcase. Her voice of reason took over.

She cleared her throat, hoping he didn't pick up on the tremble in her voice. 'Happy New Year.'

Heath glanced casually back at her, a tiny smile forming at the corners of his full, kissable lips. 'That it is, Molly. That it is. Happy New Year.'

Heath was over the moon. He'd finally had the guts to kiss her and he had felt it. Molly Jones *did* like him. He could tell from the way she had kissed him, and the look in her beautiful emerald-green eyes said everything. She had quickly recovered, though, and now looked to be pretending she had felt nothing. But he was a patient man, and was willing to wait as long as it took for her to realise *he* was her knight in shining armour.

CHAPTER

6

When she woke up Molly felt like a freight train was tearing through her head, tooting its horn loudly for good measure. She rolled over, blinking her bleary eyes, to check the time on her bedside clock. Strewth! she thought. It was ten o'clock. After waking up before dawn every morning, this was what she called a sleep in.

She was still wearing her clothes from the night before, including her boots, and her feet ached like hell. She smelt like cigarettes, alcohol and sweat. Not a good combination. There was something foreign stuck to the front of her shirt too, perhaps remnants of the sausage roll she'd devoured at some point last night. She ran her tongue over her furry teeth, thinking how much she would kill for a drink of water and a toothbrush.

Molly willed her body to stand up but the fear of a smashing headache kept her horizontal for a bit longer. Her thoughts wandered back over the events of last night, the memories stealing the breath from her. Running into Mark after all these years ... and then sharing the earth-trembling kiss with Heath. It all felt so surreal. Why did Heath decide to kiss her like that, now, after years of being mates? Especially considering he knew how close she and Jenny had been. Was it lust on his part, or loneliness, or something more? And how did *she* feel about *him*? Were the strange sensations she was experiencing around Heath because of deeper feelings, or was the longing to be loved overcoming her, making her not think straight? And Mark, just reappearing back in her life like a genie out of a bottle. For goodness sake! It never rains but it pours. What did she want to come of all of this? Anything, nothing, everything? Be careful what you wish for, she thought. Be very, very careful.

Molly allowed her mind to flicker over the lighter parts of the evening, trying to distract herself from the heavy thinking. Her head hurt too much for that right now. Good old Kenny – talk about a laugh a minute; the recollection of him running around butt-naked in the middle of the Bull Bar parking lot with his red jocks hanging off the top of his head made her chuckle. He'd then proceeded to dance like Peter Garret while singing 'Blue Sky Mine' at the top of his lungs. She even had a giggle at her own expense, remembering how she almost fell back down the front steps of her own home when she was blinded by the powerful sensor light on the verandah. Ah, New Year's Eve 2011. 'Oh, what a night' had taken on a whole new meaning.

Molly forced herself out of bed so she could go and have a long, hot shower, an extra-strong cuppa and a greasy bacon sandwich. It might help her feel a bit better. Being vertical made her head throb even more but she didn't expect any pity. She had done it to herself, even though she hadn't really drunk that much compared to what she used to.

She opened her curtains to let in the sunlight, squinting as the rays poured in like liquid gold. She could see the round yard from where she stood and David and Rose were already out there, working with one of the horses. She gazed lovingly at her daughter. Rose was sitting on the rails in exactly the same spot that Molly used to sit on when she was a kid.

David had mentioned last night that he'd be needing the round yard first thing, and then it was all hers. Molly couldn't wait to get out there and show Rose how far Buck had come in the last week. He had progressed in leaps and bounds. Gazing at Rose now, so adorable in her little boots and big shady hat, Molly felt a wave of panic at the very thought of having to tell Mark everything, and her grandparents. She sat down on the end of bed and thought seriously about what she should do, about what would be best for her precious girl.

Would telling Mark about Rose straightaway be wise? What if he never wanted to see her? Or even worse, what if he decided to get to know her and then just disappeared out of their lives? How would she explain that to her little daughter without breaking her heart? She was excited for Rose, but she couldn't bear for her daughter's heart – or her own – to be broken. Or what if Mark absolutely fell in love with Rose – who wouldn't? – and, as her legal father, winded up wanting to take her away somewhere? For Molly, that would be like somebody grabbing a knife and stabbing her in the heart.

No, Molly decided, telling Mark straightaway was too risky. She would have to get to know him better before she broke the news to him. What difference did a few more weeks make, after waiting years for him? She also decided not to tell her grandparents yet. They would only worry, and it would put too much pressure on her and the whole situation if they knew. Molly was so deep in thought she just about hit the roof when her mobile rang. She took a quick look at the number and smiled.

'Hi, Jade. How are you feeling this fine morning?' Molly said as she rubbed the sore spots on her feet.

'Hey, Molly. I'm surprised I've pulled up *pretty* good this morning. More importantly, though, how are you feeling? Especially about the whole Mark thing? Must have been a bit of a shock running into him, hey?'

'Yeah, I'm a bit stressed out about it, Jade. You know me, I worry about anything involving the opposite sex, particularly when they're the father of my child ...'

'Aw, Mol, I knew it'd be concerning you, which is normal given the circumstances, mate. Try not to let it get to you too much, though. It will all work out for the best. You've just got to find the right time to tell him. If that's what you decide to do.'

'I think I'm going to wait a little while, get to know him. What do you reckon?'

'Sounds like a great idea. Just follow your instincts and take your time. Hey, do you fancy doing something with the blokes this afternoon, once you've finished working on Buck with Rose? It might take your mind off things; let you relax for a while. Maybe we could all go for a ride down to the river and chuck in a line. It'd be nice to have a feed of fresh fish for dinner tonight.'

'That sounds great, Jade. Count me in. I should be finished around three.'

'Excellent. Can you let the guys know that I'll be around about four-ish? Would that be okay for you? I've got some goss to tell you about me and Mel as well. I'm so thrilled that I've met her!'

'Ooh, that sounds interesting. I'll see you then, mate.'

'Okay, Molly. Catch you,' Jade replied, hanging up the phone.

*

On her way to the shower Molly found her grandmother waiting for her in the kitchen with a fresh pot of coffee.

'Happy New Year, love,' Elizabeth said, smiling. 'Did you have a good time last night?'

'Happy New Year to you too, Grandma. Yes, it was a great night, but I've got a massive headache this morning. It's self-inflicted though, so no sympathy expected,' Molly said as she leant in to give Elizabeth a hug and kiss.

'Pooh! You smell like an ashtray, love! Did you smoke last night?' Elizabeth asked, sniffing the air around Molly like it was hazardous.

Molly shook her head firmly. When David had busted her at seventeen sneaking a ciggie in the stables, he'd sat her down and made her smoke the whole packet in front of him. It had worked a treat. She had gotten down to the last two cigarettes before running to the toilet to throw up. It had put her off being a smoker for life. 'No, Grandma. Not one cigarette for me last night, but the place was full of smokers. That's why I'm heading for a shower. I know I pong!' Molly dashed for the bathroom, acutely aware of how dreadful she must look, still in her clothes from last night.

After breakfast with Elizabeth, Molly headed out into the sunshine to begin her day with Rose. She found Skip on the front lawn playing with the puppies and realised that she was missing a boot. One was where she'd left it on the verandah last night, but the other one was missing in action. After five minutes of searching she found the boot amongst her grandmother's prized roses, which were looking the worse for wear. She had forgotten that puppies loved chewing on shoes. She made a mental note to leave her boots up higher next time so the little blighters couldn't get to them. She tried to straighten the roses up as best she could after the puppies' obvious frolic, mumbling to herself not to forget to fence that area off so they couldn't get into it. Grandma would have a fit if the puppies ruined her beloved garden.

Rose squealed and came running when she saw her mum, her arms outstretched, ready for a big hug. Molly crouched down to Rose's height so she could give her a big squeeze.

'Good morning, my sweetheart. Happy New Year! Have you been good for Granddad and Grandma?'

Rose nodded enthusiastically. 'I've been extra good because Grandma said she'd take me into town for some ice-cream this afternoon if I was a good girl.'

'That sounds great. What flavour are you going to have, princess?' Molly asked as she ruffled her daughter's wild hair affectionately.

'My favourite, of course! Triple choc chip!'

David wandered over, looking as though he had finished his work for the morning. Molly knew that he'd be looking forward to an early lunch and an afternoon nap before going out and spraying the crops with fertiliser tonight. There was constantly plenty to do on the farm, but David thrived on the work, forever telling Molly it made him content at the end of the day when he'd been out getting his hands dirty. It was in his blood to be out on the land everyday, just like it was in hers.

Molly smiled up at David from where she was sitting with Rose, playing with Skip and the puppies. 'Happy New Year, Granddad. Thanks so much for looking after Rose. I really appreciate it. We had a brilliant night.'

'No need to thank me. It was my pleasure. I love having Rose's company. She keeps me on my toes. I'm glad you had a good night out, love. You deserved a break. You don't get to go out that often any more.' David turned to Rose, 'Well, I'm going in now, little mate. Thanks for coming out and helping me.'

'You're welcome, GG!'

Molly stood up, one of the puppies wriggling tirelessly in her arms. 'After I finish working with Buck I'm thinking of heading out for a ride and a spot of fishing, Granddad. Just for an hour or so, that's if there's nothing you need me to do. It sounds like Grandma and Rose are heading into town for some ice-cream so I have a bit of free time up my sleeve. I might even catch some fish for dinner if we're lucky.'

'That's fine with me, Molly. Have fun. Try and catch me a barra. We'll see you later on then,' David answered cheerfully.

'See you, GG,' Rose said, blowing him a kiss. David pretended to catch it, holding it close to his heart and smiling affectionately.

*

Trev and Heath were out on the front patio of the workers' cottage when Molly and Rose got there. Trev was hosing it off and Heath was hanging out a load of washing. Molly felt a flutter in her stomach when she recalled the kiss she had shared with Heath last night. She tried to push it to the back of her mind but it refused to stay there, the sensation of Heath's lips caressing hers impossible to forget.

'Hey there, you two. How have you all pulled up today?'

'I feel fantastic!' Trev answered as he swung the hose up in the air to shoot Molly and Rose with it.

Molly tried to duck but the water got her right in the face as Rose ran and hid behind Heath's legs, giggling madly. 'You bugger, Trev! I'll get you back when you least expect it, you know!' She chuckled as she wiped the water from her cheeks.

'I dare you to try,' Trev replied lightheartedly.

Heath picked Rose up for a cuddle, laughing at Molly as she stood wiping her face. 'That's payback for laughing at me the other day when Kenny dumped the bucket of ice all over me!'

Molly jumped when she heard a loud noise start in the workers' cottage. 'What in the hell is that?'

Trev smiled. 'Um, Kenny was trying to figure out a way to clean the house quickly because it's his turn to be Sadie. He came up with the bright idea of using the leaf blower to blow all the dust out of the place. But I think he's making the place dirtier, not cleaner. You got to go and have a look for yourself, Molly. It's a crack up!'

Molly rolled her eyes. 'He's one in a million, our Kenny.'

Heath laughed. 'You got that right.' He leant over and gently placed Rose back on the ground. He was trying hard not to ask Molly about the bloke at the bar last night but it was eating him up, and he'd suffered a sleepless night because of it. Should he say anything? Was it wise to? Shit, why the hell not? He'd kissed her, for fuck's sake. Didn't that count for something? He suddenly felt strangely nervous and he avoided her gaze, instead busying himself with straightening the boots up near the front door, which he never did. What was *wrong* with him? He took a deep breath to try and steady his pounding heart. 'Last night was a corker hey, Molly? Very memorable indeed. Cracked me up when that bloody singer tried to hit on you, though. I mean, you don't even know him and he was acting all chummy with you. I could see you looked a bit uncomfortable. I don't understand blokes like that.'

Molly felt her heart stop dead in its tracks. How in the hell was she meant to reply to that? Heath had no idea just how *much* of an impact Mark had made on her life, but for some strange reason she couldn't bring herself to tell Heath. Why? She'd always told him everything. Was it because of the kiss they'd shared? Because she was falling for Heath and she didn't want to hurt him? Or was she just protecting herself? She didn't know but the urge to change the subject was almost choking her. 'Oh, um, him. Yeah, he ... um, he heard from someone that I was good with horses and he needs one of his mares worked with. That's all.' She waved her hand in the air, giggling uneasily. 'Pfft! He wasn't *hitting* on me. What gave you that stupid idea?'

Heath rubbed his chin, pretending to think deeply. 'I dunno. Maybe it was the fact his eyes just about undressed you on the spot. Or *maybe* it was the way he so slyly got your phone number within minutes of meeting you.'

Molly wished she could tell Heath the truth, but her instincts were cautioning her not to. What in the heck was going on here between them? Everything felt so tense, uncomfortable – not at all like they were normally around each other. She felt the need to defend herself, and that puzzled her. 'I told you, he needs me to work on his mare. Simple as that. I reckon you're reading a little too much into it.'

Heath raised his eyebrows teasingly. 'Am I?'

Molly ignored his questioning gaze. The whole conversation was beginning to upset her. Was it because she felt bad lying to Heath? 'Come on, Rose, let's go check out what Kenny's up to inside.'

Molly took Rose's hand and stuck her head past the flyscreen door to find Kenny blowing the crap out of everything in sight. She was sure there was more dust floating around inside the workers' cottage than out of it. Garp was hanging onto one of the lounge room curtains by his claws, his eyes wide open, looking scared to death. Kenny smiled at them, yelling over the noise of the blower in his hand.

'Hey, Molly and Rose! I think I should patent this thing as a vacuum cleaner. But instead of sucking the dust up it blows it away.' The three of them watched as a huge cloud of dust settled on the couch. Kenny scratched his head. 'Well, maybe I'll have to give it a bit more thought first.'

'That's just silly!' Rose exclaimed with a giggle as she covered her ears.

Kenny appeared to decide he had done enough and turned off the leaf blower. The ear-piercing noise, which had vibrated around the workers' cottage making it sound ten times louder than it really was, blessedly stopped. Garp dropped to the floor and ran like a soldier in the frontline towards the safety of one of the bedrooms, his ginger fur still on end. Molly and Rose headed back outside to Heath and Trev, and Kenny followed.

'Are you boys up for a ride and a spot of fishing later this afternoon?' Molly asked, avoiding Heath's intense gaze. It was making her a little skittish. What was he doing to her? And why was she letting him get under her skin?

They all nodded eagerly. Anything that involved fishing, they were there.

'Great. Jade should be here around four, and then we can all head out. I'm just going to head home and do some light training with Buck.'

*

'I wish I could come riding with you this afternoon, Mum,' Rose said, her bottom lip almost hitting the floor as she climbed up on the top rail of the round yard that was shaded by a paperbark tree. 'I miss old Jimmy so much.'

'I know, sweetheart. I miss him too. But I bet you he's up there in horsy heaven watching over you. And at least he's not in pain any more,' Molly replied softly before placing a couple of tender kisses on Rose's cheek. 'Not long now and Buck will be all yours. Then you can come riding with me again, all the time. *And* the girls at pony club are going to be so jealous of how striking he is. I mean, just look at him! He's so handsome.'

Rose smiled as she admired Buck, who was busy prancing about the round yard like a champion fighter at the beginning of the boxing match, clearly showing off a little in front of them. 'Yeah, I reckon they will be. He's wonderful isn't he?'

'He sure is, sweetheart. And the best thing is, you picked him yourself. So that makes him extra special,' Molly said, opening the lunch box she had packed for Rose. She pulled out a Vegemite sandwich and passed it to Rose, along with a popper.

Molly slowly worked her way into Buck's space, talking calmly, soothingly, softly. Over the past week she had noticed a massive improvement in him. He no longer kicked or tried to bite, even letting her walk around him without his ears pinned firmly to his head. Now Molly studied his body language and noticed his tail had stopped flicking and his eyes were no longer wide with fear. Finally, after a few more minutes, she got close enough to hold her hand out. She allowed him to take his time, deciding whether he wanted to take a step towards her. She held her breath, feeling like the whole world had suddenly fallen still. Rose was silent on the fence, watching, and Molly continued to hold her breath as she waited.

With a little hesitation, Buck dropped his head and slowly walked over. Molly's heart leapt and she cheered loudly in her head, but remained slow and calm in her movements. The horse eventually got close enough to sniff her outstretched hand. She followed his cues and slowly placed her hand on his neck. Then what she had been waiting for happened: he lowered his head and rested it against her chest. She let out a sigh of relief – he had finally decided to trust her. She pulled a carrot from her back pocket and Buck sniffed it before taking it from her and devouring it with loud chomping noises. Molly glanced over towards Rose, and the look of pure delight on her little girl's face melted her heart. She reached out and stroked Buck's beautiful chestnut coat once again. 'Steady, fella, it's okay, it's going to be okay. Steady, steady boy.'

*

Molly let out a sigh of pleasure as she hopped up into the saddle of her beloved Leroy. She could feel he was as excited as she was to go for a good gallivant around the farm. Here, in the saddle, she felt truly free. There was nothing more beautiful to her than feeling the sheer power of her horse beneath her. It gave her wings, making her feel like she could fly when galloping around the bushlands of Jacaranda Farm and beyond. Even the smell of horses made her feel grounded, connected to the earth in a way that only a horse lover could understand. Give her that horse smell over fine French perfume any day; and the best thing was, it was free.

She leant in to give Leroy a warm hug around his neck and he let out a neigh of pleasure. They were old mates now, bonded on a very special level. She had saved Leroy from a premature death when he was only three years old. Molly had spotted him aboard a road train that was parked in town while the driver took a well-earned rest at the bakery. Sadly, Leroy was destined to be the main ingredient in dog food. Whilst walking past the truck Molly's attention had been grabbed by Leroy neighing loudly and stomping his feet, causing havoc among the other horses on board. Molly had tried to shush him but he'd continued to neigh, as if begging her to save him, his big pleading eyes stealing her heart. Molly had given in, paying the truck driver a few hundred bucks to make the unruly horse her own. Molly just knew there was something special about him that nobody else could see. She had spent months on the ground with him, proving to him that she wasn't going to hurt him, just as she was doing with Buck. Once she had gained Leroy's trust, she had begun work in the saddle and he had turned into the best Australian stock horse she had ever owned.

Molly loved that horses were incapable of sending out false signals with their body language. Unlike humans, horses showed you exactly how they were feeling, every second of every day, with every centimetre of their powerful bodies, from the tips of their ears to the tips of their tails. Yes, a horse was an open book Molly found so very easy to read. All it took was patience and time; time to sit and watch them in their natural surrounds and patience to let them become mates with you when they were good and ready. That was Molly's gift, her ability to hear and understand the unspoken language between a horse and a human that connected them on a level most people could only dream of.

'Is everyone good to go then?' Trev asked, casually rolling a cigarette between his yellow-stained fingers.

'Bloody oath!' Molly replied. The sun was sweltering hot and all she wanted to do was get into the Walsh River to cool off.

Trev lit his freshly rolled cigarette with his Zippo, blowing a puff of smoke into the air, before tapping Dakota gently in the ribs to let her know he was ready to go.

Behind Molly, Heath was sitting comfortably on his gelding, JD, who he'd named after his favourite drink. Molly had found JD for Heath four years ago, out on a station in the Northern Territory when she was mustering. JD had needed little training when she found him. Even at the young age of four he was a beautiful-natured horse with station work in his blood. Molly had gotten him for a steal, seeing the owner of the station was one of her granddad's best mates.

The group of five – Molly, Heath, Kenny, Trev and Jade – rode casually for the first few kilometres, giving themselves time to chat.

Molly gazed ahead of her, always finding herself in awe of the place she called home. For miles and miles fields that were recently bone-dry were filling with fresh new shoots of green grass, thanks to the recent rain they had enjoyed. Although there wasn't enough grass as yet to be good fodder for the cattle, it certainly made the place look revitalised. Anthills built to astronomical heights dotted the landscape, created at strategic points by the ants to give much-needed reprieve from the harsh sun. The lazy squeak of a windmill pumping water from the nearby bore, supplying the cattle with vital water, travelled on the gentle afternoon breeze along with the sweet song of the birds that were perched high in the many enormous native trees. Some of the trees had been part of Jacaranda Farm for centuries, with trunks too big to wrap your arms around.

Further off in the distance high mountain peaks reached towards the skies, the trees sparse amongst the coppery-red, rocky outcrops that were dangerous to climb. Molly knew that from experience – she had once climbed them in search of hidden Aboriginal caves that an Indigenous elder had told her about. After hours of exploring she had stumbled across them, the artwork on the rock walls inside the caves absolutely amazing. It was a slightly eerie place, though. The hairs on her neck had stood on end as she ran her fingertips over the ancient paintings. Some powerful spirits still lived in the caves, she was sure of it – so much so that one visit to the sacred site was enough. Jacaranda Farm held a lot of history, especially for the local Aboriginals, and that knowledge made the land even more magical for Molly, more exquisite.

Unintentionally breaking Molly's dreamy focus on the countryside, Jade began telling her about her phone call from Melinda that morning. 'I couldn't believe it, Mol. I only gave her my number last night and I didn't think I'd hear from her for a few days, if at all. I was stoked when I heard her voice.'

'Oh, Jade. That's fantastic! I'm so happy for you. And why did you think she wouldn't call you? Have you looked in the mirror lately, mate? You're gorgeous! What did she say?'

'She wants to take me to the Tim McGraw concert in Townsville this weekend. Apparently she bought two tickets and was starting to worry that she might be going on her own. She said it all worked out for the best that she hadn't found anyone, because now she gets to take me.'

'Ooh, you lucky bugger! I love Tim McGraw. I wanted to go to the concert, but it's a bit hard with Rose. I'd feel bad leaving her for a whole weekend. You'll just have to take heaps of photos for me. I'm so jealous you'll get to see Tim McGraw live.'

'I promise I will. I got a bit gutsy and told her I didn't want to wait that long to see her again, and we've decided to catch up tomorrow night at my place. I'm cooking her dinner, so fingers crossed it all goes well.'

'You go, girlfriend! I'm so happy for you.'

'Thanks. Hey, enough about me though. How are you feeling about the whole Mark thing this morning?'

Molly fumbled with the brim of her hat, something she always did when she was anxious. 'I've decided I'm going to spend some time with him first. You know, before I tell him. I need to make sure he's a decent bloke before I drag him into Rose's life. We've survived quite well without him, so what's the rush? At least I've finally found him. That's the main thing.' Molly felt like she was trying to convince herself, not Jade, about her decision.

'Do you think you could fall for him, Molly? I mean, wouldn't it be perfect if he turned out to be the man of your dreams?'

'Yeah, well, he's certainly good-looking and seems really nice, but I'm trying hard not to think that way just yet, even though it's bloody hard. I mean, we don't know each other at all. I reckon it's more important right now to try to keep emotion out of it and look at the situation from my head, not my heart.'

'Well, whatever you decide to do, you know I support you one hundred per cent, my friend.'

'Thanks. I'm going to run it all by Trev, though, as he always gives good advice. I might have a chat to him now if you want to ride with Heath and Kenny. Do you mind?'

'Not at all, Molly. I'll keep them entertained while you talk to Trev.'

The friends parted ways and Molly ambled Leroy up alongside the older man.

'Trev? I'd love to hear what you think about something that's on my mind,' Molly said. Trev nodded complacently and then listened intently while Molly filled him in, all the while shaking his head in disbelief. He took a deep breath before answering, as if drawing on the earth's energies to give him the right answer.

'Well, that's a curly one, all right. I'm like you when it comes to being cautious about people, Molly. I've learnt the hard way in life not to trust anybody until they've earned it. I reckon you've made the right decision about not telling the bloke for now. I mean, it would be nice for Rose to know her father, but then again, he could be someone you and Rose definitely don't need in your lives. I'll keep my eye on him for you, mate. You know, check him out and get my own sense of him. Meantime, follow your gut instincts, Molly. That's the best advice I can give you. You're a smart girl and you'll do the right thing.'

Molly gave him a grateful smile. 'Thanks heaps, Trev. And please don't tell Granddad or Grandma any of this, okay? They're getting too old for this drama and I don't want to stress them out. I'll tell them myself when the time is right, I promise.'

Trev ran his fingers along his weather-worn lips. 'My lips are sealed.'

*

As the bush began to open up and the track beneath them widened, Molly gave Leroy the cue to go for a gallop. She felt his muscles tighten beneath her as he spread his stride and ran for gold. The other four followed suit, enjoying the wind tearing past them as they dashed towards their destination. Heath tried to overtake Molly, a challenging smirk curving his kissable lips, but she refused to let him past and pushed Leroy that little bit harder, grinning at Heath victoriously as he came up beside her, Leroy's nose still a feather's breath ahead of JD's. They were back to normal, acting as though nothing had happened between them, which was a relief to Molly after the tension back at the cottage. Too busy competing with each other, they were taken by surprise as Jade came flying past them, beaming gallantly. Heath and Molly laughed as Jade reached the sparkling river bank ahead of them, throwing her hat up in the air in victory. Meanwhile, it took five more minutes for Kenny and Trev to reach them. They had given up a kilometre back, quite happy to let Molly, Heath and Jade fight it out for first place.

The five of them took off the horses' saddles before leading them into the river for a well-deserved swim. Leroy loved the water and he revelled in it now, kicking up sprays of water as he dunked his head and blew water from his lips. Molly gave him a few minutes to let off some steam before grabbing a handful of his mane and gently pulling herself onto his back. She laid out flat against him, wrapping her arms around his big strong neck while he swam beneath her, making sure she kept well away from his legs, which were kicking madly underneath the water. She had been caught out once before by Leroy and it had hurt like hell. He had left a massive black and purple bruise on her shin for a week, and even now, when she thought of the pain, it made her cringe.

Molly closed her eyes, blissfully relaxed as she lay on Leroy, the speckles of sunlight filtering through the paperbark trees delightfully kissing her skin, until a splash of water snapped her out of her trance-like state. Heath grinned back at her mischievously as he splashed more water in her direction.

She squealed, trying to avoid the playful attack as she dove under the water, swimming out of the path of Leroy and aiming for Heath's legs. She grabbed hold of them, tugging him under the water. Heath pretended to struggle, his powerfully built body an obvious winner over Molly's petite frame, but he let her believe she was winning all the same. They wrapped their arms around each other, tumbling under the water playfully and coming up for lungfuls of air, laughing wholeheartedly when they did so. They were completely unaware of Jade, Kenny and Trev, who were swimming over to the other side of the dam.

The enjoyable romp continued for a few minutes, until they were both utterly exhausted. Molly floated on the water, trying to catch her breath, while Heath held her there with his hands resting under the small of her back. Their laughter slowly subsided, the atmosphere turning electric when their gaze came to rest on one another's. Heath's intense eyes told Molly everything: everything he felt, everything he wanted to do to her, everything she had been questioning since they had kissed.

Molly's pulse quickened, her breath escaping her in short gasps as she smiled shyly at him, every contour of his gorgeous face now close enough for her to reach out and touch, to kiss, to caress. The urge to do so was all-consuming and it shocked her, frightened her. Was she being disrespectful to the memory of Jenny? She turned away, and Heath gently sighed, his hands delicately moving from the soft curve of her back as he swam away from her and towards JD, his horse.

There was no denying it; things had *definitely* changed between her and Heath and she wasn't sure whether she was glad of the fact or not, even though she was now acutely aware she *was* harbouring some feelings for him. Oh shit, what a tangled web she was caught up in.

Once they all began to look like prunes the group headed back to the shade of the paperbark trees that had been planted many years ago to help stop the erosion of the Walsh River banks. After getting the horses settled, the men headed off to unpack the fishing gear while Molly and Jade set up the picnic blanket with some food. Molly had packed baked ham and pickle sandwiches, rum balls, fruit mince pies and Christmas cake, all left over from the Christmas celebrations. Trev had brought along icy-cold beers to wash it all down. Once the food was set out, the group ate to their hearts' content, leaving nothing but crumbs as evidence of their ravenous feast for the hundreds of ants to carry away.

'I reckon it's time to chuck in a line, guys and gals,' Heath said, taking off his damp singlet and hanging it on a nearby tree branch to dry in the sun. Molly hesitantly admired his well-formed six-pack for a second before turning away, not wanting to be caught perving.

'Who's up for the challenge of catching the biggest fish?' Jade asked as she got out her hand line, putting a piece of wiggling bait on the hook.

'I'm up for that!' Trev answered smugly. He had always seemed to have the luck of the Irish when it came to fishing.

'What's the prize going to be, Jade?' Kenny asked as he threw his line and it landed with a plop in the water.

'Um, how about we all put ten bucks in and the winner takes all?' Jade said after thinking for a moment.

They all nodded eagerly, and spent the next hour taking in the peace and beauty of the river as it glistened before them like a diamond in the sunlight. That was the great thing about hanging out with good mates, Molly thought, you didn't have to fill in the silences. Although she was beginning to wonder if she could really class her and Heath as 'mates' any more, for there was far more than that between them, an entire undercurrent of feelings trying to claw their way to the surface. Did she *really* want to go there with Heath? It didn't feel like a wise idea when they worked together all the time. Mind you, that was the least of her worries. The biggest worry was Jenny. Even though her friend had passed away, Molly should know better than to go lusting after a mate's boyfriend. Especially now she had found Mark. She owed it to herself and Rose to see if she and Mark had a chance ... and there had undoubtedly been a spark between her and Mark last night. She glanced up at the heavens, wishing her parents could give her some kind of sign. But then again, maybe they already had. Maybe that was why Mark had come back into her life.

Kenny was the first and only one that got a decent-sized bite. He jumped up from his position on the ground and reeled in his prize catch, smiling proudly as the group huddled around him to see what it was. It was only a catfish and no good for eating, but it was the biggest catfish any of them had ever seen.

'Well done, mate,' said Heath, patting Kenny on the back. 'We'll give you the money when we get home.'

Trev was slightly gutted that he didn't live up to his image of the master fisherman but he was a good sport. 'The look of surprise on your face when you caught that fish was priceless. That thing is a bloody whopper!' he said, smiling.

'I suppose we should pack up and head home before it gets dark, you lot,' Molly said.

'Yeah, I have to get sorted for tomorrow,' Heath added. 'David wants me to get all the picking sticks and machinery ready this afternoon so we don't have to waste time doing it all in the morning.'

'Do you want a hand, Heath?' Molly asked, packing up her fishing gear, her heart pitter-pattering as her arm brushed against his.

'Nah, I'll be right, Molly. Thanks anyway.' Heath smiled. He was trying to act cool, calm and relaxed, but on the inside he was a mess, the desire to kiss Molly's soft, sweet lips close to unbearable. But did Molly want to kiss *him* again? That was the all-important question. He wasn't completely sure. One thing he *did* know for sure, though, he wasn't going to give up the fight for Molly Jones. The woman had stolen his heart.

CHAPTER

7

The kookaburras laughed melodiously in the distance, rousing Molly at sparrow's fart. She lay in bed, enjoying her last few minutes of peace and quiet, stretching blissfully, listening intently to the sounds outside her bedroom window. The birds were beginning to wake, singing sweetly, rejoicing in the beginning of a new day – or so Molly liked to think. There'd been a light shower during the night and green tree frogs were croaking delightfully in the downpipes of the house, the echo making it sound like there was an army of them. Cicadas noisily showcased their acoustic talents, singing out at over one hundred decibels each – an insect orchestra in the bush that was Molly's backyard. She would have to take Rose foraging so they could collect all the discarded cicada shells off the tree trunks. Rose loved taking those sorts of things for show-and-tell at school – if they stored the shells in a glass jar they would last for ages, seeing as school was still a few weeks away. Rex, the rooster, cock-a-doodle-dooed, proclaiming his power over the hens and announcing to all that this was his territory for yet another day.

Molly adored listening to the sounds of the earth as it awoke. It was her way of sneaking in a few minutes' meditation before she got out of bed. Her mind was much clearer and calmer after a good night's sleep, as though she knew which direction she was headed in. The kiss with Heath had been amazing, the thought of his lips caressing hers still sending tingles through her, rousing something deep inside her. The intensity between them at the dam yesterday intrigued her. But she couldn't go there with him, not when Mark had just waltzed back into her life, not when it went against everything she believed in. And on top of all that, just to make matters more complicated, it was way too coincidental to ignore Mark's surprise arrival back into her and Rose's life. She *had* to see if there was any possibility of a future for her and Mark, if the spark she felt on New Year's Eve was worth pursuing.

Today Molly and Rose were driving the cattle over to Rob and Cheryl's place, in Malanda. Molly loved Malanda. Although it was only a ninety-minute drive it felt like another world away, and she could almost imagine she was driving through the luscious green fields of Ireland, especially in winter when it was below zero and mist covered the hills and valleys like a comforting blanket. Over in the dairy country they were blessed, with plenty of feed nearly all year round. In Dimbulah they were lucky to make it a few months after the wet season before having to buy in fodder again.

Molly could hear Rose stirring in her room next door. She jumped up out of bed and ran in to Rose, diving under the sheets to give her an affectionate cuddle, then playing the part of the tickle monster as Rose squealed and giggled in delight.

Hearing the commotion, David made his way down the hall, stopping in the doorway of Rose's bedroom, a warm smile lighting up his face. He waited until their laughter subsided, watching mother and daughter together, before grabbing their attention. 'You two kids want some chicken bum nuts on toast before you head out this morning? Grandma is making them now if you do.'

'That sounds ripper, Granddad. Thanks! We'll be out in a minute. Rose and I just need to get dressed.'

Rose stuck her thumb up in the air. 'Yeah, ripper, mate!'

David chuckled. Rose had learnt that one from Rob when she was only two years old and it had stuck with her ever since.

*

After eating their poached eggs and giving Elizabeth a big kiss Molly and Rose headed out to the truck with Skip cavorting at their feet. They always took him on their road trips. He'd sit between them on the front seat like he owned it. Now and again Rose would allow Skip to sit on her lap, his head dangling out the window, his tongue flapping around in the breeze like it had a life of its own. Rose would shriek when a bit of Skip's slobber would fly back in through the window, giggling all the same.

Under David's direction, Molly reversed the truck up to the cattle yards until she was snugly up against the loading chute. It wouldn't be long before they could hit the road – this mob of cattle was a calm lot, and it wouldn't take much to get them loaded. Being herd animals, once a few climbed on board the rest would follow.

Molly and David worked at the back of the mob, guiding the cattle towards the loading chute. Rose and Skip stayed in the truck, their two heads squashed up against the back window so they could take in all the action. Red dust filled the air as cattle filed one by one up the ramp, their bellows echoing around them. Thirty minutes later, Molly, Rose and Skip were on their way.

As the scenery flashed past outside the truck, Molly switched on the local country-music channel. She recognised a song she liked and sang along to the radio. A road trip without country music wasn't half as much fun.

Rose giggled. 'Mum, you're way out of tune!'

Molly playfully stuck out her tongue and laughed. 'I reckon I should record an album. I'd make millions!'

'I don't think so,' Rose said, shaking her head.

'Well, how about you sing along with me? Then you won't be able to hear how bad I am.'

Rose thought for a few seconds. 'Okay. But only if you put on my favourite CD.'

Molly rolled her eyes. 'And let me guess, hmm, that wouldn't be Kasey Chambers, would it?'

'Oh, don't be silly, Mum! You know I love Kasey! She's the best country singer ever!'

'I think you could be right there. You'll have to find the CD in the glove box, sweetheart. Mum's a bit busy driving the truck.' Molly had heard the CD countless times, thanks to Rose's fixation with it, but at least she knew the words of *every* song and she'd have fun singing along with Rose.

The sun was settling into its rightful place, high in the sky, beaming its magnificent rays down on the landscape. Everything gleamed in the dew that had fallen overnight, including thousands of spiderwebs aglow amongst the native trees and shrubs on the sides of the uneven dirt road. Molly gazed out the windscreen, singing along with Rose and taking in the country as she drove. She was always amazed how much the scenery changed between Jacaranda Farm and Malanda, and she marvelled in its beauty every time she drove over there.

They got to the outskirts of Dimbulah, about thirty minutes from Jacaranda Farm, waving to everyone on the roads along the way. A gesture of hello changed from the city roads to the heart of the bush, something Molly had learned about drivers in Australia. In the city, most people waved and beeped frantically if they saw someone they knew, but drive an hour inland and it was a swift wave with an effortless lift of the hand instead. Go further into the bush and a hello became a simple lift of a finger off the steering wheel; even *further* it was basically a dip of the head. It was a small thing, but observing little differences like this between town and country people amused Molly. She wondered if anyone else even noticed. The small town of Dimbulah was bustling as locals ran their errands. Some people were picking up essentials from the local store and checking their mailboxes – the postman was totally unheard of in their parts – while others stood in the street yarning to neighbours, whom they had probably not seen in a week, given the long hours they had to put in with their crops and livestock, and the distances between properties.

Rose waved out the window to old Bluey, who was sitting on the park bench in front of the town's only bank. It was his daily ritual to sit in that very spot, enjoying the sunshine and watching the goings-on. He was a lovely bloke, and Molly felt sorry for Bluey. The only place he wanted to be was on the land, but he had to be near a hospital due to failing health. He loved pulling out his black-and-white photos from the good old days when he was a ringer. These days Bluey had to live between four walls instead of out on the land in his swag. Old age had made sure of that. Molly believed that Bluey's heart had been broken by living on a small block of land with a roof over his head instead of stars. His spirit lived in the bush, and that's probably where it had stayed the day he moved into what he called 'suburbia'.

It only took a minute to drive through the main street of Dimbulah, passing the hardware store, bakery, chemist, take-away shop, hairdresser's, Jade's beauty shop, two schools – the primary and the high school – and the pub, before they were on their way out of it. They passed paddock after paddock, full of horses and cattle, their heads down as they lazily chewed on grass. There was agriculture everywhere you looked, and Molly found it comforting to know there were so many people able to make a go of life on the land. Some farmers had chosen to grow hay, cashews, coffee or ti-tree while others grew mangoes, limes, lychees, paw paws and avocados. They were the main crops in this neck of the woods, but as you went further towards Malanda, and the environment and climate changed before your eyes, so did the crops. In Malanda, the farmers chose to grow potatoes, corn or peanuts, and sometimes even macadamias.

The next small town they passed through was Mutchilba, and if you blinked your eyes you would miss it. Molly swore under her breath when she barely avoided running over one of the Mutchilba shopkeeper's cherished peacocks. Somebody had run one over a month ago and the shopkeeper, Brian, had burst into the Dimbulah pub, after having one too many beers at home, demanding that the bastard who'd killed it own up. Nobody did. It was probably one of the many caravaners that had driven through on their way to Chillagoe.

The Mareeba to Dimbulah highway, known as the Wheelbarrow Way, was a very popular tourist road. Directional signs were placed strategically along the way, turning it into a scenic drive that took travellers deeper and deeper into the region, encouraging them to stay longer and explore the rich history. The name was an apt tribute to all the mining pioneers who had walked it over a century ago. The men pushed their wheelbarrows in which all their belongings were stored. Their wives walked behind with the children, their babies in their arms. These days the road was bitumen but every year the 'Wheelbarrow Way Race' was held as a way of keeping the history alive. Teams of people got together, some dressed up in outlandish costumes, and walked or ran the 137-kilometre trek from Mareeba to Chillagoe over a three-day period. It was one of the highlights of the year for the Dimbulah locals.

As the road stretched out as far as the eye could see, the paddocks on either side of the truck began to be filled with sugarcane instead of fruit trees. The flowers on the tops of the sugarcane danced in the breeze, creating a sea of soft shimmering pink that reminded Molly of fairy floss. The trees began to change, too. Some were remarkably old, bare of leaves, their branches resembling human limbs reaching towards the skies. Others had masses of green leaves adorning every branch; to Molly these stood for life and youth. Taken together, the trees provided a perfect example of the ebb and flow of Mother Nature. Vibrant bougainvilleas grew rampant in nearly every person's yard they passed; their radiance was striking.

'Mum, they're back again!' Rose shrieked, pointing to a pair of wedge-tailed eagles on the side of the road up ahead. Rose loved birds and had a bird book at home that David had given her. She studied it endlessly with him.

Molly gazed as the enormous eagles heaved themselves up and into the air, out of the way of the oncoming truck. 'Yes, darling, they're such beautiful birds. They come every year around this time, don't they? You'll have to tell GG when we get home. He'll be really excited that they're back.'

Rose nodded, deep in thought, as the eagles flew towards the mountains and gradually disappeared from sight. 'Do you think they're flying back to their baby birds?'

'They might be, sweetheart. Eagles normally keep their nests up on the mountaintops, out of the reach of predators.'

'How lucky for the baby birds,' Rose replied distantly.

'Yes, it *is* lucky. That way the babies don't get eaten by dingoes or snakes,' Molly said, intent on watching the road.

'No, I meant they're lucky to have a mum *and* a dad,' Rose said quietly.

Molly reached over and held Rose's little hand, squeezing it tight. 'I'm so sorry that you don't know your dad, Rose, darling, I truly am. But hopefully you will meet him one day.'

Rose squeezed Molly's hand back. 'It's not your fault. I love you, Mum. We do alright on our own, anyway.'

'Yes, we do, don't we?' Molly replied, blinking back tears. 'I love you too, sweetheart, more than all the stars in the sky.'

Thank God Mark had come back into her life, she thought. Maybe now she'd finally be able to give Rose something she so badly wanted – the chance to know her father. Fingers crossed that when she told Mark, he'd be happy about having a child – a beautiful and intelligent daughter that he could love just as much as Molly did.

Molly slowed the truck down as she indicated, turning to take the back route to Malanda. They passed the Lotus Glen prison and the sugarcane mill before taking a sharp left towards Atherton. It was here that the scenery really began to change. The grass took on a deep shade of green and the cattle looked fatter from enjoying their daily feast. The red dust that blanketed everything in sight around Dimbulah was left behind and instead there was red mud, which stained everything that came into contact with it. It was perfect soil for potatoes and vegetables, and macadamias too. Molly slowed again as they approached the famous little humpy store, giving the traffic behind her plenty of warning that she was intending to pull off the road. The truck turned slowly into the cul-de-sac before coming to a complete stop, the brakes loudly releasing air.

Molly undid her seatbelt and fished around on the floor for her wallet. 'You want to come in and get some nice hot nuts and a drink, Rose?'

Rose licked her lips. 'Yes, please, Mum. I'm starving, Marvin!'

Molly patted Skip on the head. 'You stay here and mind the truck, mate, but don't worry; I'll bring you something tasty back, too. I always do.'

Skip whimpered as he slumped down on the seat in defeat, obeying his master. Molly checked that all the cattle were content in the back before heading into the shop with Rose skipping beside her.

Molly and Rose filled their shopping bags with warm macadamia nuts, homemade cookies, tropical fruit, chocolates, jams and drinks. The humpy was an icon around the Tablelands, supplying its customers with delicious local produce and homemade goodies. Molly had been coming here since she was a kid. Her favourite item in the shop was the guava jelly, which she spread thickly on her breakfast toast for a sweet treat. She made sure to grab two jars of that and also a jar of rosella jam for David and Elizabeth. Not that the jam contained birds; it was made from the red pods of a wild bush that thrived around the tropics – a very pretty bush to have in the garden and a close relation to the hibiscus.

Skip sniffed the contents of the bags, eagerly awaiting his treats as Molly and Rose settled back into the cab of the truck.

Molly pulled a biscuit from the bag and handed it to him. 'Here you are, mate.'

Skip scoffed it down in seconds, licking every last crumb from his lips.

'You guts!' Rose squealed, scratching him behind the ears. She pulled on her seatbelt and settled back with the bag of macadamias. 'These are yum,' she added, passing the packet over to Molly. 'Want some, Mum? I know they're your favourite.'

'Hmm, don't mind if I do,' Molly replied, placing the packet in her lap for easy access. Rose wriggled excitedly as she searched the bag for the next treat to devour. Molly knew that stopping at the humpy was one of the highlights of the trip for Rose, as she wasn't allowed to eat much junk food at home. Molly let out a little burp and mother and daughter both cracked up laughing. What a wonderful way to spend the day, Molly thought contentedly.

*

As they neared Malanda Molly noticed Rose begin to fidget in her seat, Rob and Cheryl's farm now only minutes away. She knew Rose couldn't wait to get there. Rose adored them both and loved visiting their place. Without checking the distance already travelled Molly knew they were close, as the temperatures had dropped enough for her to feel a little cool. Mist covered the tips of the hills that rolled out endlessly before her and she couldn't help imagining that the lush green grass was like a big electric blanket that protected the valleys beneath from the cold. It was nothing like the brown paddocks they had back home with a heat that nearly cooked her and flies that drove her absolutely nuts. The cows even looked happier over here, Molly thought. They had big, plump bellies from all the grass they could eat and, as Rose had once brought to her attention, the cows mooed like they were singing. Molly smiled as she recalled the time Rose had asked David why the cows over this way had huge black spots. GG had lovingly explained to her that it meant they were cows used for milking. He had taught her so many things over the years, even how to say the alphabet backwards, which all her friends at school thought was really cool. One day, on a drive over, Rose had even asked Molly if they could live here in Malanda. Molly had told her that it was too cold and wet and it gave you mould in your bones if you stayed too long. Rose just giggled when Molly said stuff like that, rolling her little green eyes at her like she knew Molly was just pulling her leg.

Skip barked animatedly as they pulled into Rob and Cheryl's drive. Molly chuckled at the way his whole body shook as his tail took on a mind of its own. His sister Dusty lived here and Molly knew Skip loved coming to have a frolic around the gardens with her while she and Rose did their thing. He bounded onto Rose's lap, evidently keen to escape the confines of the truck.

Cheryl waved blissfully from her spot on the front verandah, a cup of steaming coffee in her hands and the newspaper in her lap. Molly waved back as she drove past the house and towards the yards to off-load the cattle. Rob was already down there, fixing one of the gates.

'Hi, Rob,' Molly called out the window.

'Hey there, Molly, be with you in a second. G'day, young Rose. Better finish up here or we'll have all your cattle loose. Some silly bugger reversed into the gate with the tractor!' he said with a guilty grin.

'I wonder who that was,' Molly called back, laughing as she spotted Rob's tractor parked to the side, the back end of it looking the worse for wear.

*

Once the cattle were all off safely, Molly whistled to Skip, letting him know he could come down from the cab to play with Dusty.

'We better go and say hi to Aunty Cheryl then, Rose,' Molly said, shivering from the sudden drop in temperature. Her body wasn't built for the cold. It made her bones rattle and her teeth ache.

'Yay! I want to tell Aunty Cheryl about all the yummy food we ate on the way over!' Rose grinned, bits of chocolate biscuit still stuck in her front teeth.

'Oh, you'd better not do that, sweetheart. I reckon Aunty Cheryl's been flat out in the kitchen all morning making us lunch. She'll be a bit disappointed we didn't save our bellies for the feast she's prepared. Am I right or am I right?' Molly asked, raising her eyebrows in Rob's direction.

'You're spot on, love. Cheryl's been cooking up a storm in there. There's a roast chook and potato salad and Rose's favourite, pavlova with cream and strawberries. So you better make room for lunch or you'll be in right trouble with the boss of the house,' Rob said, chuckling.

*

After Cheryl's delicious lunch, Molly felt she was going to burst. She unbuttoned the top of her jeans, letting out a huge sigh of relief when the pressure eased. She rested back on her chair, uneasiness making her fidget as she waited for everyone else to finish eating. Molly was normally so relaxed in her aunt and uncle's company but today her mind kept wandering off elsewhere, torturing her with images of Mark smiling at her on New Year's Eve and Heath's penetrating gaze at the dam. She knew Cheryl could sense her preoccupation, as her aunt kept glancing sideways at her, a worry line creasing her chubby brow.

Molly's bladder suddenly started screaming for reprieve so she excused herself from the table. She had to laugh when she sat down on the loo. Cheryl had hung a little sign in the dunny that read, 'Changing the toilet roll does not cause brain damage!' What a crack-up.

She walked back into the kitchen, still feeling uncomfortably full. 'Hey, Rob, how about you hand me that tea towel and I'll help Cheryl clean up while you play with Rose.'

'Good idea. I reckon I got the better end of the deal too, getting to muck about with Rose. I love any excuse to be a kid again,' Rob said as he chucked the tea towel at Molly and disappeared out the kitchen door.

The women washed up in silence for a few moments before Cheryl loudly cleared her throat, catching Molly's faraway attention. 'So, Molly, love, tell your favourite aunty what's bothering you. You seem a little, well, distracted today. Is everything okay?'

'What do you mean? I'm fine,' Molly replied, taking a sudden interest in getting the plate she was holding as dry as possible, not wanting to look Cheryl in the eye.

Cheryl touched her on the arm. 'Don't get me wrong, you don't have to talk about it if you don't want to, but you're not yourself, love. Just know I'm here if you want a chat.'

Molly shook her head gently. 'You know me too well. I'm just having a bit of man trouble, that's all – nothing I can't handle.'

Cheryl sighed. 'Ah, men, you can't live with them, but you can't live without them. I didn't know you were seeing anyone. Who is he?'

'Oh, I'm not really seeing anyone yet. It's just a guy I'm interested in. I want to wait to see how things go before I tell anyone about him though. It might come to nothing.'

'Well, I'm dying to know who it is,' Cheryl said, ripping off her bright-pink gloves and hanging them on the tap. She turned to Molly with raised eyebrows. 'I hope you don't mind me putting my two bob's worth in but you know what? I reckon you and Heath would make a great couple. I know you might feel obligated to respect Jenny's memory, seeing you two were so close, but honestly, love, Jenny's gone now and there's nothing we can do about that, and people's lives have got to go on. Any fool can see that Heath fancies you, and he adores Rose. He's a decent bloke, and very easy on the eye, too, if I might say so. It's not Heath, is it?'

Molly gasped, unable to hide her shock, the memory of kissing Heath flooding back to her in an instant. She instinctively touched her bracelet, fumbling with it, not knowing what to say, the world feeling as though it was spinning beneath her feet. She took a deep breath, exhaling slowly. 'Heath, oh no, we're just good mates.'

Cheryl touched Molly on the cheek, creating a moment of warmth and understanding. 'Sometimes, we can be so busy looking for something, we don't recognise what we already have. And the things we dream of can be right under our noses. Remember, dear, you don't have to go searching for love – it will find you. You have to believe that. Just trust in your instincts and follow your heart.'

Molly reached out and hugged her, emotion catching in her throat as tears filled her eyes. 'I love you so much, Cheryl. Thank you for always caring about me, and Rose.'

Cheryl squeezed her tight. 'I love you too, both of you.'

*

At four o'clock Molly and Rose said their goodbyes, whistled up Skip, and climbed back into the truck. Just as Molly was about to drive away her mobile phone rang. She didn't recognise the number, and her heart almost stopped when she heard Mark's voice after she took the call.

'Hi, Molly Jones. How are you?'

'Hey, I'm great, thanks. How are you?' Molly tried hard to sound completely normal, but she noticed Rose gave her a curious look.

'I'm good, thanks. Plodding along. Hey, Molly, I was hoping you could do some work on my mare like we talked about on New Year's. How's later this week looking for you?'

'Oh, yeah, sure. You can come over on Friday if you like.'

'Great! I just need your address.'

Molly filled him in.

'Okay, got it, thanks. I'll call you if I get lost. Look forward to seeing you, Molly.'

'No probs. Catch you then.' Molly flipped the phone shut and noticed her hands were shaking. She looked across at Rose, now completely focused on playing with Skip on the front seat, and felt a tug at her heart strings. Why had she become so emotional when she was talking to Cheryl? Was it because she was dreading telling Mark about Rose? Or was it because she was afraid she was falling in love with Heath Miller?

CHAPTER

8

Lightning flashed across the night sky, illuminating Molly's room. It took her back to her childhood when, petrified of the monsoon storms that would arrive without warning, she would hide under the bed clutching her teddy bear to her thumping chest as rain hammered deafeningly on the old tin roof. Her mum or dad would come running in to comfort her, telling her that the thunder was just God moving his furniture about and the rain was him watering his gardens. She smiled at this memory of her parents as she rolled on her side and buried her head into her pillow.

Molly slept fitfully, tossing and turning for hours until she finally fell deeply into the land of dreams, a land of dreams that was filled with the faces of two very different men, one she hardly knew and one she felt like she had known for a lifetime. At about five in the morning she woke needing desperately to go to the toilet and, once she had, she couldn't go back to sleep. Cheryl's words were still rolling around in her mind, teasing her, tempting her, confusing her. She huffed loudly, pushing herself out of bed, and decided she might as well get up and make herself a cup of extra-strong black coffee. Mark was meeting her at eight so she had a few hours to get her nerves under control.

Molly flopped down on the comfortable old lounge chair on the front verandah, watching the sun come up. Skip came to sit beside her and she tenderly rubbed his head, chatting away to him as if he was a person. He was the best listener she had ever met. She watched as one of the chooks went scooting across the front lawn in an attempt to make a break for it while there were no dogs to contend with. With a start Molly recalled she had forgotten to shut the chook-pen door last night, and she prayed that nothing had gotten in the pen for a midnight feast. It was common for dingoes to come sniffing around if they knew there was live food on offer.

She grumbled as she got up from the chair – knowing she should check the chooks out before she made breakfast – telling Skip to stay where he was, or else. She didn't feel like reprimanding him this early in the morning if he were to chase the chooks. Molly got to the bottom of the steps and pulled on her boots. What a sight I must look, with frazzled bed-hair, my polka-dot PJs and a pair of boots, she thought, having a chuckle at her own expense.

Mack and Sasha yapped excitedly as she walked past the kennels, obviously eager to get out of the enclosure and get up to some type of mischief for the day.

'I'll let you guys out in a minute!' she called back to them. Sasha's tail was wagging out of control, slapping Mack in the face as he ran around beside her. Molly couldn't help but smile. Puppies were so adorable.

'Well, well, don't *you* look stunning this morning, Miss Molly Jones?'

Molly just about jumped out of her skin as she spun around, spotting Heath heading in her direction, a chook in his hands. A weird sensation washed through her body, sending her heart racing. She fought hard to ignore it.

'Thanks, Heath,' Molly said, striking a pose in her PJs as if she was a contestant on *Australia's Next Top Model*. 'This is the new work wear for the farm. Like it?'

'I don't think it would suit me, Molly, but you wear it fantastically,' Heath replied huskily, amusement written all over his face as he playfully eyed her up and down.

Molly blushed under his mischievous gaze. 'I don't know about that. I can just picture Kenny wearing it, though!' she replied, laughing, relieved the tension from two days before had eased.

Heath shook his head and smiled. 'Kenny would wear anything, or nothing.' He handed Molly the hen, which was flapping like crazy. 'I *just* saved this one from being picked up by a wedge-tailed eagle. I was sitting on the front patio having my morning cuppa and suddenly this chook went tearing by at warp speed, clucking like a lunatic. I thought maybe Skip was chasing it so I went to tell him off, and instead I found an eagle coming in for the swoop. I hit the deck just as it came in with its claws extended for the kill. It almost picked me up instead. Talk about almost giving a bloke a heart attack!'

Molly burst out laughing. 'Oh no, that's terrible! I've heard that eagles take chickens, but I've never seen it with my own eyes. Thanks for being the hero and saving my mate here, anyway,' she said, taking the chicken from his hands.

Heath smirked. 'No worries, Molly. You owe me one, though, after having to make a fool of myself in front of the blokes.'

'Sure. You let me know what I can do to make it up to you,' Molly said jovially, unable to meet his deep-blue eyes. They were making her feel giddy.

Heath cleared his throat, images of Molly making it up to him in unspeakable ways causing him to crave her even more.

'Um, well, there is one thing ... Me and the boys are planning a pig hunt tonight. The bloody things have been ripping into the mango crop and your grandfather wants us to cull a few. Not that we mind – you know how much we love pig hunting. *And* it would be a great help if you could come along to lend your expertise.'

Molly's face lit up. 'Of course I'll come along with you! What time should I be ready?'

'Meet us at the cottage around ten tonight. Is that okay for you?'

'Not a problem. Now, I better get this chook back in the pen before it has a heart attack. The poor bugger's losing feathers like they're going out of fashion.'

'See you tonight then. Have a great day,' Heath replied, grinning at Molly in her PJs as she wrestled with the chook and the pen door. God, she was beautiful. Even first thing in the morning she had the ability to take his breath away. What he would give to wake up beside her every day. It would be a dream come true.

*

Rose had decided to help Elizabeth bake cookies for the morning and Molly was silently relieved. Her daughter would be busy when Mark arrived. Molly wasn't ready to see Mark and Rose together, not yet.

Rose looked adorable in the little floral apron that Jade had bought her for Christmas. Molly made a mental note to call Jade later. She wanted all the goss on her first date with Mel and, knowing Jade, it would be a thrilling tale indeed.

Molly felt her belly turn over with nerves when she heard Skip barking out the front, letting her know there was somebody coming down the driveway. She ran into the bathroom and quickly rinsed her mouth out with some mouthwash, jumping up and down on the spot as it exploded in her mouth, making her eyes water. She glanced at her reflection in the mirror, hoping she could conceal the cyclonic emotions she was feeling deep inside, her emerald-green eyes prominent against her olive skin and jet-black hair. She practised her best smile, pleased with her poker face, before heading out onto the front verandah just as Mark was pulling in. She took a deep breath and cleared her throat as she walked towards him. 'Hey, Mark!'

'Hi. How are you on this fine morning, Molly?' he answered, flashing a sexy smile as he got out of his Toyota, his white teeth in perfect contrast to the dark honey colour of his skin. He quickly ran a hand through his unruly brown hair, his long fringe flopping back down into his chocolate-brown eyes by the time he stretched out his long legs.

Molly felt her face flush as she fiddled with the brim of her hat. 'I'm great, thanks. Looking forward to meeting this wonderful mare of yours.' She was eager to stick to the task at hand, staying in her business frame of mind. It was a comfortable place for her out in the round yard and she couldn't wait to get the small talk over and done with so she could get down to work. It meant she didn't have to focus her attention on Mark.

'You just point out where you'd like me to park, and I'll unload her from the horse float,' Mark said.

'Yep, no worries. Just park over there under the wattle tree, but I'd prefer it if I got her off the float, mate. All part of the way I work, if you don't mind.'

'Alrighty then. I'm warning you, though. She's a livewire,' he said casually as he turned on his heel and hopped back into the driver's seat.

Molly watched on as Mark parked up in the shade, her emotions calming slightly at the thought of the task at hand. As soon as he had come to a stop she walked towards the back of the horse float. 'What's her name?'

'I've called her JJ, after Janis Joplin. She's a bit of a rebel, just like Janis was.'

Molly slowly opened the back of the float, talking softly to JJ and avoiding making any loud noises or sudden movements. First impressions meant a lot with a horse, and Molly wanted to make a good one. 'Hey, beautiful girl. You ready for some work?'

JJ whinnied, shuffling nervously, her hoofs tapping on the floor like a tap dancer as she moved around the confined space. Molly eased her way into the float, talking soothingly the whole time. She carefully undid the lead rope from inside the float and gently backed JJ out. The horse took her time, assessing if there were any dangers lurking outside the float. Molly let JJ do what she needed, at the same time giving the horse gentle commands to let her know that even though Molly wanted to make friends, she was also the boss.

Finally JJ emerged from the float, and Molly could feel the tension oozing out of her as she led her towards the round yard. She was a beautiful thoroughbred, her coat the same jet-black colour as Molly's hair with a striking star that sat perfectly on her forehead as if painted there. Molly stopped and let the horse sniff the gate to allow her to get used to the surroundings, holding the lead rope with one hand while she ran the other hand over the raw timber, assuring JJ it was safe to go in. The mare, anxious, backed up a few steps and Molly allowed her the space, still in charge but respecting the horse's needs. JJ's ears were flat on her head, not a good sign, and Molly prepared herself for what might be a bit of a temper tantrum. JJ neighed loudly before rearing up in the air, aggressively pronouncing her dislike of the situation. Molly stood her ground, keeping enough space between her and JJ for safety but still holding the lead rope firmly in her hands. Out of the corner of her eye she saw Mark racing up to them and immediately held up her hand, signalling him to stop without uttering a word. Mark stopped dead in his tracks, obeying Molly's wishes, as JJ's front legs came back down to the ground with a massive thump, kicking up the dust with her feet. Molly used all her strength to keep hold of JJ's lead rope as she demanded attention from the horse with her firm, direct words. The horse went to kick but Molly saw it coming and jumped out of the way.

Molly kept up a stream of soothing talk and JJ remained still, her ears flicking forward as she began to relax and listen. After a few more minutes Molly calmly opened the gate and led JJ into the round yard without any problem.

Molly could feel Mark watching her but she ignored the urge to look over at him, instead focusing all her attention on the horse. She put the mare through her paces, lunging her on a long rope, continually changing the direction to keep JJ listening. After half an hour or so of hard ground work Molly felt it was time to put her favourite stock saddle on the mare. Mark had helpfully placed the saddle over the timber rails for her so she was good to go.

Molly tied JJ to the hitching rail, slowly rubbing the saddle blanket over her coat to let her get used the feel and the scent of it, and then positioning it carefully on her back. Very slowly, Molly picked up the saddle, allowing the mare to smell it thoroughly before putting in on. With added care and soothing words Molly buckled up the girth, being extra careful not to pinch JJ. She preferred to use a rope halter instead of a bridle, believing that a metal bit was too harsh on a young horse. There were no quick-fix solutions to changing horse behaviour so Molly was considerate, taking her time with all her movements, because establishing mutual trust between her and JJ was critical right now.

Molly heard the soft strum of a guitar and her attention was briefly drawn to Mark. He was sitting on the grass, leaning back against the massive trunk of a tall gum tree, guitar in his lap, intently jotting down something in a notebook with a cigarette hanging from his lips. Skip sat beside him, watching like an eager spectator. It was a nice picture, and Molly couldn't help wondering if Mark was writing a song. It sure looked like he was. What was it about?

She dragged her gaze back, pulling herself up into the saddle, keeping a firm grip on the reins so she could control the horse from where she sat. All her senses were alert, taking in everything JJ was telling her with her body language. She felt the horse tense up like a spring beneath her and she prepared herself for JJ's imminent buck. The mare jerked up her hindquarters, but Molly braced and planted her bum firmly in the saddle, her back feeling the brunt of the powerful jarring of every buck. At one stage, JJ had all four feet off the ground.

After a few minutes of thrashing about the mare evidently decided it would be less strenuous to allow the person in the saddle to stay on her back. JJ stood, breathing deeply, sweat making her coat shine in the sunlight like it was black silk. With gentle leg pressure Molly asked the mare to walk on. JJ took a cautious step forward. Molly leant over and gave the mare a tender rub on the neck, telling her what a good girl she was for moving forward without bucking. Molly could feel her shirt sticking to her back with sweat. Retraining a horse was so physically demanding. She had had to use every muscle in her body to stay in control. She knew she would feel it tonight, but she was happy with the progress she had made so far. She could tell from JJ's responses that she'd been schooled before. JJ just needed a bit of discipline after being turned out for so long. Molly continued to direct JJ around the yard, sending her left and right and eventually getting her to back up and drop her head. After another hour in the saddle, JJ was in need of a rest and some water and so was Molly. She was parched, her mouth drier than the Simpson Desert. It had been a good few hours' work.

*

Mark waited patiently until Molly had safely loaded the mare back into the float before speaking. 'Would you like a beer, Molly? I have a six-pack in the Toyota.'

Molly felt her pulse quicken, the thought of sitting down with Mark for a casual yarn making her slightly anxious, but then again, if she wanted to get to know him she had to make the effort and get over her nerves. 'Um, yeah, sure. Why not? The beers would be warm by now, though, wouldn't they?'

Mark smiled, obviously chuffed Molly had accepted his offer. 'Nope, icy cold they are. They're in an esky in the back. I'll just go grab them.'

Molly sat down under the gum tree as she waited for him to collect the beers, her eyes burning a hole through Mark's notebook resting beside her. She was dying to know what was written in there.

Mark appeared beside her and handed her a beer before sitting down next to her. 'You did brilliantly out there, Molly. I never thought JJ would respond so bloody well. The locals are right. You *are* a horse whisperer.'

Molly felt herself blush. 'Pfft, no I'm not! But thanks.'

'No, really. I wish I could do what you do. It's very impressive.'

Molly took a sip of her stubby then pointed the top of it towards Mark. 'I wish I could sing like you do. Now *that's* what I call impressive.'

'Oh, thanks, but honestly, I ain't *that* good,' Mark replied as he plucked a dandelion clock from the long grass and handed it to Molly. 'Here, blow this and make a wish. Who knows? It might come true.'

Molly's heart tap-danced at the unexpected romance of his gesture. She gently took the flower from him and closed her eyes, wishing with all her might that things would turn out for the best, and that she would choose the right path to follow. She blew delicately, smiling as the soft feathery flower broke up and floated effortlessly away in the subtle breeze.

Mark smiled at her as he placed his hand lightly on her shoulder and squeezed it gently. 'I'd love to know what you wished for. I know what I would have asked for. Would you like to have dinner at my place tonight? I'll even light some candles – make it, you know, romantic.'

Molly wasn't into candlelit dinners unless she knew the man exceptionally well. 'Oh, thanks for the offer but I can't tonight,' she answered, instantly seeing his disappointment. 'Would you like to come pig hunting tonight, instead?' she added hastily. She'd rather go on a first date out horse riding or pig shooting or fishing, where she felt relaxed. Not that she was asking Mark on a date. Or was she?

Mark's face lit up like a Christmas tree. 'Bloody oath! I love pig hunting! Count me in. What time do you start?'

'Oh, say about nine-thirty-ish. Give or take. I'm meeting the guys over at the workers' cottage at ten.'

How would Heath feel about Mark coming along? Over the past week Heath had proven to Molly that he had feelings for her, and the last thing she wanted to do was hurt him. To be honest, she had feelings for Heath too. Although just what type of feelings, she still wasn't certain. Heath had suffered enough heartache over the past year and she didn't want to be the cause of any more. But, on the other hand, she had to get to know Mark, and what was the harm in him coming on the pig hunt?

'Right, I'll see you back here round then,' Mark said as he opened the driver's door and hopped into his Toyota. 'And brilliant work today, by the way. Thanks. You'll have to let me know whether you'd like a cheque or cash for the work. Either way, it doesn't matter. Oh, and when would you like me to bring JJ back again?'

Molly did a quick mental review of all her jobs over the next few days. 'How about the middle of next week? I'm pretty flat strap until then.'

'That sounds good to me.' He tipped his hat and drove off down the drive, dust flying behind him.

*

When Molly got a minute from playing with Rose that afternoon, she picked up the phone and dialled Jade's number, eager to hear about her date with Melinda.

'Hey there, Molly! How are you? I was going to give you a call tonight but you've beaten me to it. We must have ESP.'

Molly smiled into the phone. 'I reckon we do, mate. We always go to ring each other at the same time. So, come on, spill the beans. I'm all ears!'

Rose handed Molly one of the Anzac biscuits she had made with Elizabeth, and Molly absently kissed her on the head as she listened to Jade.

'I'm going out to play with Mack and Sasha,' Rose whispered as she ran off down the hallway.

'Hang on a sec, Jade,' Molly said, interrupting her friend in full flight. 'Dinner will be on the table in half an hour, darling,' she called after Rose. 'Make sure you come back in and wash your hands then, okay?' Molly turned her attention back to Jade. 'Sorry about that, mate. You learn to do ten things at once when you have kids. Go ahead. I'm all yours again.'

'No worries, Molly. Say hi to Rose and make sure you give her a big mushy kiss from me too. It's been almost a week since I've seen her – way too long! But oh my goodness, Mel's amazing. She and I sat here until four this morning, drinking red wine, talking and talking – we even revealed to each other what our lifelong dreams were. It was so romantic.'

Molly was impressed. 'That's fantastic! I'm always telling you to get to know the girls better before jumping in the sack, and finally you've worked it out for yourself. A deep and meaningful can be just as great as sleeping together, if not better, I reckon. Did she stay over?'

Jade laughed. 'I knew you'd ask that! No, she actually went home. I'll admit I tried to get her to stay, but she refused. She did give me a kiss on the lips before she left, though, and I felt like I'd died and gone to heaven ...'

'Hmm. This one sounds like a real keeper. Not in it just for one thing. I hate men like that – I've got no time for them. Let's just hope Mark isn't one of them.'

'Hey yeah, have you seen him since New Year's?'

'He was here today with his mare. I didn't spend a lot of time with him because I was working, but I'm going pig hunting with the boys tonight and I've asked him to come along. I'll see if he can keep up with me out on the hunt!'

Jade laughed. 'Trust you to have your first date with him out pig hunting, Molly Jones. Gotta love ya!'

'Yeah, well, you know me. Always been the romantic type of gal.'

'Have fun, but just make sure you follow your heart, my dear friend. You don't want to rush into anything, and break your heart or someone else's in the process. Oh crap, look at the time; I better get moving. I have a massage client coming in ten minutes and I haven't even got the table set up yet. Why don't you and Rose come over for dinner on Thursday night? You can fill me in on your big pig hunting adventure then?'

'That sounds great. We'd love to. We'll see you around six, okay?'

'Brilliant. See you then, Molly. Love you!'

'Love you too.' Molly sat for a moment, staring at the phone, trying to rub away the tension building in her neck. What did Jade mean by telling her to follow her heart? And whose heart was Jade afraid she might break in the process?

CHAPTER
9

Heath opened the door of the workers' cottage and Molly saw his broad smile dissolving as he spotted Mark in the passenger seat of Molly's Land Cruiser. 'What's he doing here?' he asked gruffly, the muscles in his chiselled jaw tightening.

Molly tried hard to ignore his tone, a little taken aback. Heath had never spoken to her like this; in all the years they'd known each other they had never even had an argument. But she couldn't be angry at him for it. He didn't know anything about Mark being Rose's dad – she knew Trev wouldn't have told him. So could it be jealousy speaking? Or was there something else on his mind? It pained her immensely to not be able to tell him the entire truth but she just couldn't, not right now, not until she had spoken to Mark. 'I invited him along. Seeing he's new to town, I thought it might be great for him to meet you guys, you know, so he can make some mates out here in Dimbulah.'

After a tense moment, Heath nodded and smiled back at her. He was too afraid to speak in case he exploded. Him friends with

Mark? Molly had to be kidding! He yelled out to the guys, who were out the back, gearing their dogs up with chest plates and the GPS collars that were five hundred bucks a pop, ready for the chase. They had only started using the GPS trackers in the last few months and the devices were absolutely brilliant. They had a range of seven kilometres, meaning the group knew where their beloved dogs were at all times, which in turn made it easier for Molly and the guys to find them *and* catch the pigs.

Trev had two experienced pig dogs, Jocks and Tyson. They were both eager beavers when it was time for them to sniff out the pigs, knowing their role like it was second nature. Molly found it hilarious whenever Trev called out to Jocks. It sounded like he was looking for a pair of underpants, not a mean, keen, hunting dog.

Kenny's dog, Diesel, was a Rhodesian ridgeback, an enthusiastic hunter but also one of the most loving dogs you'd ever meet. Quite often Molly would find Skip and Diesel playing together at the dam. They were best buddies.

Heath's dog, Boozer, was a Bull Arab. He was bred purely for pig hunting. Once the dog had his gear on he was raring to go, eager to begin his ritual of sniffing out the scent of the pigs, chasing them down and holding them until Heath could get to him and deal with the massive beasts.

When the dogs were loaded into the back of the Cruiser the three guys jumped up into the tray themselves. 'Right when you are, Molly!' Trev yelled, tapping on the roof to let her know they were all in safely.

'Let's hit it then,' Molly called back as she started up the old girl. It coughed and spluttered for a few seconds, throwing a big puff of black soot out of the exhaust and into the huddle of men on the back. Molly laughed as she watched them wave their hands about frantically in a useless attempt to chase away the thick smoke, which was almost blacker than the night sky above them. The Cruiser set off down the dusty track as the full moon cast its brilliance across the paddocks. Once Molly's eyes adjusted to it, it was like driving around in broad daylight. It was a perfect night for a pig hunt.

Molly felt a flutter in her belly. She was always keyed up to get started and get her hands dirty, hunting down the pigs that ruined their vital crops. It was a sport you either loved or hated, she reflected. There were no in-betweens. Those who loved it, loved everything about it, but she knew others were repulsed by pig hunting. She reckoned that many of those people had no idea what it was like to lose the whole harvest, in one night, to a group of hungry feral pigs. It was heartbreaking.

Molly's next-door neighbours knew all too well the destruction pigs could wreak. They were pumpkin farmers – and pigs *loved* pumpkins. When the pumpkins were near to being harvested, Fred and Kathy spent sleepless night after sleepless night sitting in their Land Cruiser, guns loaded, ready to defend their livelihood. In Molly's part of the world, pig hunters were valued, not shunned.

*

On the back of the truck, Heath, Kenny and Trev watched the moonlit landscape pass by, not a sound in the world beyond the engine and the dogs' excited panting.

'I don't know why she had to bring him along,' Heath huffed, motioning to the cab of the truck with his thumb.

'Come on, Heath,' Trev said. 'We don't even know the bloke yet so we've got to give him a fair go. I've got my eye on him, though, don't you worry. I'll make sure he's worthy of Molly's company.'

'He'd better not hurt her. I'll break every one of his bones if he does.' Heath punched a fist into his open hand.

'Just try to be civil to the bloke, for Molly's sake. You don't want to upset her now, do you, mate?' Trev pleaded.

'I'll try, but I'm not promising anything.' Heath scowled.

Trev raised his eyebrows. 'Why are you so put out by him being around her, anyway? You haven't got the hots for the boss's granddaughter, have you buddy?'

Heath looked away.

Trev exhaled loudly. 'Oh shit, you do. So, what are you going to do about it, mate?'

Heath ran his hands over his face in frustration, sighing loudly. 'Fucking nothing. I can't do anything. I've had plenty of chances to tell Molly how I feel and now it looks like she's met someone else. My loss is his gain, as they say.'

Trev shook his head. 'I don't know what to say.'

'I reckon he looks a bit girly in his baggy jeans and flower-power shirt. Not really pig-hunting gear. He looks like a Hawaiian cowboy. Gone are the days where men were men and pansies were flowers,' Kenny said, grinning, trying to ease the tension, and all three men burst out laughing.

*

Molly parked up the back of the paddock, just inside the nets that protected the fruit from birds and bats, but not from pigs; the pigs barged right on through, leaving gaping holes in the nets that needed sewing up on a weekly basis. The hilly terrain spreading out behind them was rugged, the absolute definition of what people called hard country. Native trees grew on the sharp, rocky mountains, some covered in bright flowers, proof of their resilience in the unforgiving country that surrounded Jacaranda Farm.

They let the dogs down off the back, the animals' body language showing they were strongly picking up the scent of the pigs. Molly spotted fresh tracks that were wider than her boot in the dirt, and enthusiastically pointed them out to the men.

They motioned for their dogs to go, following on foot and trying hard to keep up with them on their passionate pursuit, but lost them within seconds. Heath skidded to a halt, ordering everybody else to stop. He assessed the luminous screen of the GPS he held in his hands, meticulously evaluating the distance and position of all the dogs.

Off in the distance there was a high-pitched squealing, which sounded like a colossal pig. The group ran in that direction, Heath calling out directions as they went. The adrenaline was pumping and Molly could feel her heart beating like thunder in her chest. Nobody spoke. The critical thing was to get to the dogs before the pig got the chance to fight them off. Molly had seen her fair share of injuries to their hunting dogs. Some were so bad that dogs had to be put down, which broke Molly's heart. Luckily, that rarely happened.

Molly couldn't believe her eyes when she saw the pig the dogs were holding down by its ears and cheek, their teeth hunkering down into the boar's flesh. It must have been well over 150 kilos.

Trev pulled his enormous hunting knife from the leather sheath on his belt, the moonlight flickering off the razor-sharp blade, and plunged it deep into the boar's heart. It was over in seconds. All went jarringly silent, except for the heavy panting of the dogs. A cheer erupted and the group crowded around to evaluate the size of the boar. It was the biggest Molly had ever seen.

'What a beauty, hey!' Kenny said.

'I reckon, but strewth I'm unfit! I'm sweating more than a pregnant nun in confession!' Trev wheezed. He lit a cigarette, blowing smoke rings from his lips and sighing in pleasure. Molly shook her head at the absurdity of his lighting up when he was complaining about his fitness level.

Heath slapped Trev on the back. 'Good catch, mate. I'll have to get a photo of this one to send to my parents. They'll be gobsmacked when they see the size of it.'

'What do *you* reckon, Mark?' Molly asked, wanting to include him in the conversation.

Mark was still trying to catch his breath. 'Fucking fantastic! Man, that was fun.'

Heath rolled his eyes. Even Mark's voice annoyed him. He knew he was being childish but he couldn't help himself. Molly Jones should be his and Mark was treading on his territory. What did the guy have that he didn't?

'Well, I reckon there are more where this guy came from. Let the hunt continue!' Molly said triumphantly, utterly wrapped up in the thrill of the chase, completely oblivious to Heath's jealousy, which was gaining momentum by the second.

They spent the next few hours running around the bush like a group of highly-trained soldiers. The total catch at the end of the night was three, an excellent haul for one night's pig hunt. The dogs could have kept going all night, but Molly and the men were weary from all the running about and decided it was time to head home and hit the sack.

Molly noticed her boot was torn and leant down to inspect the damage while the men loaded the dogs back up into the Cruiser. She caught Mark out of the corner of her eye staring at her bum for *way* too long. She straightened up, feeling very self-conscious, but also flattered that he found her attractive. Then she glanced over at Heath, and could tell by the fierce look in his eyes and his clenched fists that he had seen it too. She quickly ushered Mark into the Cruiser before Heath did something he might regret. Flipping heck, she didn't know how much more of being torn between two men she could take. It was exhausting *and* emotionally draining.

CHAPTER
10

Molly pulled into Jade's family's farm, hitting a water-filled pot hole in the drive that would have swallowed a small dog whole. A spray of putrid mud flew in Molly's window, leaving a trail of red earth dripping down her cheek and onto her new shirt. She wiped it away quickly, cursing under her breath, as she directed the Land Cruiser this way and that, trying to avoid the places where the dirt road had completely washed away. She could feel the tailgate slipping and sliding all over the place, as though she was driving on ice. The monsoon season had well and truly arrived, earlier than normal, and the rains had come down hard in the past couple of weeks.

Rose screamed as a massive black snake slithered across the road in front of them. Molly checked in the rear-vision mirror, hoping she had run the thing over, but it was nowhere to be seen. Snakes were fast, damn fast. She'd heard stories at the pub of people who thought they'd run a snake over only to find it wrapped inside their tyre arch when they pulled up. The very thought made Molly's skin crawl. She could handle snakes, but not when they came anywhere near Rose. Jacaranda Farm was an hour from the closest hospital and a snake bite to a small child could be lethal. Jade, on the other hand, loved snakes. She believed humans and animals were all connected, and went out of her way not to harm any living creature that made its way into her house. Molly found her way of thinking slightly weird, but endearing all the same. Jade's biggest fear was spiders, although she tried not to kill them unless completely necessary. Even moths and ants were sacred in Jade's hippy home.

Molly tooted her horn as she pulled up outside the front of the old corrugated-iron cottage, waving to Jade, who was hosing thick red mud from her car on the lawn near the front door. Jade had done an amazing renovation job on the cottage, and anyone who walked through the front door was surprised by the contrast between the outside and the inside. Jade had made the old place into a home, saving a place that was on its last legs, and filled it with her colourful, quirky furniture.

Molly loved hanging out at Jade's. She always felt at peace the moment she stepped through the door. Jade had made the place so warm and inviting, it felt like a sanctuary where Molly could just forget her troubles.

Molly had barely pulled into the drive before Rose was out of the passenger door and running towards Jade. Molly laughed as Rose whipped the hose out of Jade's hands and chased her around the yard, drenching them both in the process, giggling hysterically. Molly made sure to stay out of the war zone, not wanting to get wet, enjoying watching her two favourite girls having fun.

They all headed inside to the enticing smell of beef roasting in the oven. Molly almost had to wipe the drool from her lips. Her favourite meal of all time was a good roast, and Jade cooked the meanest one she had ever tasted.

Jade and Molly pottered around in the kitchen, rum and Cokes in hand, while Rose fed Ruby, Jade's pet cockatoo, strawberries in the lounge room. Molly took a sip of her gloriously strong drink. Jade always knocked her socks off with the amount of rum she put in the glass, but it didn't matter – she and Rose were staying overnight.

'Dinner looks brilliant! I can't wait to tuck in,' Molly announced, examining the amazing-looking roast beef that Jade had just taken out of the oven.

'Thanks, Mol. Can you carve the beef?' Jade asked her, handing over a knife. 'We've got all the trimmings too, of course: roast veggies, gravy – and I even took on the challenge of Yorkshire puddings, which look to me as though they're going to work!' Jade bent down to look through the glass oven door at the small Yorkshires rising. 'I've tried making them before but most of the time they end up looking like burnt pancakes and I've had to chuck them in the bin. I must've had that magic touch tonight.'

'You did go to some trouble for us. You're the bestest mate ever,' Molly mumbled through a mouthful of crispy beef fat, unable to resist peeling the crunchy skin off and scoffing it as she was carving the succulent meat.

'Dinner's served, sweetheart!' she called to Rose as she put the beef down on the dining table. She ducked into the living room to make sure Rose had put Ruby safely on her perch, her beak covered in strawberries, and led Rose to the bathroom to wash her hands before dinner.

Finally they were seated and Molly's eyes widened with hunger as she served herself from the feast before her. While they ate, Rose talked about everything she'd been doing during the school holidays, and Jade listened with interest as Rose described her adventurous days out on the farm.

Looking at Rose's bright eyes and animated face made Molly so happy. I can't be doing *too* bad a job as a mum, she thought suddenly, the guilt she constantly carried around about Rose's lack of father subsiding for the briefest of moments. Fifteen minutes later their plates were basically licked clean and stacked on the kitchen sink, and the trio relocated to the coziness of the lounge chairs. Jade flicked on the television so Rose could watch some cartoons. *Tom and Jerry* was on, and it took Molly back to the days when she was young. She and Jade used to sit and watch the very same cartoons together while gorging themselves on lollies and biscuits.

Suddenly, Molly felt something huge and furry crawl across her arm. She flung herself off the couch like she was leaping from a burning building, frantically trying to brush the gigantic huntsman spider away whilst shrieking at full volume. Finally flicking it off, she watched as it flew through the air, seemingly in slow motion, and landed on the couch next to Jade. Jade – who'd finally caught on to what was wrong with Molly after watching the spider land smack-bang beside her and scurry her way – also leapt from the couch, screaming like a mad woman and ripping her clothes off. In less than a minute, Jade was standing in the lounge room in just her underpants and bra while she brushed her skin off hysterically. Rose rolled around on the floor in fits of laughter.

'Watching you two dancing around like a pair of idiots is way funnier than watching the cartoons on telly!'

'You cheeky thing, Rose! That spider scared the life out of me!' Molly scolded half-heartedly.

'Me too! The bugger was looking for somewhere to hide in my clothes,' Jade said, giggling as she picked her strewn clothes up from the floor, shaking them all out thoroughly and getting dressed again.

'Do we know where it went?' Molly asked, looking around warily.

'It's probably hiding from you!' Rose said.

'Yeah, well, I wouldn't blame it after that,' Molly replied, giving up on the search and turning her attention to Rose. 'Sorry to end your fun, sweetheart, but you need to get ready for bed. It's nearly nine o'clock.'

Rose crumpled up her nose. 'Oh, Mum! I want to stay up with you and Jade.'

'Sorry, Rose. It's past your bedtime already,' Molly replied, touching Rose gently as she took her hand and led her into the bathroom to do her teeth. Afterwards she tucked Rose into bed in Jade's spare room. 'Good night, beautiful. Sweet dreams,' Molly said, giving her a kiss.

'Night, Mum. Love you,' Rose replied, yawning.

'Love you too. I'll leave the night light on for you.'

Molly snuck out of the room, knowing that Rose was probably almost asleep before she even reached the door. She took a quick glance back, her heart melting as she admired the innocent beauty of her daughter. When she got back to the living room she flopped back down on the couch beside Jade.

'So, are you looking forward to going to the concert this weekend?'

'I can't wait. It'll be great to spend some more time with Mel. We've talked every day since she was here for dinner.' Jade stared off into the distance, as though in deep thought, then turned back to Molly. 'Hey, I've been dying to ask, but I wanted to wait until Rose had gone to bed. How did it go out pig hunting with Mark?'

'Yeah, it was good. We had fun.'

'That's great, Molly! I hope you two hit it off, if that's what you truly want, of course.'

'Do you *really* hope so?' Molly asked, taking a sip of her drink.

Jade tipped her head to the side. 'What do you mean? I only want the best for you, and Rose.'

'The other night, on the phone, you told me to follow my heart and to be careful not to break anyone's in the process. I've been trying to figure out what you meant ever since.'

Jade looked sympathetically at Molly. 'Oh, mate. I'm sorry. It's just, um, how do I put this? I saw you and Heath kissing on New Year's. And let me tell you, sparks *flew*. I'd have been burnt to a crisp if I was standing beside you.'

Molly shuffled her feet nervously, her voice almost a whisper. 'I didn't think anyone saw that. Besides, it was just two mates wishing each other Happy New Year's.'

Jade laughed dismissively. 'Now, come on, Miss Jones. It was *way* more than that. Don't deny yourself the truth. The way he touched your face when he kissed you ... he obviously adores you. The question now is, how do you feel about him?'

Molly took a deep breath, finally allowing herself to accept what she already knew, and feeling safe enough to let her guard down in front of Jade. Tears sprang up in her eyes. 'Oh, Jade, what am I going to do? I have feelings for him too, but it's complicated, and I'm *so* scared. I feel like a bitch even thinking about Heath in any way other than a mate. I mean, Jenny and I were like sisters.'

Jade's eyes filled with compassion. 'Oh mate, don't you *ever* talk like that about yourself. You're such a kind and considerate person, which is why Heath adores you and it is also why Jenny would approve of him falling in love with you, and you with him.'

'Thanks, Jade, I appreciate the kind words. If only I could make myself accept them as true. But it's not the only reason, even though it's a biggy. There are other important things ... like the fact Heath and I have been friends for so long and I'm afraid we might lose all that if things go pear-shaped between us. And all these years I've been hoping Mark would somehow come back into my life – and now he's here! I feel like I *have* to see if there's a future for me and him, don't you think? I've had his child. I owe him and Rose that much.'

Jade reached out and took Molly's hand. 'I just want you to be sure you're seeing Mark for the right reasons. He can always be Rose's father without you needing to be his wife, you know.'

Molly nodded. 'I do know that, but it would be nice, wouldn't it, to all be a family together? So I really want to get to know Mark and see if there's anything between us – other than the sexual chemistry, which we established seven years ago. I need something deeper from him now, a connection on a level that creates love, not lust. I mean, there's no denying that he's hot in a rockstar kind of way, and I got the feeling last night that he feels the same about me ... On the pig hunt I caught him looking at my butt *way* too long.'

'You do fill out a pair of jeans nicely. You can't blame the guy.' Jade laughed.

'Shucks, thanks!' Molly giggled, wiping her tears.

'So, are you seeing him again anytime soon?'

'Yeah, I'm going to do some more work with his mare next week. I think I might offer to go to his place this time, if he has a round yard. It'd be good to see how he lives and how he keeps the place he's looking after. It might give me some more insight into the type of bloke he is.'

'Good idea. I reckon you can tell a lot about a person by the way they live. Take your time with everything though, Molly. I mean, Heath isn't going anywhere. Just be careful around him with Mark. It'll be hard for him and he's been through enough this past year without having his heart broken again.'

'I know. Believe me, the *last* thing I want to do is hurt Heath. He's one of my best mates.' Molly exhaled loudly. 'Anyway, enough stressing about men. Time for us girls to have some fun!' She tipped her glass upside down. 'I'm empty. Let's get a refill!'

*

A few drinks later, and feeling somewhat tipsy, the women decided to relive their youth and run around the backyard in an effort to catch cane toads. Jade wanted to eradicate a few, and being the peace-loving hippy that she was, she didn't believe in killing them. She insisted on putting them into a massive bin, ready to dump them at the edge of the property the following morning. Molly tried to explain between fits of laughter that the toads would just bounce their way back but Jade refused to change her views on what she referred to as 'cold-hearted slaughter' – knocking them over the head with a golf club, which was what Molly had suggested.

Molly spotted a toad the size of a baseball glove bounding across the lawn and ran after it with Jade's long-handled pooper-scooper in hand. Suddenly a bandicoot tore out of the bushes and scuttled across her bare feet, scaring the living daylights out of her and sending her flying backwards into Jade's large outdoor fishpond. She landed with a gigantic splash as the goldfish fled in every direction, panicked by the colossal obstacle that had just landed in their normally serene pond. Molly resurfaced with aquatic weeds wrapped around her face, spitting the fishy-tasting water from her mouth as she tried to peel a waterlily from her head.

In between fits of laughter, Jade grabbed Molly's outstretched hand, slipping on the wet grass as she tried to help Molly up.

'Shit, Jade! Who put this thing here?' Molly shrieked as she stood on wobbly legs, dripping in the foul-smelling water.

Jade took a few deep, giggly breaths, trying to regather so she could speak. 'You know that pond has been there since we were kids, Molly! You fell into it when you were twelve, too! This time was *waaay* funnier though!'

Molly tried to look serious. 'I was thinking environmentally. I thought I might save water by not having to have a shower before bed tonight, Miss Jade.'

'Yeah, right. Pull the other leg, mate! Your sense of balance is just whacked out from all the rum and Cokes!' Jade giggled. 'Now, we better get you a towel so you can dry off.'

Molly got a whiff of the odour on her clothes. 'If it's all right with you, I might have a shower. I smell like a trawler that's been at sea for months.'

Jade wrapped her arm around Molly's shoulder and sniffed her hair, retreating instantly. 'Mm, not a bad idea ... I don't want my sheets smelling like a fisherman has slept in them.'

*

Molly felt at peace as she and Rose left Jade's the next morning. It was such a relief to have finally talked about what was happening with Mark. She hadn't realised until last night how much she needed to talk to someone about it. Thank goodness for Jade, she thought. She put her sunnies on to protect her eyes from the bright morning sunshine, all the while enjoying the sun's warmth as it caressed her skin. Rose followed suit, putting her loveheart-shaped sunglasses on and giving Molly a big cheesy grin. Molly's heart swelled with love for her beautiful daughter. She was determined to give her little girl the best life possible. If that meant making things work with Mark so that Rose could grow up with both her parents, then that was exactly what Molly would try to do. She of all people knew how badly a child wants and needs their mother and father, and her feelings for Heath would have to stay where they were, buried deep down inside her.

CHAPTER

11

David clicked away on the camera as if he was the paparazzi as Rose paraded around in her new school uniform, beaming from ear to ear. Molly couldn't help admiring her daughter's beauty as Rose pulled on her backpack, preparing for her first day back at school after the long Christmas holidays. Molly could hardly believe she was starting Grade Two. It seemed like only yesterday that Molly was changing nappies and having sleepless nights getting up to breastfeed.

Molly pulled into the drop-off zone at the front of St Anthony's primary school and jumped out of the Land Cruiser, running around to meet Rose at the passenger-side door. She took her daughter's little hand and walked her to the door of the classroom, leaning over to give her a big cuddle and a kiss on the cheek.

'Now, you have a lovely day at school, sweetheart. GG's going to pick you up this afternoon because I'll be at work.'

'Okay, Mum. Love you.'

'Love you too, Rose,' Molly whispered in her ear. She watched as Rose disappeared into the sea of squealing children. Molly waved to the teacher, a mate from years ago, then headed back to the car and drove off towards the property where Mark was living.

Molly had been working steadily with JJ over the past couple of weeks and had decided it was time to take her out for a trail ride. Mark was joining her on one of his mate's horses and they were going to have a picnic by the dam. She found herself really looking forward to the day.

Molly had been pleasantly surprised when she had first visited where Mark was housesitting. He obviously took great pride in the home he was taking care of and everything was in its place, not at all like the bachelor pad she was expecting. Unless he'd had a major clean up because she was visiting? He had also been on his best behaviour whenever she had gone there to work with JJ, even treating her to a few home-cooked lunches. Nothing had happened between them, apart from a bit of harmless flirting, which had been nice.

As the weeks passed Molly's guilt over not telling him about Rose was becoming unbearable. It wasn't that she hadn't spoken about Rose. On the contrary, she'd made a conscious effort to tell him how wonderful Rose was and filled him in on all the adorable things she did and said. He seemed to enjoy hearing about Rose, even appearing keen to meet her. But Molly had not plucked up the courage to introduce them yet. Mark was certainly proving to be a decent bloke, and Molly found herself seriously considering telling him today.

Mark was waiting for her at the stables when she arrived. She parked under the shade of the ironwood trees and made her way over to him.

'Morning, Molly.'

'Hey there, Mark. How are you?' Molly replied, admiring his warm smile.

'I'm fantastic. Looking forward to the ride today and seeing how JJ goes. You've done a brilliant job with her, Molly. She's a completely different horse now to when I first got her. She even stands still when I'm cleaning her hoofs.'

'Nah. She's the same horse. She just needed someone to understand her, that's all. I'm glad you're happy with her, though,' Molly said as she helped him put the saddle bags on. 'These bags weigh a ton! What have you packed us for lunch?'

'Oh, a bit of this and a bit of that, with a few beverages to wash it all down. Nothing too fancy but it'll hit the spot at lunch time.' Mark wiped his dirty hands on his jeans and took a quick look around the stables. 'Right, I think we're good to go.'

'Excellent. It's a perfect day for a leisurely ride, with those endless blue skies and just a few clouds floating about to give us some shade,' Molly said as she looked to the heavens above, squinting from the sun.

'It's *always* a good day for a ride I reckon, Molly,' Mark said as he pulled himself up in the saddle of the gelding. 'Rain, hail or shine. Especially with you.'

*

Heath felt the sap from the mangoes burning the sensitive skin on his lips. He instinctively rubbed them with his fingers, wincing when he realised he'd probably just put more sap there. He wasn't often stupid enough to get sap on his face, always aware to keep it well away from his eyes when he was picking, but today his thoughts weren't on the job at all. They were on Molly.

He reflected back to last night, when over a few beers Molly had casually mentioned she was going for a horse ride with Mark. Heath had felt jealousy rising up from his heart and into his throat, threatening to cut off his airways. He had quickly made the excuse that he needed to use the loo, escaping into the soothing darkness of the night towards the outside toilet. He had slumped down on the ground, hanging his head in his hands, the thought of Molly being out of his reach making him breathless with heartache.

All he wanted to do was hold her close to him, to tell her how much he felt for her. But why bother when she had eyes for another man? He had dug deep within his soul, trying to find the courage to let go of her, just like he'd had to do with Jenny. If there *was* a God, why was he being so damn cruel? Molly obviously didn't feel the same about Heath, choosing to ignore all his efforts and instead focusing her attention on Mark. She could clearly see something in Mark that he couldn't. He *needed* to find a way to stop loving her, or the jealousy might turn him bitter and that would destroy his and Molly's friendship. She meant too much to him for that to happen. It was important that Molly and Rose remained in his life, even if it meant watching Molly fall in love with another man. As long as she was happy, that should be all that mattered.

He had sat there for so long, preoccupied by his thoughts, that when he had got back to the workers' cottage Molly had gone home. He had retired to bed, defeated by the torrent of emotions he was experiencing, falling into a fitful sleep crammed with bad dreams. And he had woken to begin the day feeling exactly the same, his feelings for her still there, still consuming him.

'You with us today, mate?' Trev called from the other side of the huge Bowen mango tree.

'Yeah, sorry, just having a bad day, that's all,' Heath called back as a mango slid from his long picking stick and plummeted to the ground, splattering as it hit. 'Shit!' he grumbled.

'No worries. We all have our bad days, buddy,' Trev replied, a rollie hanging from his parched lips as he heaved a heavy crate of mangoes off the ground to chuck up on the back of the old farm ute.

Heath clobbered a march fly that was feasting on his forearm, its serrated mandibles leaving a massive welt the size of Mount Everest and itchy as hell. Just another bite to add to the hundred he had already endured today. Everything was annoying him and he just wanted to punch something. What was he going to do to get over her?

'Smoko time!' Kenny called from the cherry picker. It was positioned high up in the sky as Kenny reached out with his picking stick, wobbling on one leg to grab the final mango from the top of the tree he was working on. Kenny may have been a laid-back kind of guy but when it came to smoko time he was always on the ball, counting down the seconds to the fifteen-minute break they had to sit in the shade of the trees and rest their legs.

The call for smoko was music to Heath's ears. He wandered over to the back of the ute and unpacked the cane smoko basket which, as always, held a flask of coffee strong enough to keep you awake for a week, and a packet of Arnott's assorted biscuits. He filled three plastic mugs with the steaming coffee and flipped three crates upside down so he, Trev and Kenny had somewhere to relax in the shade of the mango trees. He sat down with a groan, his legs weary, watching as Kenny carefully lowered the cherry picker down to the ground then stepped out through the small safety gate with caution.

'You look so serious when you're coming back down to earth now, Kenny. That fall a few months back really put the wind up you, mate, didn't it?' Heath said, dunking a butternut biscuit in his coffee and losing half of it to the bottom of the cup. He huffed. It just wasn't his day, or week, or month for that matter.

'It taught me a lesson or two. Trust *me* to be the one to have an accident like that. I felt like a right tool.' Kenny grinned as he wiped his dirty hands on his already grimy jeans before grabbing a handful of biscuits from the packet to munch on.

'Yeah, I reckon. Only you'd be capable of forgetting you were still up in the air and not on the ground before you stepped out the gate and fell five metres. Not to mention landing on your pinkie and breaking it.' Trev chuckled.

Kenny held his little finger up in the air and wriggled it, a cheeky smile crossing his lips. 'It's made a full recovery though. I was a bit worried that I was going to lose the capacity to pick my nose with it.'

'Good on you, Kenny.' Heath chuckled as he counted his blessings for having such great mates around to give him a laugh. Lord knows he needed it at the moment.

*

Molly was relieved when she spotted the dam shimmering in the distance. She was boiling up in the merciless heat and couldn't wait to dive into the cool water. A few ducks floated peacefully on the dam, ducking their heads occasionally for a nibble of what lay beneath. Two wallabies drinking on the far side of the water sensed the movement of the horses and made a mad dash to the safety of the thick scrub beyond, vanishing within seconds.

Molly and Mark dismounted the horses and left them to rest under the shade of a massive red gum, making sure they could reach the water for a long drink. Gorgeous waterlilies with magically buoyant leaves and spellbinding dusty-pink flowers covered nearly half the dam's surface. It astonished Molly how strong the leaves were – allowing frogs to freely bounce from leaf to leaf across the water – and she loved how they worshipped the sun by day and closed up in floral slumber at night. It was amazing. The workings of nature constantly charmed and mesmerised her, making her feel so fortunate to be surrounded by its astounding beauty every day.

'Wow, this place is just beautiful, Mark! What a place for lunch. I'd rather be here having a picnic than eating at some flash restaurant any day,' she gasped, her eyes wide as she took in the view before her.

'I thought you'd like it. There's just something magical about it, I reckon.' Mark smiled as he unpacked a tub of potato salad and a barbecued chook along with buttered bread rolls and paper plates to eat it all on.

Molly smiled affectionately back at him; she was starting to feel so comfortable in his company. She decided today was the day – she was going to tell him about Rose – and this was the perfect place to do it.

They tucked into the food, licking the creamy potato salad from their lips as they chatted easily, chasing away the flies that seemed determined to stick to them like superglue.

'So, Molly, I've been meaning to ask you, how would you feel about us going on an *official* date sometime?' Mark asked casually between bites of his chicken roll.

Molly nodded, smiling. 'I'd love to, Mark. How about dinner down at the Bull Bar, sometime this week?'

Mark looked chuffed. 'Great! That's a date then, as long as that lesbo barmaid steers well clear of me.'

Molly nearly choked. 'You've got to be joking, right? Don't tell me you've got something against lesbians?'

'I just don't agree with it, that's all. So, I'd rather not be around them.'

Molly held his stare, her blood boiling. 'I'm sorry to hear that. My best mate, Jade, is a lesbian, and it hasn't been easy for her. Too many people are quick to judge when they don't even know the person in the first place.'

Mark looked astonished. 'Oh, crap. I really put my foot in my mouth then, didn't I? Sorry, Molly, I didn't mean to offend you, or Jade for that matter. I just can't get my head around two women *or* two men being together. It makes my skin crawl.'

Molly looked away, saddened by his point of view. Did this change the way she felt about him? Should it? She didn't know what to think. They sat in silence for a few minutes, neither of them knowing what to say until Mark shuffled over next to her, taking her hand in his.

'I can see I've really upset you and I'm truly sorry. I promise to keep my opinions about it to myself from now on, okay?'

Molly looked at him, squeezing his hand, wanting to believe him. 'Okay.'

'Good. Let's just get on with enjoying the day.' He leant in and pulled Molly close, and before she knew what was happening, Mark laid a lingering kiss on her lips. Molly felt her head spin, and blushed as Mark pulled away. He smiled at her and rested his hand on her thigh as he continued chatting, like the kiss was no big deal.

'So, how did your little girl go on her first day back at school this morning?'

'She loves going to school so there were no dramas.'

'She sounds like a real little cutie. I hope I'll get to meet her one of these days.'

'Oh, um, well, maybe on the weekend I can bring her over for a swim in the dam? She'd love that.'

'Ah, no rush, Molly, there's plenty of time for that,' Mark replied offhandedly, swishing away a fly from his face. 'I'm just enjoying spending time with *you* at the moment. So tell me, what's the story with her father? Does he still live around here or did he take off?'

Molly froze, panic rising up in her throat. She wanted to scream out the words she'd been dying to speak for years, but they were all a jumble in her head. She took a deep breath, trying to steady herself. She knew what she had to say would shock Mark to the core.

Mark obviously noticed her shaking. Reaching out, he gently put his hand on her back.

'I'm sorry, Molly. You don't have to tell me anything. It's none of my business. I'm way out of line for even asking. Just forget I did.'

Molly picked up a twig and began scraping at the ground with it like she was digging her way to China. She rummaged around in her mind to find the right words, keeping her gaze glued to the earth, not wanting to look Mark in the eyes for now. 'No, Mark. I'm the one in the wrong here. There's something you really need to know about Rose.' Her voice was almost a whisper and she wondered if he could hear the quiver in it.

'What do you mean?'

Molly found the strength to look up and into his brown eyes, her soul desperate to see into his. 'Remember that night we shared seven years ago, Mark? Well, my little girl is your daughter.' She bit down hard on her lip, holding her breath, waiting for his reaction.

Mark's jaw dropped open as a look of sheer panic crossed his face. He shook his head from side to side in a daze. Molly put her hand on his arm but he sternly flung it away, glaring at her. He scrambled to his feet and moved out of her reach, like she was a poisonous snake about to bite him.

'What is it you want from me, Molly? How do you know she's mine? You had no problem having a one-night stand with me, so how do I know you didn't do that at every bloody rodeo, with every other Tom, Dick and Harry?'

'You were the only man I had sex with that *whole* year, Mark, so you have to be her father! I know it's a hell of a shock, but I thought you had the right to know. And I was hoping you'd be at least a *little* happy about it. Rose is a beautiful little girl.'

'You expected me to be *happy* about this? You suddenly telling me I'm the father of a kid, your kid? You must be delusional! I don't want a serious relationship, with you or any other woman for that matter. I'm just here for a good time, not a long time. I don't want the responsibilities of fatherhood or a committed relationship. Fuck! You should've told me this when you first met me again, not a month down the track! Who in the hell do you think you are keeping this from me? I don't want to talk to you about this right now. I can't think straight. I'll talk to you in a few days, once I've calmed down,' Mark roared as he stormed towards his horse, leaving Molly crying uncontrollably on the picnic blanket.

She felt like he had just stuck his hand in her chest and ripped her heart out. Rose was a part of her and she loved her with every breath that she took. She was worthy of her father's love, but now it looked as though Mark wasn't capable of giving it to her and by the sounds of it he was only after one thing, like most blokes. She watched as he galloped off like a madman, a trail of dust rising behind him. What was she meant to do now? Run after him? Stay here? Molly's tears fell freely, her sobs filling the air as she cried and cried because her little girl's father might never want to know her.

CHAPTER

12

A blue-tongued lizard dashed across the road and Molly instinctively swerved. The Land Cruiser fishtailed as she fought to regain control of the steering. Her nerves nearing breaking point, she pulled over on the side of the dirt road, just before the turn-off to Jacaranda Farm. She turned off the ignition and looked at herself in the rear-vision mirror. It wasn't a pretty sight.

She had stayed by the dam for hours, not wanting to face Mark back at the stables. She didn't know what to say to him. Thankfully, he was nowhere to be seen when she had finally arrived back, so she had put JJ back in her paddock and made a fast getaway.

She didn't want anyone to see she had been upset, especially Rose, so she pulled a packet of wet wipes from the glovebox and did her best to wipe away the tears from her eyes and cheeks. Her emotions changed from one second to the next, making her feel as though she was on a rollercoaster without a safety harness. She stared back at her reflection, still in shock from the way Mark had lashed out at her. Thinking back to his reaction she felt overcome with anger, claws of bitterness scratching away the layers of her heart. How dare he accuse her of sleeping around at every rodeo she went to? And how dare he try to seduce her just to get her between the sheets? The constant attention and charm that she thought was a sign of him *really* liking her was just a facade. Thank God she hadn't been stupid enough to succumb. And what about Rose? She deserved so much better than this. So much more from the man that was her biological father. Feeling a burning desire to escape the confines of her truck, she swung open the door and stumbled out into the long grass, breathing the fresh air deeply into her lungs. Normally, she would be cautious of snakes with such thick scrub underfoot, but today she challenged them to try to bite her.

She slowly walked back to the car and leant against the passenger door, trying to rub the throbbing headache from her temples. She had always known there was a possibility Mark would react badly to the news, but it had been so much worse than she'd ever imagined. Maybe she was right to have been so cautious in the first place? Perhaps they *were* better off without him? Grief tugged heavily at her with that very thought. Was Rose going to have to grow up as Molly herself had done, without her father? No, she wouldn't allow that to happen. She couldn't. Molly angrily shook her head and kicked the back tyre with her boot, mentally slapping herself for believing there might be a fairytale ending with Mark. Only in the movies were there happily-ever-afters. It was never that easy in real life. She had begun to let her guard down – and look what had happened. She wished she hadn't run into Mark again. Her life had been happy and peaceful before all of this. God, what a mess she'd made of everything ...

*

When Molly pulled up at the homestead Rose and Heath were playing with Skip and the puppies on the front lawn. It brought a warm smile to her face watching them together. Heath was brilliant with Rose, always happy to spend time with her, teaching her about everything from why there were clouds in the sky to why she must *never* hop in a car with a stranger. Heath looked over and gave her a quick wave before being bowled to the ground by an over-excited Skip and practically licked to death by him and the puppies. Rose giggled, clapping her hands in delight.

Molly took a quick glance at herself, happy that the redness had almost gone from her eyes and cheeks, before hopping out of the Land Cruiser and running over to join in the fun. She grabbed Rose and gently tackled her to the ground, laughing as Rose got her own back and began tickling her in the ribs. Heath joined in, pinning Molly's arms down and assisting Rose until Molly begged for mercy, screaming that she would wet her pants if they didn't stop. She sat up, playfully slapping Heath on the arm, tears of laughter still streaming down her cheeks.

'Strewth. Talk about ganging up on someone!' she said, still trying to catch her breath.

Rose giggled. 'Sorry, Mum, but it *was* funny watching you squirm like a witchetty grub on the grass!'

Heath nodded enthusiastically. 'Tell me about it.'

Rose wrapped her arms around Molly, giving her a tender hug. 'I love you, Mum, with all my heart.'

Molly swallowed down hard, ridding the lump from her throat. 'I love you too, princess, more than all the water in the ocean.'

Heath pointed to Skip, who was doing his business right in the middle of the front lawn. 'Better watch out for those barker's eggs he's giving birth to. Nothing worse than stepping in a big, warm pile of dog poo.' He wrinkled his nose at Rose. 'Come to think of it, I better go grab the shovel so I can get rid of it before someone does. Knowing my luck it'll most probably be me.'

Molly screwed her face up. 'Dirty bugger! Thanks, Heath, you're a champ.' She turned her attention to Skip. 'Can't you do your business somewhere else, you grot?' Skip barked back at her before running off to chase Mack and Sasha around the garden again, his tail wagging furiously.

Rose sat down on Molly's lap as they watched Heath walk towards the garden shed. 'Mum, you know what I wish? I wish Heath could be my dad. He'd be the best dad ever.'

Molly gently turned Rose's face towards her so she could look deeply into her daughter's emerald-green eyes, a mirror image of her own. 'I'm so sorry you don't know your dad, Rose, but Heath loves you like a dad and that's something very special to be thankful for. One day we *might* find your *real* dad, but for now, we have to be thankful for having each other. Okay?'

Rose's eyes filled with sadness. 'I know, Mum. I just really wish I could meet my own dad one day. I know he left before he even knew you were going to have me. And I know you've looked for him. But all my friends at school know *their* dads. It's not fair.'

'You will, sweetheart, you will. I will do my very best to try and make your wish come true. Promise.' Molly tenderly wrapped her arms around Rose, wishing she could take the pain away, knowing there and then that she had to find a way to bring Mark and Rose together even though part of her wished to never see Mark again.

Heath wandered back into view with the shovel in hand and Molly stared dreamily at him. Rose was right – he would make a wonderful dad *and* a perfect husband for some lucky woman one day. Molly secretly wished things could be different but life was never that easy. And she was too messed up at the moment to get into a relationship, what with Mark coming back into her life; she didn't want to drag Heath through all the crap she was going through. He'd dealt with enough. No, now wasn't the time to fall head over heels in love. Instead she had to focus on Rose and what was best for her. As she understood, there were always webs of reality weaving their way through your everyday life, making it impossible to have what you wanted *all* the time. Some days you were the spider, dancing upon your beautifully spun web, and other days you were the prey, stuck fast to the web and unable to move from its grasp, no matter how much you struggled to break free. And right now, she felt like the prey, struggling to break free of her past so she could get on with her future. A future that she had no clue as to what was in store.

Once Heath had cleared up after Skip he came back over to the two girls. 'Hey, ladies, us blokes were thinking about going to the drive-in this weekend to watch *Toy Story 3*. Are you up for going?' Heath winked at Molly, letting her know he was really aiming the question at Rose.

Rose leapt from Molly's lap and jumped up and down on the spot. 'Oh, can we, Mum? Can we? Pretty please, with sugar on top!'

'Of course we can, sweetheart.'

'Yippee! Thanks, Mum. Thanks, Heath. You guys are the best!' Rose squealed.

'You're more than welcome, little buddy,' Heath replied.

'Mum, why don't we ask Aunty Jade to come too?'

'I reckon that's a beaut idea, Rose. We'll give her a call later on to see if she wants to come along.'

'Okay, Mum, done deal,' Rose said, giving them a thumbs up. 'Now, I have to go and tell GG and Grandma.'

Molly and Heath watched as Rose raced up the front steps and into the house, accidentally slamming the screen door behind her in her haste. 'Sorry!' they heard her call out.

'She's a doozy, that little girl of yours,' Heath said, smiling fondly.

'Yeah, she is, isn't she?' Molly said proudly. 'Thanks for doing this for her, Heath. I really appreciate it.'

'Doing what?'

'Saying you wanted to go and see *Toy Story 3*. I know you've only offered to go for Rose's sake.'

'Oh that! No worries.' Heath lowered his voice to a whisper, covering his mouth with his hand as if he was about to reveal a state secret. 'Believe it or not we really *do* want to see it. I've even heard it's 3D. It's going to be a hoot wearing those crazy glasses.' Heath looked at her seriously. 'Don't tell anyone, though. Us blokes have got a reputation to uphold around these parts.'

Molly gave Heath a friendly hug. 'I'm so lucky to have you in my life.'

Heath wrapped his arms around her. A soft, sweet scent of shampoo drifted towards him, making him want to run his fingers through her hair. 'And I'm lucky to have you and Rose in *my* life too.'

Molly pulled away, quickly wiping back tears. Heath gently touched her cheek. 'Hey now, what's all this about?'

Molly shook her head. 'I don't want to worry you with my dramas. I'm sorry. I've just had a horrible day.'

'I'm all ears, Molly. Please trust me. You can talk to me about *anything*. You know that,' Heath replied tenderly, his voice caressing her heart.

Molly sniffed, trying hard to take stock of her emotions. She felt a burning desire to tell Heath the truth. Besides, he knew the whole story about how she had fallen pregnant, that she had never seen the guy again since that night at the rodeo. He really did have a right to know. Didn't he?

'Mark is Rose's father, Heath. That's why I've been spending time with him, getting to know him.'

Heath gasped, everything suddenly making perfect sense, his eyes flaring in understanding. He reached out and tenderly squeezed Molly's shoulder, his eyes full of compassion. 'Holy hell! I had no idea. So what's the problem?'

'Well,' Molly said, looking down, 'until today, he didn't know he was Rose's father. I told him when were out riding and he lost it. He stormed off, basically saying I could be lying, telling me he didn't want to talk about it and making it *very* clear that he was only with me for a quick fling.'

Heath's face twisted with rage. 'That bastard! Saying that to you! And he doesn't know how lucky he is to have Rose! Do you want me to go and have a little talk with him? I promise I'll be civil, even if it kills me.'

'No, Heath! This is my battle and I need to deal with it. Besides, I know you too well. There's no way you'd be able to remain civil in this situation. You're too close to Rose and me to be an outsider in it all,' Molly replied, touched by Heath's offer.

Heath took her hand, looking her straight in the eyes, his love for her undeniable in his warm gaze. 'I respect that, Molly. And I'll stay out of it, for now. But if he hurts you or Rose, he'll be a very, very sorry man. You and Rose mean the world to me.'

'I know we do, Heath. You mean the world to us too.'

Heath smiled and gently touched Molly's face, wiping her tears away with his fingertips. 'Just know I'm here, whenever you need me. Okay?'

Molly cleared her throat and took a deep breath. 'Thanks. I know you always have my back and it means a lot.'

Heath shoved his hands in his pockets, a smile lighting up his face. 'Hey, I have an idea, Molly. I have to head up to Mum and Dad's place next weekend, just for two nights, to help my brother with some bull catching. David said he can do without me for a few days and it'd be nice to catch up with the family. Why don't you and Rose come along too? It might do you good to get away for a few days and Mum would love to see you both. She's always asking about you two.'

Molly took a few moments to think about it. She didn't want to give Heath the wrong idea by going out to his parents' station with him, or did she? Damn it! She wasn't sure of anything any more. She *had* been there a number of times with him before, so it wasn't out of the ordinary. It was always an adventure out bull catching, and Rose *loved* visiting Heath's mum Alice who spoilt her rotten. Yes, it would take her mind off things here for a while, and give Mark some time to cool off, too, before she spoke to him again, which she knew she had to. She wasn't giving up on the notion of him being a part of Rose's life that easily. She couldn't. It meant too much to Rose. 'That sounds great, Heath. We'd love to come along with you. Thanks.'

'Fantastic. I'll give Mum a call tonight and let her know – she'll be thrilled. We'll take Buck along for the journey too, if you like. We can hitch the trailer on the back of the Toyota. It'll be good for Rose to bond with him a bit more, now that you're happy with his progress. Rose must be getting pretty close to riding him; he's developed into a trustworthy horse, thanks to all your hard work and dedication. Maybe she might even be able to ride him out there.'

'That's a great idea, Heath. Rose is going to be so excited. I just want to take Buck out for a trail ride over the next week, before Rose gets in the saddle. He's performing well in the round yard, but as you know, it's a whole different ball game once you get the horse out into the scrub, where there's a load of distractions.' Molly glanced at her watch. 'Speaking of Rose, I better get in and get her into a bath. It's coming up to dinner time and it's my turn to cook tonight.'

'Yep, no worries. Oh, before you go, your granddad wants us to muster the cattle tomorrow for the saleyards as the meat prices are good at the moment. It's going to be a bit tough as the scrub is really thick out there, but it'll be nice to have a break from picking. Are you coming along with us?'

'Count me in. I'd love a day out mustering.'

Molly gave him a smile before turning and heading towards the homestead as the sun began to set on the horizon. Her horrible day hadn't ended so horribly after all.

*

Heath watched Molly head off, and wandered back to the workers' cottage. He was over the moon that Molly and Rose would be coming with him. The understanding of why Mark had been so prominent in Molly's life was easing his heartache, giving him hope that something *might* be possible between him and Molly. He let his thoughts wander repeatedly over the fact that Mark was Rose's father, infuriation at Mark's reaction crashing against his chest like a raging sea. Mark had no idea what he had given up, but Heath sure did, and if it was he who had been Rose's father, he would have felt like he was the luckiest man in the world.

CHAPTER

13

Molly loved the early-morning starts when she went out mustering with the men. To watch the sun rise gloriously in the sky as she settled into the saddle for the day was always exhilarating. She smiled as Leroy whinnied beneath her. 'You guys good to go then?' she asked, pulling the rim of her akubra down and swatting the persistent flies away from her face.

'Ready when you are, boss,' Trev replied, heaving himself up and into the saddle.

Kenny smiled broadly, his breakfast of bacon and eggs still hanging onto his teeth. 'I'm always ready.'

Heath nodded as he gave JD a yank on the reins and a few sharp orders to steady up. 'I reckon JD's going without us if we don't make a move soon. He's got bloody ants in his pants today. We'll follow you, Molly, seeing as you know which unlucky buggers are going to be on someone's dinner plate.'

Molly laughed. 'Oh, good on you, Heath, make me sound like the grim reaper, why don't you? We all eat meat, don't we? I think some people just forget how it gets onto their plates. Hopefully I get to keep some of the tails this time. I'm hanging out for a good ox-tail stew.'

'Yum, my mouth's watering just thinking about it,' Heath replied, licking his lips. 'Don't you worry. I'll go and pick the tails up from the slaughterhouse myself if it means you're going to cook your famous ox-tail, mushroom and Guinness stew.'

'Who said anything about sharing?' Molly teased as she tapped Leroy in the ribs, galloping off. The men followed, trying their best to steer clear of each other's trails of dust.

As Molly cleared the thick scrub that surrounded the main part of the property she spotted a large mob of cattle in the middle of a clearing, well away from the trees that would make for an easy getaway. She smiled smugly at the luck of it until she laid eyes on a brawny bull standing in the middle of the mob, its disposition changing the minute it caught sight of her. It clearly wasn't happy, kicking vigorously at the dusty ground and snorting loudly to warn her off. Molly remembered the aggressive bugger from the last time she mustered this area and knew that he wasn't afraid to charge. The bull had massive horns that could easily kill a horse and she didn't want Leroy, or herself for that matter, to get hurt. She kept a tight hold on the reins, letting Leroy know he was to stay put, or else.

Trev, Kenny and Heath took their positions around the huddle of bellowing cattle, keeping their eyes firmly fixed on the hostile bull, readying themselves for whatever he wanted to throw at them. They tried to keep their distance, not wanting to antagonise the bull, but at the same time well aware they had a job to do. And if that meant dealing with an argumentative bull, then that's just what they'd have to do. It was all part and parcel of being a stockman.

The outside world faded away as they focused all their energies on the job at hand, their senses acutely alive as they eased their way closer and closer to the herd, attempting to edge them in the direction of the yards where they would be sorted out tomorrow. The bull seemed to be losing some of its aggression as it began to follow the other cattle. Then, without warning, it broke ranks and made a frenzied dash for freedom towards a nearby cluster of trees, sending the mob into utter disarray. Thick clouds of dust and the bellows of calves filled the air as cows ran helter-skelter in panic, causing absolute chaos for Molly and the men.

Kenny gave an almighty whistle and signalled his decision to chase the wayward bull as the others did their best to take control of the cattle. Molly shouted after him, calling for him to wait for help, but he couldn't hear her over the rumble of cattle and horses' hoofs on the hard earth. Her instincts screamed at her to follow Kenny; she knew he would need help with such an unruly beast. She gave the reins a sharp flick, letting Leroy know to break into a gallop with the added aid of her spurs.

She bolted after Kenny, holding the reins with one hand and her hat on her head with the other. The bull abruptly changed directions, swerving all over the place like a car out of control. Molly heard Trev cracking his roo-hide whip behind her as she wheeled Leroy sharply around and continued the chase.

Kenny was behind her now – she could hear the thunder of Frank's hoofs just metres away. Kenny rapidly passed her, his face full of sheer determination to catch and corner the disobedient beast. Molly couldn't help but smile at his long lanky form as he overtook her.

The bull drew close to a rocky outcrop that dropped twenty metres to the ground below. It skidded to a halt as Kenny and Molly vigorously pulled their horses up so they didn't slide over the cliff themselves, both of them breathing heavily from the energetic pursuit. Not uttering a word to each other, they kept their attention entirely on the strong-willed beast now only metres from them.

The bull realised it was cornered. If it backed up a certain death would follow, but to go forward it had to deal with Molly and Kenny. It assessed its choices, turning and looking in the direction of the drop and then staring back menacingly at Molly and Kenny, its nostrils flaring as froth spluttered from its mouth.

Molly and Kenny tried to slowly walk the horses around behind the bull, allowing them to push it forwards towards Trev and Heath off in the distance. Abruptly, the bull charged Kenny, its deadly pointed horns aimed straight for Frank's chest. The horse reared up, neighing loudly in panic. Molly watched in horror as Kenny was thrown from the saddle; his face contorted in terror as his body flew through the air and slammed onto the dangerously rocky ground. Time ticked by painfully slow, everything moving in slow motion. Molly let out a heartfelt cry. Kenny might be badly injured or even worse, dead.

Frank galloped off, the leather reins dragging on the ground behind him. The bull stood beside Kenny's prone form, determining its next move.

Out of the blue Heath came tearing in on JD, yelling determinedly for Molly to back off. He had to protect Molly and Kenny – Kenny was defenseless and there was no way in hell Heath would let Molly get hurt. The bull looked ready to kill, and Heath wasn't going to risk losing a mate or the woman he was madly in love with. He would protect Molly with his own life if need be. He galloped straight towards the bull, and, after a moment of hesitation, it retreated, much to his relief. Finally facing defeat it made a mad dash towards the huddle of cattle.

Molly and Heath jumped down from the saddle and ran over to Kenny, who was lying deathly still on the ground. Heath touched Kenny's throat and Molly prayed he would feel life pulsing beneath his trembling fingertips. Both Molly and Heath jumped back with fright as Kenny abruptly came to and sat up, swinging his arms frantically and screaming blue murder. They ducked his wild and reckless blows as the shock of what had just happened threw Kenny's survival mode into overdrive. Heath tried to grab Kenny's arms, shouting for him to calm down, telling him it was all okay now. Molly could see blood oozing from Kenny's nostril and she worried that he had done damage to his head in the fall.

Kenny took a few seconds to realise that the threat was gone and his two best mates were the ones he had been trying to knock clean out. Molly noticed he looked dazed, and now that it was safe to approach him again she did so, placing her hands on his.

'Are you all right, mate? You've had a pretty bad fall.'

Kenny rubbed the massive egg that had popped out of the back of his head then took a good hard look at his hand. 'Well, no blood, so that's a good sign, hey.'

Molly pointed to his nose. 'You got a bit of blood coming from your nose.'

Kenny wiped at it with his sleeve. 'Oh, that. No worries about that, Molly. I get a nosebleed whenever I get *really* stressed out. Always have done, ever since I was a kid.'

Molly shook her head. 'Really? I've never seen you get a nosebleed before.'

Heath chuckled. 'That's because Kenny *never* gets stressed out.'

Kenny nodded in agreement, licking his dry lips. 'You got that right. I'm as dry as a Pom's towel right now, though. Could anyone spare a torn and broken man a nice drink of cold water?'

Heath smirked. 'Sure thing.'

Molly gave Kenny a quick hug before standing up and heading over to her saddle bag. 'I'll grab my water for you, buddy. Just give us a sec. You keep sitting there until you feel a bit better.'

Kenny slowly pushed himself up off the ground, ignoring Molly and Heath's persistent pleading for him to stay sitting, checking his limbs for any deep cuts or broken bones as he stood. 'I reckon I'm all right. My head feels like I've been slogged with a sledge hammer, but it's nothing a few painkillers and a shot of whisky won't fix.'

Heath walked around behind Kenny to check out his head. 'Faaaark! You've got yourself a corker of a lump there, mate. No wonder you've got a massive headache. Maybe you should go back to the workers' cottage and have a bit of a rest?'

Molly overheard the conversation as she headed back to the guys with her water bottle. 'I reckon that's not a bad idea, Kenny. Maybe you should get Grandma to check it out when you get back too, just to be safe. It might be a smart move going to see the doc after a fall like that.'

Kenny picked his hat up off the ground and bashed it against his leg a few times to shake the dust from it. 'Nah, I'll be right. Stop fussing. I'll miss out on all the action if I go home to bed.'

'As long as you're sure you're right. I think we've had enough action for today.'

They all turned as they heard Trev's whip cracking like fireworks in the distance.

'We better go and help him out – the poor bloke's mustering all the cattle on his own over there,' Heath said.

'And one crazy-arse bull too,' Kenny said, shaking his head in disbelief.

'Hopefully Frank has calmed down a bit so we can find him for you,' Molly said. 'Heath, you go and give Trev a hand, if you don't mind, and I'll have a quick squiz around for Frank. He won't have gone too far, knowing him. He's probably just hiding over in the scrub somewhere.'

Heath nodded. 'Righto.'

Kenny watched them both get settled back in the saddle as he sat under the shade of a paperbark tree. 'Don't forget about little ole me!' he called after them.

*

Molly wiped the dust from her face and licked her parched lips while helping push the last of the cattle into the yards. Her mouth and throat were dry from all the dust she had inhaled throughout the day and her back ached like crazy.

The sun was just setting on the horizon, painting the sky magnificent shades of orange and red as the last cow wandered languidly into the cattle yards. Molly smiled when she locked the gate behind it, happy with the number of cattle they had rounded up. The cattle would be sorted in the morning and then either sent off to the saleyards with David or set free to fatten up a little more. She looked over at Kenny, who was gingerly sliding his way off Frank.

'How are you feeling, buddy?' she called out while she dismounted Leroy, feeling the blood start flowing into her numb behind.

Kenny screwed his face up as he tried to walk, limping badly on his right leg. 'I feel like I've been run over by a steamroller and then the bloody thing has reversed back up over me a few times. I need a stiff drink, I reckon. That'll make me feel a whole lot better.'

'Sounds like a plan to me. Have a *few* stiff drinks and then you won't feel a thing, and even better, you'll sleep like a baby.'

'You coming in for a drink?'

'Nah, not tonight, Kenny. I want to spend some time with Rose. Are you coming to the drive-in on Saturday night? It should be a hoot.'

'Bloody oath I am. I love going to the drive-in. I can't wait to wear those 3D glasses as well. I'm going to look so damn cool.' Kenny grinned.

Heath and Trev trotted into the stables, their weariness evident. Heath let out a long groan as he slid down from the saddle, his spurs clinking as his boots hit the ground. Molly couldn't help admiring him as he removed his hat and ran his strong hand over his short hair. He was gorgeous, especially when he was covered in dust and sweat; it made him look so manly, so desirable.

'You must be knackered, Molly. You've outdone us blokes with all the galloping about you did today. Mighty impressive, I must say,' Trev said, giving in to a yawn and stretching his tired limbs high in the air.

'Thanks, Trev. I do try my best,' Molly answered, stoked that Trev had noticed how hard she had worked.

'I second that. You kept us on our toes today,' Heath added with a wink and a grin.

Molly felt herself blush and she quickly turned her head, pretending to be engrossed in her saddle bags, which were empty already. 'Well, someone has to keep you lot on your toes. Mind you, my back is bloody killing me. I reckon I'll need an Epsom-salt bath when I get home to help relieve it.'

'I can give you a massage if you like. Apparently I have magic hands,' Heath said, his smile so alluring Molly virtually lost all feeling in her legs. Part of her wanted to say yes, every inch of her yearning to feel his hands caressing her ... but as usual her logical mind stepped in, images of Jenny haunting her. She fought with reason, the silent battle making her want to scream. She was so sick of not knowing what to do.

Heath looked over at her, waiting for a reply, cottoning on to the fact she was at a loss for words and unable to make up her mind.

He held his hands up in the air. 'Purely for medicinal purposes, nothing else intended. You have my word.'

Molly went to answer, and then hesitated as she bit at her fingernail. 'Not tonight, Heath. I did promise Rose we would watch a movie together, but I'll hold you to the offer. Is it okay to take a raincheck for now?'

Heath smiled broadly. 'Not a problem. You enjoy your night with Rose.'

'I'm off to have myself a warm shower and a bit of grub,' Trev said with a quick wave.

'Me too. Then I'm going to have a drink with my mate, Jack Daniels,' Kenny said as he followed Trev out of the stables.

'That sounds like a plan to me, Kenny!' Heath called after them. He leant into Molly and she felt her breath quicken, her fingers gripping the leather reins in her hands like she was hanging from a cliff. 'Night, Miss Molly. Sweet dreams,' he whispered in her ear, smiling affectionately before turning and walking away.

'Same to you,' Molly called out after him, her heart still pitter-pattering against her chest.

*

Molly brushed her teeth before heading off to bed, dragging her feet along the timber floors like they were small boulders, her hand holding the thumping pain in the bottom of her back. It ached like crazy after galloping around the countryside all day. How she wished she could let Heath soothe the pain away with his so-called magic hands. She had no doubt he would be able to enchant her with his touch. That's what terrified her. She switched off the light and climbed into her bed, sighing with pleasure as her body relaxed into the mattress. She had thoroughly enjoyed spending the day out with Heath today, and she couldn't wait to spend the entire weekend with him out on his parents' station with Rose. What might happen out there? Would the wall she had built up around herself, the one that Jade kept telling her she had to get rid of, stay solid? Or would Heath send it crumbling to the ground? She closed her heavy eyelids, not having the energy to think about it all any more, and drifted off to a peaceful sleep.

CHAPTER
14

Buck's hoofs clip-clopped rhythmically over the rocky terrain as Molly carefully guided him through the thick scrub, feeling completely at ease on his back, her months of patiently working with him coming to fruition. She could tell his senses were on alert, his ears flickering while he listened to the birds singing from the treetops and the whispering sound of the wind as it ruffled the leaves, but he was calm and relaxed. Reaching a creek crossing he paused, hesitant about stepping in the water, the situation new to him. Molly eased him on, confirming with her voice that he had nothing to worry about. He trusted her and took a small step forward, blowing his lips gently and letting the cool water wash over his legs. He got to the other side and Molly leant back in the saddle, gently pulling on the reins, motioning for him to stop. He followed her cue, dropping his head slightly as he waited. Molly leant forwards and stroked his neck.

'Good boy. You're doing so well. I'm mighty impressed that you're doing everything I'm asking of you.'

She loosened her grip on the reins a little, feeling comfortable that he was listening to her and following her instructions. She applied gentle pressure with her legs, asking him to walk on, wanting to get him into the open so she could take him for a gallop. They reached the edges of the scrub where the fields were aglow with glorious sunlight and Molly gave him a tight squeeze with her legs. Buck obeyed, picking up the pace, his hoofs pounding the earth as he opened his stride. Molly smiled broadly, the beauty and magic of the moment filling her with pride for the amazing horse Buck had become. After long months of gruelling training and endless devotion she had no doubt in her mind that he was ready, ready for Rose to finally ride him and make him her own.

*

That night, the three girls sat like peas in a pod in the front of Molly's Land Cruiser, surrounded by the bags of Minties, Chicos and Maltesers they had bought for the drive-in. Jade wiggled her feet while balancing five steaming pizza boxes on her lap.

'Far out, these are hot! Can we at least tuck into one of these garlic breads, Molly? I'm starving and the smell of this food is driving me nuts!' Jade was already opening the hot foil of the buttery garlic bread. She stuffed a piece in her mouth. 'Do you want a piece, sweetheart?' she garbled to Rose through a mouthful of food.

'Yes, please!' Rose replied.

'Hey, you two, don't forget the driver here,' Molly said, chuckling at Jade and Rose as they juggled hot pieces of garlic bread in their hands.

'So, tell me all about how you and Mel are going, Jade,' Molly asked between bites.

'Really well. In fact, even better than that! I cannot believe how lucky I am to have met her. She's wonderful.'

'Oh, Jade! That's great news. I'm thrilled for you both. You deserve to find true love, and it's beginning to sound like that's exactly what it is between you and Mel. Do you *feel* like it's true love?'

'Yep. Not that I've felt true love before, but I reckon this is it. I have so much fun with Mel. She's a great lady to hang out with. And she's so caring about me and interested in what I want out of my life.'

'That's so good. I'm so happy for you. I know you've both been waiting for the right time, but it *has* been five weeks ... Have you had a sleepover yet?' Molly asked, raising her eyebrows, insinuating things to Jade that she didn't want to mention in front of Rose.

'Ah, yes, we have ... and boy, oh boy! I'll fill you in later on what happened, though, hey,' Jade answered, grinning like a naughty child.

'Yes, good idea, you can fill me in on your pyjama party later.' Molly chuckled.

'Have you heard from Mark?'

'Nope,' Molly replied, not wanting to talk about him in front of Rose.

'Hmm,' Jade said slowly, shaking her head.

In front of Molly's Land Cruiser they could see Heath, Trev and Kenny in Kenny's Holden ute, fold-out sun lounges and beanbags bouncing around in the back. Both cars joined the long queue of utes and cars at the turn-off to the Rodeo drive-in. It was a popular outing for the locals on a Friday and Saturday night. Rose giggled in anticipation and Molly smiled tenderly at her daughter, happy she was making her little girl's night by taking her to the drive-in with the boys.

They finally reached the tiny ticketing booth where a cheerful man greeted them all from the window of the small besser-block building. Molly spent a minute reaching back and forth through the window, exchanging money for their tickets and back-to-the-future-looking 3D glasses. She swatted at the hundreds of tiny insects congregating under the seriously bright fluorescent lights that lit up the ticket booth, thanking the friendly man as she drove forward. She dimmed her headlights as they moved into the drive-in's parking area, scanning the darkness for Kenny's ute.

'There they are.' Jade pointed.

'Ah, yeah, I see them,' Molly replied, maneuvering the Land Cruiser in beside them, making sure she parked as close to the speaker on the pole as possible.

'Hey, you three, fancy seeing you here!' Heath said as the girls piled out of the front. 'And I see you brought us all dinner, how wonderful of you,' he added as he helped Jade place the pizza boxes on the bonnet.

'I even made sure I got your favourite, super supreme with extra garlic, mushrooms and pepperoni.' Molly grinned.

Heath licked his lips enthusiastically. 'Thanks, Molly. Appreciate it. You're always so thoughtful.' He turned to pick up Rose and she gave him a cuddle. 'You ready to watch the movie with these cool-looking glasses on?' Heath asked, waving them in front of Rose.

Rose took the glasses and put them on, grinning from ear to ear. 'Yep! These are a bit weird, though. They're making everything look all wobbly. How am I meant to watch the movie when everything seems like I'm looking through a bowl of Grandma's strawberry jelly?'

Molly laughed. 'Darling, they don't work their magic until the movie actually starts. How about we set up camp in the back of the Cruiser? That way we can all sit back and demolish some pizza while we enjoy *Toy Story 3* together.'

The guys helped the girls set up their sun lounges along with their pillows and blankets before grabbing a share of dinner and hoisting themselves up into the back of Kenny's ute just as the opening credits started to roll. As the massive screen came to full animated life Molly basked in the cool country-night air, with millions of glimmering stars acting as the ceiling of the outdoor theatre. No sign of storms, which was a relief. That would most certainly have brought an abrupt end to their fun adventure.

The occasional fruit bat swooped this way and that, creating a shadow ten times its size across the gigantic screen. Molly found herself distracted from the movie when a stray kangaroo, clearly lost, bounded through the rows of parked cars trying to find its way back to the scrub. Children giggled and scurried out of its way as adults tried to turn it away from their cars and out of the drive-in. For any visitor to the area looking for a truly outback experience, this was the place to come, Molly thought.

'Hey, Molly, do you have any Rid? The mozzies are making a real meal out of my legs,' Jade whispered, scratching so hard Molly thought she was going to take a layer of skin off.

'Yeah, it's in the glove box, matey. Can you bring it back with you so Rose and I can use it too?'

Jade jumped down from the back, pulling a frightening face.

'If I don't return they've carried me away!'

'Mosquitoes can't carry you away, Jade!' Rose replied, as if Jade didn't know anything.

Molly lifted her glasses and had a peek over at the three men, chuckling to herself at the sight of them. All three were being swallowed up by their beanbags as they munched away hungrily on their pizzas with the crazy-looking 3D glasses on. She felt a warm fuzzy feeling when her gaze fell on Heath; he looked so sexy, as always. She reflected on the tender look in his eyes when he'd told her how much it meant to him that she and Rose were in his life, and it sent a flood of emotions running through her. What was she so damn afraid of when it came to Heath? He was one of her best mates so she should be able to trust him, to lay all her feelings and fears on the line. But maybe that was exactly why. And she had to admit it, love wasn't one of her strong suits. Her most recent experience with Mark, and her bad experiences with guys before him, were brilliant proof of that.

'Mum! Are you watching the movie or are you going stare at the guys all night?' Rose whispered, snapping Molly out of her trance.

'Yeah, Molly! This film is fantastic!' Jade added as she jumped back up and got settled into her sun lounge.

'Oh, sorry you two,' Molly murmured and she turned to face the screen. At that moment, one of the cartoon characters threw a ball and it came flying straight for her. She instinctively ducked, laughing along with Jade and Rose at the realistic special effects enhanced by the glasses.

Close to the end of the movie, Molly heard thunderous snoring coming from the direction of the guys. 'Hey, you lot. Which one of you buggers has fallen asleep?'

Kenny looked over at her, stuffing a handful of popcorn into his mouth. 'That'd be Trev. All the excitement has worn the poor old bugger out. Not as much of a party animal as he used to be.'

'Well, poke him in the ribs or something. We can't hear the movie over his snoring! He'll be annoying everyone else too.'

'Gladly,' Heath whispered back as he prodded Trev fair in the ribs.

Trev sat bolt upright looking vague and confused, with his 3D glasses hanging haphazardly off his face. 'Shit, where am I?'

'You're at the drive-in, Trev, remember?' Heath laughed.

'Yeah, and some of us are trying to watch the film,' Jade called back, giggling.

The end credits signalled it was time to pack up and the crowd slowly began to make their way out of the drive-in. By the time Molly pulled up out the front of Jade's house Rose was fast asleep on Jade's lap. Jade gently eased her way out of the passenger door.

'Night, Molly. Thanks for taking me along to the movie. I hope you hear from Mark soon, and if not, maybe you should go over and see him when you get back from Heath's parents' place, hey? It's going to drive you nuts otherwise. I think it would be best for both of you if you sat down like the adults that you are and laid all the cards on the table. Life is never easy when emotions are involved, and I know you're really confused at the moment. Just make sure you're true to the real you, and it will bring blessings into your life that you never imagined possible,' she said softly, not wanting to wake Rose.

'You're right, mate. A beautiful way to put it, and it makes loads of sense, as always. If I don't hear from Mark by the time I get back from Ironbark Station I'll make my way over to his place to try to talk to him. But, you know, I'm not going to get down on my knees and *beg*. That'd be pointless. He has to *want* to be in Rose's life. Thanks for coming along tonight. It was fun, as always,' Molly whispered back.

'If I don't see you before you go out to the station, have fun and follow your heart – not your head – and make sure you give Alice a big hug and kiss from me,' Jade said kind-heartedly as she waved Molly off.

'I will, Jade. Promise. I can't wait to go. Rose is even counting down the sleeps. It's going to be lovely having some time away with her. Catch you later, mate.'

Molly carried Rose into her bed and got her settled under the sheet, gently kissing her on the cheek. 'Love you, my angel,' she whispered as she brushed a tuft of hair away from Rose's face. 'Sweet dreams.'

She switched on Rose's night light and quietly sneaked out the bedroom door, smiling affectionately as she took one last look at Rose sleeping. Her maternal instincts overwhelmed her, making her determined to talk some sense into Mark. Surely, if he met Rose, he wouldn't be able to help but fall in love with her. How could *anyone* not love such a sweet and innocent little soul such as Rose Jones?

CHAPTER

15

The Toyota Hilux thundered along the dirt road, the occasional patch of corrugation sending shuddering vibrations through the cab and items flying from the dashboard. Rose giggled as she caught a wayward packet of butterscotch lollies, shoving one in her mouth, as she continued to play a game on Molly's iPad. Molly looked through the back window, checking that the horse float was still safe and sound; she worried that Buck might be finding the journey a little bumpy. Not that she could do much about it; the roads were more like bush tracks out this way, covered in deep crevices, and Heath was driving as carefully as he could.

The scenery had changed dramatically along the way, the landscape becoming more dry and barren as they got deeper into the outback, and although it was harsh and unforgiving country, Molly thought it held within it a magical, untamed beauty. They had already been travelling for two hours with only one more to go, and Molly couldn't wait to reach Ironbark Station. She always felt a world away from her everyday problems out there, and John and

Alice made her and Rose feel so very welcome. It would be the ideal place for her to sit back and relax, to allow herself time to think about what had happened over the last couple of months. Because at the moment she was so confused.

It was hard to believe that Christmas was only two months ago. So much had happened since then and she honestly didn't know which direction she was heading in, what path her life was going to take. Was it just because she was craving a family life, feeling vulnerable because of Mark, that she was looking at Heath in ways a friend normally wouldn't? She glanced over at Heath, her thoughts taking her back to the night she had kissed him, to the afternoon they had spent frolicking in the dam, her legs going weak once again as she relived his lips on hers.

'What is it, Molly?' Heath asked, feeling her eyes burning a hole in him.

Molly shuffled uncomfortably in her seat and hastily tried to think of something to say. 'Oh, um, I was just wondering why you didn't stay out working on the station with your family?' It was a question that had often crossed her mind, yet she had never asked him before.

'Well, cattle farmers don't always make a lot of money, and it was hard work for my parents trying to bring in enough to support us all. I hated seeing them struggle so much just to put food on the table. So, seeing I was the youngest, and my older brother had more of a right to take over the station, I thought it was only fair of me to go and find work elsewhere. That's when Jenny and I packed our bags and headed for Jacaranda, ready for a new adventure.'

'That would have been a hard decision for you,' Molly replied, admiring Heath's thoughtfulness, but not at all surprised by it.

'It was at first. But now I don't mind at all – I like working on Jacaranda Farm. You guys are like family to me.'

Molly nodded slowly as she absentmindedly ran her fingertips over the horseshoe design on her bracelet. 'Yeah, we are like family, aren't we?'

'For sure. David is like my second dad. I'm lucky to have a great boss like him.'

'He appreciates having you around, Heath; you're a very hard worker. He'd hate to lose you. You'll always have a job there, for as long as you want it.'

'I hope so, because I'm not thinking about going anywhere anytime soon.'

'Glad to hear it,' Molly said with a smile.

*

When Heath pulled into Ironbark Station Molly and Rose jumped down from the cab, stretching their legs pleasurably. The massive homestead sat like a tropical oasis in the middle of the stark landscape, thanks to Alice's green thumb. Large patches of beautiful native lavender graced the front picket fence, the aroma hanging heavily in the air, with red, white and pink roses filling the garden beds. Molly grinned as Alice erupted from the front door, a smile from ear to ear as she ran towards them.

'Heath, Molly, Rose, it's so great to see you all!'

Heath gave his mum a loving hug. 'Hi, Mum! How are you?'

'I'm great. Still putting up with your father's nagging, but other than that I'm *fine*,' she replied lightheartedly as she hugged Molly and Rose. 'Now, come inside and I'll put the kettle on. Your dad and brother should be home any minute, seeing it's almost dark.'

'We've just got to get Buck settled into the stables, then we'll be in, Mum.'

'Okay. How about you come with me then, Rose? I'll get you settled in too,' Alice said, taking Rose's hand. 'I've made up the spare room for you and your mum and I have some yummy biscuits inside that I've baked especially for you, as long as you don't go eating too many and spoil your dinner.'

'Aw, goodie!' Rose replied.

*

Bright and early the next morning, the bashed-up bull buggy hurtled through the dense scrub as they dodged colossal anthills left, right and centre. Heath sat stony-faced at the steering wheel, his muscular arms ripping the buggy from left to right, while Molly hung onto the Jesus bar for dear life, her knuckles whitening as the wind almost ripped the saliva from her mouth. Mustard-coloured dust rose out around them, making it almost impossible to see. Molly's heart pounded against her chest, her pulse was racing, the thrill of the chase was filling her with adrenaline – and she loved every second of it. Heath maneuvered the open-top four-wheel drive with precision, his years of growing up on a cattle station showing. There was no way in hell Molly would've been able to drive – she'd have crashed into something hours ago. Ironbark trees whipped past them, the branches scraping ear piercingly against the metal of the buggy as they closed in on the feral bull. Molly instinctively ducked as a low tree branch came terrifyingly close overhead, all her senses on high alert, knowing quick thinking and fast reactions were crucial right now.

Gary, Heath's brother, was in the back, ready to pounce on the scrubber bull when the moment arose. Which it did, in one swooping, action-packed minute as Heath finally got close enough to the bull to knock it over with the bullbar, pinning it beneath it, taking care as he did so to prevent too much bruising to the bull. Gary and Heath leapt effortlessly from the buggy and in a few fluent movements both of them were on the ground beside the bull, the leather bull strap between Gary's teeth so all hands were on the powerful beast as they struggled to get a hold of the bull's legs.

Molly stood up in the buggy, her breath caught in her throat, as she watched Heath buckle the strap around the bull's hind legs, making it impossible for the bull to get up. She found the way Heath handled himself so undeniably sexy ...

It was all over in a matter of seconds. The scrubber bull kicked and snorted, its aggression evident as it tried to hook Heath with one of its razor-sharp horns. It barely missed and Heath jumped backwards, landing on his butt and chuckling as he wiped a smear of blood from his forearm and transferred it onto his grubby jeans.

'Are you right, Heath?' Molly gasped, finally remembering to breathe, a flash of panic bolting through her as she realised Heath had scarcely missed being badly hurt. She couldn't bear to imagine him in physical pain, her heart breaking with the very thought.

Heath waved his hand casually in the air, a wayward smile lighting up his rugged features. 'Yeah, I'm fine, it's only a cut. Feisty bloody bugger, this one is!'

'A drop of blood's never killed anyone. Besides, you'd probably be feisty too if someone was trying to tie *your* legs up,' Gary added with a smirk as he made sure the bull was in the shade of the trees then jumped back into the buggy. 'Come on, Heath, let's head home. My belly's rumbling. I'll come back and pick this one up in the cattle truck after a quick morning tea. Don't let me forget the bloody saw blade this time so I can trim his horns down before we winch him up on the truck. Those things are lethal.'

Molly rubbed her stomach. 'I'd forgotten about food in all the excitement, but now you've mentioned it, I'm bloody starving too.'

Heath jumped over the side of the buggy and slid into the driver's seat, his face covered with dirt. Molly felt the urge to reach out and wipe the smudges from his face. 'Well, we've been out here since before sunrise, Molly, so it's no wonder you're hungry. But I'm sure Mum and Rose have been baking all morning and there'll be plenty of tasty goodies to feast on once we get back.'

Molly looked down at his torn shirt sleeve and on impulse she reached over, gently touching the place ripped by the bull's horn with her fingertips, wishing she could magically heal the spot the blood was seeping from. Heath caught her gaze and something flickered in his deep-blue eyes that made her belly flutter and her heart delightfully skip a few beats. She pulled her hand back, his skin burning her fingertips, the moment stirring a strange emotion deep inside her, unnerving her, making her blush. She turned and fixed her eyes on the bull, its body heaving as it took deep shuddering breaths.

*

Molly, Heath, Gary, Alice, John and Rose chatted amicably about what had been going on in their lives since they had last caught up. It had been close to five months since they'd last seen each other, so the conversation never lulled, and Molly loved it. The Miller family were such welcoming, close-knit people, and it was wonderful to be around them. The kettle whistled loudly and Molly pushed herself up from the dining table, her chair scraping behind her on the tiled floor. Filling six cups with hot water, she then placed two teaspoons of sugar in each, her spoon clanking loudly against the sides as she stirred them. She made sure she prepared a hot chocolate for Rose too.

'So, Rose, would you like to go out for a ride on Buck this afternoon?'

'Oh, Mum! Finally! I'd love to,' Rose replied delightedly as she stuffed the last piece of her lamington in her mouth, leaving a trail of chocolate and coconut around her lips.

'She's been telling me about Buck all morning,' Alice said, standing to help Molly carry the cups back to the table. 'It sounds to me like she's very proud of you for saving him from being sent to the meatworks by that grumpy station owner at Silverspur Station.'

Molly smiled warmly. 'That was all her doing. I just took it on to train him so he could be a great horse for Rose.'

Alice softly placed her hand on Molly's back. 'You're such a great mum. Good on you, love.'

'I'd agree with that,' Heath said, smiling.

'So, Molly, how was your morning out bull catching?' John asked as she passed him his coffee.

'It was fantastic! I love being out there.'

'Ah, that's music to my ears, a woman who enjoys the rough and tumble of bull catching. There should be more of your kind out there,' John said, waving his arm in the air. 'My Alice loves it too, that's why I married her.' He winked in Alice's direction.

'Oh, come on, you married me because I won your heart with my cooking,' Alice replied with a smirk.

John chuckled as he dunked a homemade chocolate-chip biscuit in his tea. 'Bugger, you discovered my secret. I thought I'd kept it hidden from you all these years.'

'Well, no rest for the wicked. I'm off to collect the bulls we caught this morning. Don't want to leave the buggers out there too long. It's a hot day. I'll take my coffee with me, if you don't mind. You coming, Dad and Heath? I'll need a hand to winch them up on the back of the truck,' Gary said, getting up from the table and grabbing the last lamington from the tray.

'Cor, Gary, talk about rushing a man,' John replied, trying to drink his coffee quickly and succeeding in scorching his tongue.

'Come on, Dad, where are your beans today? We've got work to do. Let's go!' Gary replied lightheartedly, repeating a phrase John had said to the boys on countless occasions when they were growing up.

Heath laughed at his dad and brother's banter. 'Yep, coming. Just give me a sec to finish my coffee. I'll meet you out front once you've sorted the cattle truck out, hey.'

'No worries.' Gary stepped out the back door.

'I have an exciting night planned, ladies,' Heath said, addressing Molly and Rose.

Rose clapped her hands. 'Ooh, goody! What is it?'

'Well, how does a movie and popcorn night sound?'

'So much fun!' Rose shrieked, almost falling backwards off her chair in excitement.

'Heath, that's wonderful of you. Sounds great,' Molly said, smiling.

A few loud blows of the air horn out the front announced that John and Gary were good to go. Heath excused himself from the table and gave Rose a kiss on the cheek. 'Enjoy your ride, sweetheart. I'll see you and your mum back here tonight, and then we'll be off back home in the morning.'

Rose's smile quickly turned into a frown. 'Oh, I don't want to go home! I'm having too much fun here.'

'We have to go home, darling. GG and Grandma will be missing us and you have to go back to school on Monday.'

'All right, then, if we have to.' Rose huffed as she got down from the dining table and put her plate and mug on the sink.

'Right, now go and get your riding gear on, Rose. Buck's waiting for you,' Molly said, ruffling Rose's hair.

'Yippee! I'll be back in a sec,' Rose said eagerly as she took off down the hallway, instantly forgetting her disappointment at going home.

Molly watched Rose disappear down the hallway and into the bathroom then turned her attention back to Alice. 'She loves coming to visit you, she never wants to go home.'

'Aw, that's lovely to hear. She's such a dear little thing. I love her to bits. She's the closest thing I have to a grandchild, really.' Alice stopped fumbling with the handle of her coffee mug, her eyes full of anguish as she looked back up at Molly. 'Sorry if that sounds a little strange. I mean, I know you and Heath aren't an item, but since losing Jenny and the baby, all I can think about is having a grandchild in the family. I'm not having any luck with Gary, he can't even find himself a girlfriend out here in the sticks. All the good ones are already taken.' Alice smiled, sighing softly before continuing. 'We were all so happy when we found out Jenny was pregnant; I'd even redecorated one of the spare rooms in preparation for when we got to babysit. And then, well ... she died. And along with her I think a part of Heath died too. I worry about him you know, a lot. How's he been doing?'

'He seems to be doing okay, Alice. He keeps himself really busy at Jacaranda and lately he even seems to be enjoying life again. It's good to see. He was down in the dumps for a long time, understandably so. We were all really worried about him there for a while, but he's a strong man and he pulled through. I think the counsellor helped him immensely. Lord knows the counsellor helped me.' Molly wiped tears from her eyes. The memory of Jenny dying in her arms, fretting about her unborn baby until she took her last breath, was still raw and painful. She tried not to think about it too much, but when she did it was still as heartbreaking as the day it had happened.

Alice pulled a few tissues from the box on the dining table and passed them to Molly. 'Oh dear, I'm so sorry, love. I didn't mean to upset you. Silly old fool I am. I keep forgetting that you were the one with her when it all happened. It must have been terribly hard on you.'

Molly blew her nose loudly. 'Don't be sorry, Alice. I know you didn't mean to upset me. It *was* awfully hard at the beginning, I had nightmares for months. I've dealt with the demons now, though. I just really miss Jenny, that's all. She was always with me, every day, out on the farm, helping me train the horses. We were basically joined at the hip.'

Alice reached across the table and took hold of Molly's hand, squeezing it sympathetically. 'Yes, we all miss her, love, very much. She was a beautifully spirited girl, just like you. But you know what? Life goes on. And I just hope that Heath finds a woman that he can fall in love with as madly as he was in love with Jenny. That would make me a very happy lady.'

'He will, Alice, don't you worry. Heath's a wonderful man. There aren't many women out there who could resist his charm. When he's ready to fall in love again he won't have any trouble finding a lovely lady. I'm sure of it.'

'I hope you're right, love,' Alice said as she slid her chair back and got up from the table, gathering empty cups and dirty plates. 'You know what, Molly? I reckon Heath has feelings for a woman already, and I have an inkling that this woman harbours feelings for him too. I'm just not sure this woman knows how to react to it. But I hope she figures it out soon, because I really like her.' Alice looked up at the ceiling in contemplation. 'No, actually, I adore her. She'd be so good for him.'

Molly felt the sword of jealousy stab her in the heart at the thought that there could be another woman in Heath's life and one that she wasn't even aware of. Although she couldn't have him, she didn't want anyone else to have him either. Selfish, yes, she admitted, but she was only human. She tried to act unperturbed by picking up pieces of coconut from the table. 'Oh, and who might that be?' she asked casually.

Alice smiled warmly, her eyes filled with compassion as she leant over and kissed Molly on the cheek. 'You, my dear. It's you. And you know what? It's okay to fall in love with him, Molly. Jenny would be so happy. She loved you like a sister.'

*

Molly watched Buck's body language closely as she lunged him in the round yard. Even though she knew he was ready for Rose to ride, she was still on guard, just in case. Alice's words were still rolling around in her mind but she couldn't let them distract her. Rose's safety right now was of top priority. There was no room for error once Rose was up in the saddle. The horse looked relaxed, at ease – a totally different horse to the one she had first met all those months ago. Comfortable with her decision to let Rose ride him, she tethered him to the hitching rail and began saddling him.

'Stop sucking in air, you big boofhead,' Molly said, as she tightened his girth strap. Buck sighed, as if understanding what she was saying, blowing his lips gently in defeat. Molly motioned for Rose to join her and Rose came running, her face lit up.

'You ready, Rose?'

'Ready as ever!' she shrieked.

'Right then, stand on this drum here and let me help you up.'

Rose slid into the saddle with ease, her year at pony club giving her confidence as she took hold of the reins. Buck stood quietly, ready for instructions. Rose beamed down at Molly, the sun's glare making her squint. 'What should I do first, Mum?'

'Just walk and trot him around the yard, sweetheart, and get him used to you being on his back. See if you can get him to back up and drop his head. Show him you're the boss, okay? Then, once you're comfortable together, you can get him into a canter.'

Rose gave Buck a squeeze, edging him forward, talking soothingly to him. Molly stood back, giving her daughter space, proud of the way Rose was handling him. She made her way over to the shade of an enormous paperbark and got comfortable, leaning back against the white trunk, happiness filling her with the thought that she had made at least one of her little girl's dreams come true.

*

Molly handed Rose a warm cup of Milo and snuggled up beside her on the couch as Heath put the movie *Flicker* into the DVD player. A bowl of popcorn sat on the coffee table along with a few blocks of chocolate, so they were all set for the movie night Heath had planned. Molly was impressed with his thoughtfulness – he'd even made sure to bring along a horse movie for Rose and a girly flick for her. She wasn't sure how they would make it through two films, considering it was already eight o'clock, but it was lovely to sit back and relax.

'Night, you three. We're off to bed to watch the telly in our room,' Alice said, giving Rose a kiss. 'Gary's staying over at his mate's tonight too – saves him driving when he's been drinking – so no need to leave the door unlocked for him.'

'Oh, okay. Aren't you and John joining us?' Molly said.

'No, love, we're old farts now and need our beauty sleep. We'll catch you all bright and early in the morning.'

Rose fell asleep halfway through her movie so Molly gently lifted her from the couch and carried her off to bed. She wandered back out to Heath and got cozy beside him, pulling a blanket from the back of the couch and spreading it over her. Even though it was hot during the day in the outback, at night it got very chilly.

She felt a little strange snuggling up on the couch beside him, especially after what Alice had said. Because deep down she knew Alice was right. Heath was falling in love with her and she could be falling in love with him; she just didn't want to admit it. She was comforted by Alice's words, which echoed Jade's and Aunty Cheryl's. Jenny had loved Molly like a sister. Maybe she had been thinking about it all the wrong way? Maybe it was okay for her to love him. Molly sighed mentally. She just needed a little time to mull it over, to really allow herself the freedom to sense her true feelings.

'Right, you ready to watch the next movie?' said Heath, the remote control at the ready.

Molly smiled. 'Sure am.'

'Hang on a tick, I might just go and grab a blanket for myself, it's bloody freezing.'

'You can share mine if you like, there's plenty of it,' Molly replied, spreading the blanket out over Heath. She groaned as she moved over, her back still sore from mustering.

'What's up?' Heath asked as he got comfy beneath the blanket.

'Oh, nothing, it's just my back. It's still a bit sore. I reckon I must have strained a muscle when we were out mustering.'

Heath grinned, wriggling his fingers in the air. 'Right then, time to cash in on that raincheck, I reckon.'

Molly felt her body temperature instantly soar as she imagined him touching her bare skin. 'Ah ... only if you're sure.'

'Of course I'm sure.' Heath leapt from the couch, dragging the blanket from Molly then placing it on the carpeted floor. He pulled the cushions from the couch and strategically scattered them about the blanket, then patted it. 'Come on, lie down here. I'll give you the massage before we start the next movie.'

'Can I go and put my sarong on first? It'll make it easier to get to my back.'

Heath shrugged. 'Whatever makes you comfortable. I'll set the little fan heater up so you don't freeze to death. Hey, I'll even warm up some oil. I think there's a bottle of almond oil in the bathroom cupboard.'

A few minutes later, Molly groaned pleasurably as Heath poured warm oil onto her back then began to firmly massage her sore spots. His hands felt like they were leaving red trails, the heat coming from them decadent against her bare flesh. She could feel his hot breath on her back as he exhaled deeply, the sensation sending luscious shivers all over her. With skin on skin the yearning inside that she had controlled until now began to grow, pleasurable tingles igniting places that made her want to roll over and tear all Heath's clothes off. But she couldn't; not yet, not here. So, in the privacy of her mind she imagined herself making unrestrained, passionate love to him, her strength of will no longer able to ward off the cravings. She thanked God he couldn't read her mind.

'There you are,' Heath whispered in her ear, his voice so husky she could tell he too was fighting off unknown desires.

She bit her bottom lip as she gathered her sarong and rolled over, her eyes searching for his in the dimly lit room. Heath sat beside her, wiping his tattooed hands on a towel to get rid of the excess oil. 'Did that do the trick?'

Molly nodded coyly. 'Uh-huh. It felt unbelievable. Thank you.'

She wriggled up to sitting and tied her sarong in a knot at the front, Heath only centimetres from her. The atmosphere between them was electric, the sexual tension in the room irrefutable. All Molly wanted to do was to kiss him all over, but instead she stood and made herself comfortable on the couch once more.

Heath got comfy beside her, smiling wickedly, the longing in his eyes almost choking her. 'Shall we watch the movie now?'

Molly's voice evaded her, her stomach doing backflips as she fought hard to catch her breath. 'Mmhmm.'

The movie started and all Molly could think of was how close Heath was to her, and how good he smelled. Her eyes drooped and she realised she was falling asleep, and tried to open her eyes wide to concentrate on the screen. The next thing she knew, she jerked awake, a heartbeat thumping softly against her cheek and an arm draped over her. The movie had finished and Heath had fallen asleep too.

She suddenly remembered where she was, feeling self-conscious that she had fallen asleep on Heath's shoulder. She slowly edged herself off the couch, trying hard not to wake him, part of her wanting to stay in the comforting warmth of his arms, but the level-headed part of her reminding her that she wasn't ready to make this decision. She gently pulled the blanket up over him and stood for a few moments watching him as he slept, imagining what it would feel like to kiss him again, to make love to him.

'Stop torturing yourself, girl!' She tore her gaze away from Heath, turned off the television, and tiptoed down the hallway to join Rose in bed. Heath Miller's magnetism was winning her over, and she wasn't too sure how much longer she could deny it.

CHAPTER

16

As Mark's dirt drive came into view, Molly fought the urge to turn around and drive straight back home. It was ten in the morning on a Thursday, so she was sure Mark would be up and about; most country people were out of bed before the sun had even had time to rise and he only played in the band on Friday and Saturday nights so it wasn't like he'd been out working late. She mulled over what she would say to him when he opened the door to her – that is, if he had the balls to. It had been two weeks since she had spoken to him last and that was when he'd stormed off and left her crying by the dam. She felt as though she had given him more than enough time to cool off, and as the days passed without a word she couldn't help thinking it was selfish and gutless of him not to face the reality of the situation. She had left a couple of messages for him over the last couple of days, since coming back from Ironbark Station, but he hadn't responded. Molly was torn between fury and despair. How could Mark choose to ignore the fact that he had a beautiful little daughter?

Her maternal instinct had clicked into top gear now and she was feeling extremely protective of Rose. She couldn't care less if Mark didn't want anything to do with Molly herself. It was a realisation that had surprised her at first, but she had come to the conclusion that she could never love a man as selfish as he was anyway. All she wanted to do today was explain to Mark how important it was to Rose to know her dad.

Molly pulled up under the shade of the enormous old mango trees, out of sight of the house, and looked at herself in the rear-vision mirror. She gave herself a quick pep talk about staying calm and strong, even though she felt a bit silly for doing so. She took a deep breath before heading towards the front of the house. An old blue Nissan Patrol caught her eye as she rounded the side. It was parked up beside the Fiat tractor under the shade of a big steel shed. Something twigged in her mind: she had seen the car around town before, and she racked her brain trying to remember whose it was, but couldn't. She shrugged her shoulders, deciding it wasn't any of her business anyway.

Molly's boots clomped on the timber verandah as she approached the front door. She strained her ears, listening for any signs of life in the house, hesitating for a moment before she knocked in case Mark was still in bed. Her bursting in on him asleep might put him in a bad mood even before she got to talk to him. She stood with her hands deep in her jeans pockets and pondered what to do. She felt a sudden rush of necessity to talk it all out with Mark so she reached out and rapped hard on the door.

Molly stood there for what felt like ages before she heard rushed footsteps coming towards the door. She held her breath, her stomach churning. She could hear the door being unlocked from inside and when she opened her mouth to say hello to Mark, was shocked when she was instead greeted by a young woman.

The woman was dressed in skimpy knickers and a man's Bonds singlet. She had obvious bed hair and smudges of black mascara beneath her eyes. She stared at Molly with disdain, visibly annoyed that she had been woken up. Molly realised it was the new woman who worked at the fish and chip shop in town and swiftly regained her composure.

'Hi. Is Mark about?'

'Yeah, he is, but he's still asleep. I was too, until you came knocking,' the young woman replied with a forced yawn. Molly guessed she'd be in her early twenties, if that. She got a strong whiff of stale alcohol on the woman's breath and stepped back a little. 'Well, um, maybe I'll come back later then.'

'That might be a good idea, maybe at a decent hour next time. Some people do like to sleep in, you know,' the woman retorted with irritation, looking Molly up and down as if *she* was the one standing at the doorway with hardly anything on.

Molly felt her temper flare and she swallowed down hard, determined not to yell at this rude girl standing before her; it would be a waste of her breath if she did. 'Actually, now I think about it, I reckon you should go and wake him up. I have to talk to him about something very important,' Molly said as calmly as she could.

'Oh yeah? Well maybe I don't want to wake him up.'

'Fine, I'll wake him up myself,' Molly hissed, her anger finally getting the better of her as she pushed past the woman and into the house, bumping straight into Mark, who was standing in the hallway in his boxer shorts looking very hungover.

'Have you been standing here the whole time?' Molly gasped, astonished that Mark had stooped low enough to get this woman to open the door so that he didn't have to talk to her.

'Yeah, I have been, Molly. I give up. You caught me,' he replied as he threw his hands up in the air in defeat. 'I thought you'd have gathered I wasn't ready to talk to you after not returning your calls, but obviously not, seeing you're here at my house, waking me up too, I might add.'

Molly could feel tears threatening to fill her eyes but she held them back, refusing to let Mark see her cry again. All she wanted to do at that moment was run, but she stood her ground and took a few deep breaths before speaking, very slowly, through gritted teeth.

'Well, now that I *am* here can we at least talk? If you decide you never want to speak to me again after you've listened to what I have to say then I promise to leave you alone. But at least hear me out. This isn't about me and you, Mark; this is about Rose, our six-year-old daughter. So how about acting like an adult and not being so goddamn selfish?'

'Oh my God! You have a child!' the woman shrieked.

Mark nodded, his annoyance plain to see as he rolled his eyes and sighed loudly. 'Okay, Molly. I don't want an argument this early in the morning and I think you need to hear some home truths about me too. Let me at least go and wash my face so I can wake up first. Have a seat out on the verandah, if you like. I'll make us both a cup of coffee – the stronger the better, I'm guessing.'

Molly didn't answer him; she couldn't speak another word, the shock of the situation getting the better of her. She could feel the woman behind her sticking daggers into her back and she desperately needed to get outside and breathe some fresh air before she turned around and punched her lights out. 'Nice meeting you,' Molly muttered sarcastically as she pushed past her and back out onto the verandah.

She glanced at the cozy chairs on offer but found it impossible to sit down, choosing to pace the hardwood floor instead as she waited for Mark to emerge from the house. She sounded like a horse with her boots clip-clopping on the timber boards, but the rhythm of the movement strangely calmed her down a little.

Mark came out fifteen minutes later, looking a little more decent now he was dressed, with two steaming cups of coffee in his hands. He handed one to Molly before sitting down in one of the cane chairs. 'Are you going to sit down, Molly, or are you going to keep pacing? It's making me uncomfortable,' he said, tapping the chair beside him.

Molly pulled the chair so it was as far away from Mark as it could be without her resorting to sitting out on the lawn and yelling to him over the rails. 'Sure, I'll sit. Now tell me, why have you chosen to completely ignore the fact that you have a daughter?'

'I thought *you* were the one who was going to do all the talking. So go ahead, talk. I'm all ears,' Mark replied gruffly, taking a sip from his coffee.

Molly cleared her throat. 'Okay then, I'll go first. Maybe I was wrong not telling you about Rose straightaway, but I didn't know you from a bar of soap and I wanted to make sure you were decent enough to be in Rose's life. I thought, after spending a few weeks with you, that you were a reliable, honest bloke, so I decided the time was right to tell you. I must admit now, though, I'm starting to question my judgement. Was I way off course?'

Mark glared at her but Molly ignored him and kept talking, needing to get it all out now that she had begun. 'I love Rose and she means the world to me. I thought I was doing the right thing. It's not her fault that I chose to wait, Mark, so don't make her suffer the consequences. It was just me being protective of her heart. She always talks about how she would love to meet her dad one day and I know it would make her so happy if she could.' Molly gently shook her head. 'But that day down by the dam, the way you reacted, and then not returning my calls ... I'm concerned that you'd rather not be in her life. I need you to at least *try* to think about how much it would mean to her if you got to know her and shared her life with her. Please, at least do that.'

Mark looked down at the floor, clearly uncomfortable. He was silent for a few moments, as if trying to find the right words. 'I suppose I need to say this without beating around the bush. I *never* wanted to have children, Molly. I really like my free and easy lifestyle. It suits me. That's who I am. I don't know if I can handle the responsibilities of fatherhood and it scares me to death just thinking about it. I'm just not cut out for it. I don't know what else to say to you. That's why I reacted the way I did and haven't rung you back. I knew what I had to say wouldn't be what you wanted to hear. I'm sorry.'

Now Molly was the one who was silent. Her mind was spinning and she felt like her heart was about to tear in two. She pointed towards the door of the house. 'So, you'd rather have the freedom to bring home random girls like that, and party all night. Is this what you're trying to say to me, Mark?'

Mark nodded. 'I suppose, in a way, it is. I really do believe that Rose will be better off without me in her life. For more reasons than I'd like to admit.'

'So why did you want to take me out on a date when you knew I had a child, given you don't want children cramping your style?'

'Well, to be frank, I hadn't thought that far ahead, Molly. I wasn't looking at having a serious relationship with you. I'm not one for commitment. Sorry if you felt any differently.'

Molly was disgusted that she had kissed him by the dam. He was just another one of those guys who only wanted one thing, ruled by what was between their legs. What had she been thinking going anywhere near him? He'd had her completely fooled, that's for sure. 'So, what you're saying is that you *don't* want to get to know Rose?'

Mark took a sip from his coffee and contemplated what Molly had just said, taking his own sweet time to answer. She wanted to reach out and shake him, tell him that he didn't know what he was giving up, but instead she tucked her hands under her legs as if sitting on them would control her urges.

'You probably won't believe me but I've thought about this a lot in the past couple of weeks. I just can't get my head around the fact that last month I was a free agent and then this month I'm a father. I'm afraid of not living up to society's expectations of what a father *should* be. I don't want to have a life with white picket fences and a family sedan. Hell, I don't even want to get married.' Mark shuffled his feet along the floor and took a deep breath, exhaling slowly as he rubbed his temples. 'When she's old enough to take care of herself I can see myself being in her life, but for now, I just can't do it, Molly. I'm sorry but I'd rather be brutally honest now than try to be part of Rose's life, only to hurt her. Like I said, I truly think she's better off without me.'

Molly stood up, giving him a look of absolute pity, and then walked away. She was utterly drained and had nothing more to say. He wasn't worth speaking to any more anyway. She couldn't *force* him into Rose's life. He was right, he would just end up hurting Rose, and that was the last thing she wanted. She wondered if he would regret this one day. When he was old and grey, when his looks had faded and his charm tarnished, when he had no family to share his life with, maybe he would look back on this day and realise that he had made the biggest mistake of his life.

CHAPTER
17

A march fly latched painfully onto Molly's arm as she laid it out with one hard slap, wiping away the spot of blood it had left with the cuff of her shirt. She smiled as she watched Kenny, Heath and Trev get dressed in their beekeeping garb, white suits with elasticised ankle and wrist cuffs plus gloves, veils and hats. They looked like mad scientists out of some science fiction movie.

Molly had been sure to wash the outfits twice before the men put them on. Any stings that were retained in the suits from last time would continue to send out an alarm pheromone that caused aggressive behaviour in the bees, often provoking a stinging frenzy. Molly had also learnt from her beekeeping course that most of the bees were females – and well, like most females, you didn't want to give them a reason to defend their home and families. The females were the ones that did all the hard work and collected all the pollen, so they were very protective of their hives.

Kenny was extra nervous about having to move the hives as he had been attacked by the bees once before and was forever haunted by the memory. Molly had insisted that he not help today, seeing as he was so worked up about it, but he was determined to get over his fear of bees, saying the only way he could do that was to go out and have a face-off with them.

They had to move the bees every so often, depending on what part of the farm they wanted the bees to pollinate. The insects were a very important part of fruit farming and most farmers had hives scattered around their properties. It increased the yield of the fruit, which helped put more money in the farmers' pockets. The added bonus was the fresh honey, which had a hint of mango flavour in it from the bees visiting all the mango flowers. Molly and Rose loved it drizzled over ice-cream for a sweet treat. It was heavenly.

Trev, Kenny and Skip jumped up in the back of the Land Cruiser and Heath slid into the front with Molly. She felt a shiver course through her entire body as his hand brushed hers. Molly knew he must have felt it too, as he looked over at her and smiled playfully. They had been flirting with each other since they'd come back from Ironbark Station, the atmosphere between them intense, the pair of them teasing each other to the brink. She had taken everyone's advice on board – Aunty Cheryl's, Jade's and Alice's, and the fact that all three women believed it was okay for her to fall in love with Heath was starting to sit well with her. It was exciting, and she was enjoying the playful seduction, the secret fleeting looks that she and Heath would share throughout the day and the way they would deliberately brush past each other.

She started the engine and headed towards the back of the property where the hives were presently being kept. She had mowed the area nearest the dam earlier that morning so the bees' new home, three kilometres away, was ready to go. It was very important to make sure the hives were close to water so they had plenty to drink. Another vital point was to make sure the hives were moved more than two kilometres from their previous location, or the bees would go back to where their home *used* to be. Bees orient to their hives by physical landmarks, not by some extraordinary radar. Even though Molly was allergic to bees she loved keeping them on the property, and found their way of life fascinating.

As she drove down the paddock Molly glanced over towards Heath. He was the perfect example of a real man, rugged and strong – such a contrast to Mark. And Heath was so loving and unselfish, whereas all Mark thought about was himself. A selfish person could never love another, she contemplated.

With that simple but influential comparison, Molly found her thoughts wandering back to the last time she had seen Mark. It had been almost a month since that awful morning on the verandah, and she had not heard a word from him since. It was like he didn't even exist, and in a way she was happy about that. Rose was certainly none the wiser, getting on with her life like any normal six-year-old girl, with a perpetual smile on her face and a passion for life. For the first time, Molly began to understand that Rose had all she needed in life just as she was, and that she didn't *need* her real father. The fact that Mark would probably break Rose's heart made her even more determined to keep him away from her. She decided to tell Rose about him only once she was old enough to understand it all. Molly no longer carried around the guilt and shame of not knowing the father of her daughter – that chapter in her life was closed, and it felt damn good. She smiled softly as she remembered how worried Heath had been when she told him what Mark had said to her that day down by the dam, and the way Heath had held her close, she had felt so secure in his arms, as though nothing could hurt her, as though his love alone would protect her.

'Shit, Molly! Watch out!' Heath hollered as Molly caught a glimpse of a kangaroo the size of a boulder bounding directly into her path. She didn't want to slam the brakes on as that would send Trev, Kenny and Skip hurtling off the back so instead she swerved in between two mango trees, wincing as she heard the branches engraving deep grooves into her beloved Land Cruiser. Not that the Cruiser didn't have its fair share of scratches and dints already.

'You blokes okay up the back?' Molly called out as they came to a standstill, the terrified kangaroo bounding out of sight.

'Yeah, mate. Bugger me dead, that was one of the biggest roos I've ever seen!' Trev called back.

'It looked as though it'd been taking steroids,' Heath said, chuckling.

'I'm jealous. I'd love to have muscles as big as that roo's. Then the chicks would really dig me!' Kenny laughed.

'It's better to have a woman that loves you for your mind, not for your muscles, Kenny!' Molly called back, giggling, as she reversed back into the mango drill and towards the beehives.

Dusk was looming as they arrived at the hives and Molly sat safely inside her Land Cruiser with Skip, watching the men at work. It was a perfect time of the day to be moving hives as dusk was when the bees shut up shop and moved indoors for the night. Occasionally, a few rogues would still be hanging around the outside so you just had to be careful not to disturb them.

She'd have loved to have been out there with them in a crazy suit herself, but she had spent a night in a Cairns private hospital when her face had puffed up to the size of a watermelon after a bee sting. Her lips had been so swollen it looked as though she had overdosed on Botox. She chuckled to herself. It was funny now, but at the time it had been quite scary. She'd been out helping David move some of the hives when *wham*! A bee had gotten into her suit somehow and stung her right on the face. Within a minute she began to feel her face swell. Heath, Trev and Kenny had struggled to keep straight faces when they had first walked into the hospital room, letting their laughter rip as soon as Molly told them to stop acting like it was a life-or-death situation. She had copped it from them for weeks afterwards, but it was all in good fun and she didn't mind having a good laugh at her own expense.

Trev gave a few short raps on the roof once he, Heath and Kenny were all up safely on the back of the Cruiser, letting her know they were good to go. Molly started the engine, driving very slowly, cringing every time she couldn't avoid a bump in the dirt track, constantly checking her rear-vision mirror to make sure the hives were still inactive and the men weren't getting stung.

Skip sat beside her, panting heavily, causing the windscreen to fog up. 'Are you right there, buddy? Stop breathing so hard! I can't see three metres in front of me.'

Skip just looked at her and barked. She rolled her eyes at him and switched the air-conditioner on full bore with the vents pointing towards the windscreen. The fog cleared up in seconds as Molly enjoyed the cool breeze blowing around her face, feeling a bit guilty that the men were stuck on the back, sweltering in their protective suits in the heat. They had to be cooking out there.

When they finally arrived at the spot she had chosen the men carefully lifted the hives off the back of the Land Cruiser and carried them over to the metal stand Molly had made up for them. They were moving in slow motion, trying their best not to get stung. And then, just as they placed the last hive down on the stand, it happened. Kenny squealed shrilly, running like a bat out of hell towards the dam, slapping at his crutch like a lunatic. The act in itself looked mighty painful and Molly grimaced as she watched him hit the water with a massive splash, a gigantic spray of water swallowing him up for a few seconds. Perhaps a bee had somehow gotten into his suit. She wound down the window to check. 'Is he all right, guys?'

Heath and Trev were laughing so hard they found it impossible to answer, instead choosing to wave their hands in the air as if to say he was fine. Molly found their laughter contagious and burst out laughing herself just as Kenny emerged from the water, resembling a swamp monster rising from the depths of the muddy floor below. He was dripping with mucky water, his suit clinging to him like glue, lily-pad tentacles wrapped all around him. He was having trouble walking now that the suit was weighed down with water and he took big, long steps as he made his way back towards them. He looked like a half-drowned Neil Armstrong attempting to walk on the moon. Molly was breathless with laughter.

'A bloody bee stung me fair on the scruffies! I don't know how the hell it got in there but it went straight for the family jewels and it hurt like nothing's ever hurt before! I reckon they're going to swell to the size of small rockmelons,' Kenny shouted, shuffling painfully from foot to foot while holding onto his groin for dear life. 'It feels as though some bastard's dropped a match down my jocks and my pubes are on fire.'

'Ouch. Bloody hell, mate. That's got to hurt, big time,' Heath said. 'I'd offer to pluck the stinger out but I ain't going anywhere near your hairy balls. I don't care how much of a great mate you are.'

'You put on quite a show there, Kenny. I nearly wet my dacks!' Trev added, wiping away the tears that were running down his face.

'Tell me about it,' Molly said, still chuckling.

'Great mates you lot are!' Kenny said, a smirk forming. 'Now get me home so I can put some ice on my balls before they explode. I can feel them swelling even more as we speak.'

'Oh, going visual, Kenny. Not a pretty sight,' Molly replied with a look of mock horror spreading over her face.

'Oh, ha-di-ha-ha!' Kenny said, his face creasing up.

Molly found herself smiling the whole way back to the workers' cottage. She felt so free, so alive, and so happy. The world needed more laughter in it, and more love, she thought, peeking over at Heath.

CHAPTER
18

Skip began to bark insistently as Molly pulled on her rhinestone Ariat boots and hopped about madly on one leg. She heard a toot out the front of the house. She quickly brushed her long dark hair and took one last look in the mirror, applying soft-pink lip gloss as she ran down the hall and out onto the verandah, making sure to lock the door securely behind her – everyone else was already at the rodeo. Heath and the guys had left early that morning as he was riding in the bull comp and needed to be there to prepare.

She couldn't wait to see him in the centre ring. He knew how to give it his all and boy, he looked good in his chaps, spurs, boots and cowboy hat. It was enough to drive a woman wild. Not that she needed *that* to drive her wild. She was finding Heath harder and harder to resist, and her need to keep her emotional distance from him was no longer consuming her. She had come to accept that Jenny would approve of her and Heath getting together. Why wouldn't she? Jenny had known that Molly didn't look at love lightly; it was something she took very seriously. If Jenny *was* looking down on them, which Molly liked to believe she was, she would know that Molly would take care of Heath, and that she would love him unconditionally.

It had been two months since she had last seen Mark and in that time she had accepted that it would have never worked between them anyway. They were way too different. Mark had no direction, no concern for anyone else other than himself, and was only after one thing when it came to women. Molly found that extremely unattractive. He *had* taught her one very important thing, though: just how deeply she wanted to be in love, to have a brother or sister for Rose, to find her knight in shining armour. It was time for her to acknowledge her dream and to not let anything or anyone stand in the way. Maybe Cheryl had been right. Maybe the love of her life had found her a long time ago and she had just been too blind to see it.

She smiled as she heard the country tunes blaring from Jade's car stereo, her belly fluttering with anticipation at the night ahead. Jade had offered to drive to the Chillagoe rodeo this year as Molly had driven last year. They always took turns. Melinda waved cheerfully from the passenger-side window of the Toyota Hilux and Molly waved enthusiastically back. She sternly told Skip to stay put on the verandah, reminding him that he was the king of the castle for now and he had to take care of Jacaranda Farm. His ears drooped as he sat down on his rug, clearly miserable at being left behind. Molly leant down and gave him a loving scratch on the head and he instantly cheered up, his tail making tapping sounds on the timber floorboards as he fervently wagged it.

Grabbing her swag from beside the door, Molly ran down the steps and out to the girls, keen to hit the road. She was looking forward to taking Rose on some of the rides this afternoon, especially the dodgem cars; they always had a blast. David and Elizabeth had taken Rose with them before lunch so they could watch the wood-chopping competition. Molly wished she could have gone with them, but she'd had to work on one of the neighbour's horses.

'Hey there, Molly. Are you ready for a great night?' Jade screamed over the music, grinning madly.

'This cowgirl is up for anything! Giddy up!' Molly replied as she slid in beside Melinda.

'Well, in that case, tonight is going to be full of fun!'

'Yeehaaaa!' Molly hollered out the window as they drove off in a cloud of red dust. She chuckled as she caught a glimpse of Skip on the verandah, his head cocked to the side, looking at the three of them as if they were bonkers.

*

Jade ended up having to park half a kilometre from the rodeo entrance, under the shade of a big old Queensland waratah tree. There were four-wheel drives and utes lined up as far as the eye could see and Molly guessed there were more people at the rodeo than actually lived in Chillagoe. But, like themselves, a heck of a lot of rodeo lovers made their way to the little country town on the fringe of the vast Australian outback for its biggest night of the year. The Chillagoe rodeo was quite famous in its own right amongst rural and city dwellers alike. It wasn't at all like the big Mareeba rodeo, which Molly also loved with a passion; it was more of a family bush rodeo where you could sit much closer to the fast-paced action than you were able to in the grandstands at the Mareeba rodeo grounds. The riders were that close you could basically smell their adrenaline, making you feel more a part of the action.

'Oh yum, I can smell loads of gastronomical delights!' Molly pronounced as she stepped out of the Hilux, sniffing the air exaggeratedly.

'Yeah, my mouth is watering just thinking about devouring a huge plate of those spare ribs dripping in gooey hickory sauce,' Jade said hungrily as she wrapped her arm around Molly's shoulder.

'I'm grabbing myself a dagwood dog covered in tomato sauce and then I'm going to top it off with a waffle with lashings of whipped cream!' Molly declared, licking her lips.

'I'm not going on any rides with you two after all that food,' Melinda said, laughing.

Jade unhooked her arm from Molly's and gave Melinda a quick hug. 'Give me an hour for the food to settle and we'll be hooning around in the dodgem cars with no worries, Mel!'

They made their way down the road, towards the scores of sounds and smells emanating from the rodeo grounds. A man's twangy voice was booming over a microphone, country music floated all around them, crowds were cheering, children were screaming with excitement and the smell of cattle and horses wafted delightfully in the air.

'Hey, Jade, remember last year when they had to cancel the night's events because termites had chewed through the lighting poles and they'd fallen over?' Molly said, the memory making her smile.

'Are you serious?' Melinda asked.

Jade laughed. 'Oh, I'd forgotten! Only in the bush could something like that happen.'

They joined the long line of people waiting to pay their entrance fee. Molly pulled out her mobile and dialled her granddad's number.

'Hello, love.' David's voice was hard to hear over the sounds of people clapping and cheering around him.

'Hi, Granddad. Whereabouts are you guys?'

'We're sitting on a picnic blanket over on the right-hand side of the arena. I'd hurry up if I were you, though, love. Heath is getting ready to ride in the next half hour or so and Rose is just about wetting her pants she's so excited.'

Molly felt her belly flutter at the mention of Heath's name. 'Okay. We're just paying to get in and I have to grab some food, then we'll be there. Would any of you like something to eat or drink while I'm at it?' Molly asked, looking at her watch.

'Hang on, love, I'll just ask.' Molly listened as in the background Rose rattled off all the food she wanted. 'Rose would like some fairy floss, a frozen Coke and a dagwood dog, if that's okay. Seeing as she's not eaten all arvo I reckon she's going the whole hog today. Grandma and I will go and grab something soon so don't worry about us. You'll have your hands full with Rose's order by the sounds of it.'

'Ok, Granddad. No worries. See you in a few minutes then.'

'See you soon,' David replied.

'Heath's going to be riding soon, girls, so we'd better get a move on.'

The three girls made their way over to the food vans and grabbed as much food as they could manage to carry, making sure they got Rose's, before squeezing their way through the crowd. Molly spotted Rose leaning up against the timber railings, her eyes glued to the poddy riders in the centre ring. The crowd cheered as children under the age of twelve, and sometimes as young as three, rode calves in the same way as the adult riders rode bulls. One of their gloved hands was strapped down firmly to a bull rope while the other was up in the air, as they swayed and moved with the bounding calf. They only had to stay on the poddy for six seconds instead of eight. For safety reasons, two men ran beside the calf, ready to catch the children if they fell. Molly loved watching them. The kids looked so cute dressed up like cowgirls and cowboys. Rose had tried it a few times but found it a bit too scary, telling Molly she'd prefer to watch. Molly just admired her for giving it a go in the first place.

Molly smiled as she, Jade and Mel sat down on the blankets Elizabeth and David had spread out in an excellent spot close to the action. Jade and Melinda said quick hellos before tucking into their food. Molly handed David and Elizabeth a coffee each.

'I couldn't come empty handed when I was going to devour all this food in front of you. Has Rose been behaving herself?'

Elizabeth nodded. 'She's been an angel, as always. She's so mesmerised by what's going on in the arena that we haven't really moved from this spot all afternoon.'

'She does love rodeos. Bit like her mum, hey,' Molly said, smiling as she looked towards Rose, who still hadn't noticed she was there. 'Hey, Rose. Are you going to come and give your mum a cuddle?' she called out.

'Mum!' Rose squealed as she ran towards her. 'Heath's coming on soon. I can't wait to watch him!'

'I know, sweetheart. Me neither. It's exciting, isn't it?'

The spectators hushed as a well-dressed, deep-voiced presenter came out onto the centre ring and announced the commencement of the bull riding. The crowd demonstrated their pleasure with whistles, clapping and cheering. Molly had butterflies in her belly as Heath waved to her from his perch high up on the timber railings beside the chutes. She waved back, mouthing the words 'good luck'. He gave her the thumbs up, slid down onto the dusty ground and disappeared out the back. Just before he stepped out of sight, Molly gazed at his muscular frame, his chaps flapping in the breeze framing the curves of his gorgeous butt. She felt a burning desire rush through her as she imagined sliding her hands inside his shirt and over his powerful chest. She never would have believed she could feel like this about Heath. But now, here she was, her heart skipping a beat whenever she saw him, her body aching for his touch. The kiss she had shared with him had changed everything, there was no denying it, and there was no turning back. Her lust for him was driving her insane. She had even been dreaming about him. His manly tattooed hands would slide over her tingling skin – just like they had on the night he'd massaged her – sending shock waves through her entire body, while his gorgeous full lips caressed her own. His deep-blue eyes would swallow her whole as he explored her mouth with his tongue, flicking it over her lips, teasing her to the point of no return, caressing her erect nipples with his fingertips and kissing her belly as he made his way down to taste her sweetness. Then abruptly she would wake, aching for him. It was sexual bliss and torture all rolled into one, especially when she had to work with him during the day. She had often caught herself admiring how his back rippled with strength as he did hard manual labour on the farm. How he smiled so sexily at her from beneath the rim of his hat, his eyes hinting at just what he'd like to do to her if he ever got her behind closed doors.

Jade leant over and whispered in her ear, snapping her out of her trance. 'How about you just pull your eyeballs out and stick them to Heath, might make it a bit easier for you.'

Molly felt her face flush as she giggled and covered her mouth in coyness. 'How do you know I was perving at Heath? It could have been any one of those cowboys back there,' she whispered, pointing to the chutes.

Jade grinned mischievously and leant in to whisper in Molly's ear again. 'Go for it! He's gorgeous, inside and out. Don't let him slip away or you'll regret it.'

The crowd roared as the first bull came bounding out of the chutes, all four hoofs of the ground. The young cowboy hung on for dear life, his form proving he was new to the sport. He made it to the four-second mark then fell from the bull's back, his feet hitting the ground first as he ran for the safety of the railings. Molly applauded his effort, along with the other spectators. You had to be tough to be a bull rider and she admired him for getting out and giving it a go.

'Mum! Heath is on next!' Rose squealed as she ran for the railing with her fairy floss.

Molly watched on, her body tingling with anticipation as Heath mounted the snorting, bucking bull inside the enclosure. She knew from her experience behind the chutes that Heath would be making sure his gloved hand was firmly in the grip of the bull rope while planting his bum fair and square on the back of the massive beast. It was all for the eight-second thrill, and the prize money, and Molly knew all too well how a person could crave that massive adrenaline rush. She got a taste of it when she was working with the horses and they bucked.

Heath nodded. The men at the front of the gate pulled a rope and the gate swung open, releasing the massive bull out into the arena with Heath planted firmly on its back. He moved like he was at one with bull, always ready for its next buck. The seconds ticked by like they were hours as the swarm of spectators stood and cheered Heath on, giving Molly goosebumps all over from the sheer passion of their support for him. The buzzer rung out and Heath released his hand from the rope. He jumped from the bull, scampering for the closest rail so the bull didn't turn and collect him with its deadly horns. The rodeo clowns ran in to divert the bull's attention, directing it towards the exit gate of the arena. Molly smiled proudly at Heath as he threw his hat up in the air and bowed to the adoring crowd, then turned in her direction to give her a smile that would melt any woman's heart. And melt Molly's heart it did.

CHAPTER
19

Once the centre-ring action had come to an end the families began packing up to leave, making way for the hardcore partygoers who were staying on for the night's festivities.

Molly gave Rose an affectionate kiss on the cheek. 'Have you had a good day, sweetheart?'

'I've had a great time, thanks, Mum. I especially loved riding in the dodgem cars with Heath while we chased you and Aunty Jade about. It was fun crashing into each other,' Rose replied with a contented smile, giving in to a big yawn.

'I'm glad you had fun, because that's what a rodeo's all about. Now, you behave for GG and Grandma and I'll see you first thing in the morning, okay?'

Rose nodded and wrapped her arms around Molly. 'Okay, Mum. Love you.'

'Love you too,' Molly replied adoringly. She gave Elizabeth and David a quick hug. 'Thanks for offering to take Rose home with you and letting me stay here to party with the girls. You're the greatest! Love you both.'

'Not a problem, Molly. You have a good time, dear, and drive home safely in the morning,' Elizabeth replied as she slid into the passenger seat.

Molly waved as David, Elizabeth and Rose pulled out of the rodeo grounds' car park. She watched their tail-lights vanish into the sea of other vehicles then turned to Jade and Melinda with a mischievous smile. 'It's time to party, ladies!'

'Woohoo!' cried Jade.

'Rum and Coke time! Last one to the bar has to shout the first round!' Melinda yelled as she sprinted towards the bar.

'Oi! That's not fair, Mel. You got a head start!' Jade called after her as she took on the challenge.

'I'll beat you both to it!' Molly shouted as she ran breathlessly past the pair of them, arriving at the bar twenty seconds before Mel and Jade and running smack-bang into Mark. Her wide grin instantly dissolved as Mark leant on the bar and gave her a drunken smirk.

'Well, howdy doody, Misssssss Molly, fancy running into you here. How's it going?' he slurred, just as Jade and Mel joined Molly at the bar, out of breath and giggling like a pair of schoolkids. 'Do you want to have a drink with me?'

Molly hadn't seen Mark drunk before and it wasn't a pretty sight. 'Looks like you've had a few too many already, Mark. Start the party early, did we?'

Jade put a protective arm around Molly's shoulder. 'Are you okay, Molly?' she asked, looking daggers at Mark.

'Yeah. I'm fine, Jade. Just in bad company here, that's all. How about we go around to the other side of the bar, order ourselves a few drinks, then go and find the guys, hey?' she replied, staring straight at Mark.

'Hey there, Jade. Oh yeah, Molly told me you were a lesbian. How's that going for you? I reckon you just haven't met the right bloke yet, babe. No way in the world you'd choose to be a muff-diver if you'd ever got it on with a *real* man. Although, now I get a good look at you, I'm pretty sure no real man would want to get with a lesbo like you anyway ...'

Jade reached out to slap Mark's face, but Molly grabbed her hand just in time. 'Leave it, Jade. He's not worth it.'

Mark just laughed, adding fuel to the fire. Molly pushed Jade back gently, standing between her and Mark. She dug her finger into his chest, wishing she could gouge his heart out and crush it like he had hers. 'How dare you talk to Jade like that! Learn some respect or stay the hell away from me.'

'Oh, fair go, Molly! I ain't no axe murderer!' Mark protested before he tried to catch the barmaid's attention by wolf-whistling.

The young woman behind the bar smiled and came towards him. 'Hey there, babe, another round of whisky on ice?'

'Yep, please, Tasha. Thanks, sweetpea.'

'My pleasure, as always,' the girl replied, batting her eyelashes at him.

Molly felt sick as she watched him flirt with the young barmaid. Mark was such a player and a darn good one at that, having even fooled Molly into believing she could have a meaningful relationship with him – all to get her in the sack. What a sucker she had been. She should have known better than to trust him. Her alarm bells should have been ringing when he had taken off at the Mount Garnett rodeo. What decent man does that? He obviously knew the barmaid well, seeing they were on a first-name basis, and she could tell they had probably slept together too. Mark turned to speak to Molly as the barmaid sauntered off to get his whisky. 'So, can I buy you that drink?'

'I don't think so,' Molly replied sternly, turning her back on him and walking away with Jade and Melinda.

Jade gave her a friendly rub on the back. 'Don't let him ruin your night. Like you said to me, he isn't worth it.'

Molly nodded. 'I know. I'll steer well clear of him, pretend he isn't even here. I've done that for seven years so I'm pretty good at it. I'm so sorry he said that to you.'

'No worries, Molly, I've dealt with it for most of my life – I can handle it. It just shocked me when he said it, that's all. He's nothing to me, so I really don't care what he thinks,' Jade said with a smile.

While Jade ordered them a round of drinks Molly tried to shake the feeling of bitterness, searching the sea of faces in front of her for any sign of Heath, Trev or Kenny. She felt a man's arm slide around her waist from behind and, thinking it was Mark, she turned around and walloped him fair on the head.

'Ouch, bloody hell, Molly! You've got one mean right hook!' Heath yelped as he jumped back in shock and Trev doubled over in laughter beside him.

Molly gasped and covered her mouth. 'Heath! I'm so sorry! I thought you were someone else.'

'I bloody hope so,' Trev said, chuckling.

'I don't know who you thought I was, but I can tell from the force behind that blow that you don't like them one bit.' Heath rubbed his head gingerly. 'Who *did* you think I was?'

'I just ran into Mark at the bar and he's more than a little drunk. I thought it was him being a smart-arse,' Molly replied as Jade handed her an icy can of rum and Coke. She took a huge swig, enjoying the sweet taste as it trickled over her tongue.

Heath looked around the crowd, obviously trying to spot Mark, the pulse in his temples throbbing. She grabbed his hand. 'Don't go being a hero. I can look after myself. He won't bother me after the cold welcome I just gave him. Let's just celebrate your victorious ride, okay? I'm so proud of you! Tonight's meant to be about good times with great mates. I don't want a fight to ruin it all.'

Trev raised his beer in the air and then took a massive slug of it. 'I'll drink to that.'

Molly giggled. 'You'd drink to anything, Trev!'

Heath placed his hand protectively on Molly's cheek. 'Okay. As long as he keeps away from you I'll keep away from him. But he'd better not try anything. I don't need much of an excuse to knock him out, believe me.'

The band began to play 'Cotton-Eyed Joe' and Jade squealed with pleasure. 'Come on! We have to dance to this one. It's a country classic!'

Jade and Mel dragged Molly towards the bootscooting mob. Molly tried to pull Heath along as well, but he stood his ground and shook his head emphatically. 'I'll stay here and mind our spot.'

Molly felt the music wash over her as she danced like there was no tomorrow. After a couple of songs Kenny came bounding towards them, his arms flying around as he danced like a crazy monkey. He was so uncoordinated that Molly couldn't help but giggle. Kenny didn't mind, he just laughed along with her while flaunting more insane dance moves.

Two hours later, Molly was back at the bar standing with Heath. She had finally managed to lure him onto the dance floor and he'd actually impressed her with his moves. She hadn't seen Mark again and she noticed the barmaid that had been flirting with him earlier was missing too. They were probably off in the bushes somewhere. She winced at the thought.

She jiggled on the spot, trying to cool off as sweat dripped down her back, throwing back a shooter and smiling as a drop ran down her chin. Heath reached out and gently wiped it away. They held each other's eyes, the passionate fire between them building. Heath seized the moment, leaning in to whisper in her ear.

'Want to go for a walk somewhere quiet? I really need to tell you something.'

Molly nodded. Without uttering a word, she took Heath's hand and led him out into the night, away from the mass of revellers. The music began to fade into the distance as they strolled further into the darkness.

Once they'd reached a place where they could be private, Heath stopped. He took Molly's hands in his and faced her. The moonlight lit up her face and there was a depth in her eyes he had never seen before. He took a second to find his voice, clearing his throat. 'God, you're beautiful.' He reached out and ran his hand down her face, tracing her lips, feeling her warm breath caress his fingers.

Molly found it hard to look into his eyes. She felt like she was falling and was afraid he wasn't going to catch her. She looked down at the ground and kicked at it nervously with her boot. 'You're not too bad yourself.'

Heath gently pushed her chin up so she was facing him. 'I want you to see me when I say this. I can't hold it in any more. I want to be with you always, Molly Jones. I want to kiss you, touch you, love you ... ' His husky voice washed over her like warm honey.

She gasped. Her feelings were so intense they were almost choking her. She was speechless, a million words running through her mind but none of them finding their way out of her lips. She drew in a deep breath, needing to explain before they went any further. 'I'm in love with you too, Heath. It's just, well, I felt guilty at first because of my bond with Jenny. I thought it was wrong of me to have feelings for you.'

'Oh, Molly, I felt guilty too, at first, because of the relationship you and Jenny had and because of the love I'd shared with Jenny. But then I reasoned with myself – Jenny loved you, and she'd love you to be with me, and me with you.'

Molly wrapped her arms around herself, happy tears filling her eyes. Heath had said exactly what she needed to hear from him.

Heath reached out and wiped her tears. 'I'm so sorry, Molly. I've said the wrong thing. I shouldn't have ...'

Molly reached out and grabbed him, pulling him into her as she hungrily kissed him. Heath wrapped his strong arms around her waist and picked her up off the ground, his tongue caressing hers as she moaned in ecstasy. He ran his warm lips down her neck and Molly let her head fall backwards as she wrapped her legs around his waist and her arms around his broad shoulders, enjoying the feeling of his stubble as it ran down her throat. Heath kissed her breasts and she shivered as she felt his warm breath caressing her nipples through her shirt. Molly could feel his yearning for her through his jeans and she groaned in satisfaction at the thought of feeling him inside her. She ran her nails up his back and down his chest. He nibbled on her neck and then breathed huskily into her ear.

'Let's not do this here, Molly. Not like this. You mean too much to me to have a quickie in the dust of the rodeo grounds. I want you so badly right now, but let's not let it happen here. Let me plan a getaway for us, by the ocean. How does that sound to you, gorgeous?'

Molly held his gaze. 'That sounds beautiful. That's one of the reasons I adore you, Heath. You are the most thoughtful man I've ever met. *And* the sexiest.'

Heath kissed her hard on the lips and let out a massive sigh.

'We're going to have to wait a few minutes before we head back, though. I kind of have a problem.'

Molly giggled, her legs still firmly around his waist. 'Yeah, I can kind of feel that, Heath.'

She slid back to the ground and Heath gently cupped her face with his strong hands. 'What's your granddad and grandma going to think about all this?'

Molly looked deep into his eyes. 'They'll be fine. They both think so highly of you. You'll just need to keep this quiet until I talk to them, okay? I want them to hear it from me first.'

'Of course. And then *I'd* like to talk with David and Elizabeth, so I can tell them how much you and Rose mean to me.'

Molly smiled. 'I'm sure they'd love to hear that.'

Heath pulled her into a warm embrace. 'You know, you've just made me the happiest man alive, Molly Jones.'

'And I'm the luckiest woman in the world to have found you,' Molly told him.

CHAPTER
20

The kitchen clock ticked loudly above Molly, echoing throughout the dark, quiet house. The sound was comforting, familiar. She dropped two heaped teaspoons of sugar into each of the three cups of black tea, stirring gently as she thought about what she was going to say. She was so excited about telling Granddad and Grandma about Heath – she knew they would be thrilled. She'd been hanging out to tell them but she just hadn't had a chance since the rodeo. Both her grandparents had left soon after she arrived home to go to Cairns for a few days to catch up with friends and attend a few appointments. She had wanted to wait until they all had time to sit down and celebrate the great news, not to say it in passing as Granddad and Grandma were racing out the door. It was too important for that. They had both arrived home this evening, refreshed and revitalised, and it felt like the perfect time to tell them.

After the barbecue tomorrow night, to celebrate the official end of the mustering season, Heath had planned a night away for Molly and him at Pretty Beach and she was longing to spend a whole night with him. It was going to be absolutely wonderful. Jade was happy to have Rose for the night, and of course Rose was really looking forward to sleeping over at Aunty Jade's. It was all set. Not that Jade knew why Molly needed her to babysit – nobody knew. Molly wanted to tell her grandparents the news first, out of respect for them both. She would fill Jade in on the great news at the barbecue, and she couldn't wait to see her friend's reaction. Jade was going to be stoked.

Molly took a deep breath, feeling nervous all of a sudden, and picked up the three steaming cups from the kitchen bench and placed them onto a tray along with a couple of gingernut biscuits, pausing to admire the full moon out of the window. A shooting star flew gloriously across the night sky and she made a wish, hoping and praying it was going to come true as she padded silently down the hallway, making every effort not to wake Rose. The flyscreen door creaked wearily when she stepped through it onto the verandah. David looked up at her from his favourite comfortable chair and smiled while Elizabeth removed her glasses, placing the magazine she was reading on the side table.

'So, love, have a seat and tell us what's on your mind. Something's been niggling at you for the past week or so, I could tell,' David said as Molly passed him a cup of tea.

Molly handed Elizabeth her cuppa then sat down on the nearby couch and called Skip over. He jumped up beside her, tail wagging, and she scratched behind his ears absentmindedly. 'Well, Granddad, Grandma, I'm in love.'

'Oh darling, that's wonderful!' Elizabeth said, her smile lighting up her entire face.

David's face lit up as he leant forward in his chair, almost spilling his tea with excitement. 'Oh, love. I think that's the best news I've heard for ages! Mind you, it is kind of sudden. I haven't really seen you going out on dates with anyone.' Molly watched as his brow furrowed in thought. 'So tell me, who is the lucky man?'

Molly felt her stomach do a triple backflip and land somewhere in her throat. She didn't know why she felt so nervous. Maybe because it was so important to her that her granddad and grandma approved? Or maybe she was worried what they might think of her dating Jenny's boyfriend? 'It's someone you know very well, actually.'

'I see. Hmm.' David held Molly's gaze. 'It's not Jade, is it, love? I mean, don't get me wrong. I have nothing against gay people and you know I adore Jade. But I wouldn't want that for you and Rose, being the old-fashioned man I am.'

Molly giggled. 'No, Granddad! I'm not gay. What made you think of that, you silly bugger?'

David chuckled as he leant back in his chair. 'All right, come on then. Tell us who it is before I die of curiosity.'

'Okay, here goes. It's Heath.' Molly found herself smiling broadly just saying his name. 'Oh, Granddad, Grandma, I so want you both to be happy for us!'

'Woohoo!' Elizabeth shrieked as she grinned at Molly. Her delighted expression made Molly giggle.

David sat quietly. Molly knew he would be rolling it over in his mind, not wanting to say a word until he'd had a chance to process his thoughts. He was a firm believer in thinking before speaking, and had often reminded her of that fact when she was going through her unruly teenage years. She held her breath, waiting for some kind of reaction. A smile began to form at the corners of David's mouth and within seconds he was beaming from ear to ear.

'Molly, I'm honoured you care so much about what we think. Heath is a good and decent man. Look at Grandma, she's thrilled.

She's always said you'd make a lovely couple, but I thought she was playing cupid. I knew there was a strong bond between you and Heath, but I could never work out whether it was anything more than just terrific mateship. Well, to be fair, I could tell he fancied you but I wasn't sure how you felt about him. How long has this been going on, if you don't mind me asking?'

'There have been feelings there for a while now, but neither of us had done anything about them, until a week ago. And of *course* I care what you both think. You're the most important people in my life, along with Rose of course.'

'Ah, Molly, it's just wonderful! I've always wanted you to find a man who would support you and look after you, someone who has dreams and aspirations for the future, and someone who might come to love Jacaranda Farm as passionately as we do. Most importantly, I prayed you'd find a man to love you and Rose the way you deserve to be loved. Heath is this sort of man. I've seen the way he treats Rose and he loves that little girl with every bit of his being.'

Molly placed her cup on the floor and ran over to hug David. It wasn't often that he opened up emotionally, and she was deeply touched.

David pulled back and placed his wrinkled hand on her cheek. 'I could tell from the look on your face when you spoke about Heath just then that he's very special to you. As long as he makes you happy, I'm a very happy man. Now, we'd better go to bed, Elizabeth, or we're going to turn into a pair of pumpkins.'

'It's not *that* late, Granddad! It's only nine-thirty.'

David stood from his chair, stretching his arms high in the air as he wandered over to help Elizabeth out of hers. 'Way past my bedtime, Molly. I'm normally snoring like a trooper by this stage. Ask your grandmother, she'll confirm that. The poor thing's had to sleep beside me for close to fifty years.'

'Hear, hear!' Elizabeth chuckled as she edged her way out of the seat.

'Oh, don't you worry. I don't need to ask Grandma. We can hear you all through the house!'

David shook his finger at her as he walked inside. 'Now, now, Miss Molly Jones. Don't get too cheeky. I can still ground you seeing as you live under my roof.'

Molly ran her fingers over her lips, pretending to zip them up, her eyes shining with happiness.

'Night, Granddad. Night, Grandma. Love you.'

Elizabeth gently cupped Molly's cheek. 'I'm overjoyed with this news, Molly. Love you too, dear.'

She watched as her grandparents headed through the screen door, arm in arm, before turning to Skip. 'So, what do *you* reckon about Heath and I being together?'

Skip barked his reply and Molly nodded as if she understood him. 'Yeah, I reckon it's great too!'

Molly sat for another hour on the verandah, sipping a glass of red wine, letting the peace and tranquillity of the night wash over her. She thought about all those years she had dreamed about finding Rose's father again, believing that that was the only way her life would ever feel complete. Yet Heath had been right there all along, laughing with her, working with her, protecting her – sharing all her ups and downs. She had so many happy memories with him, and yet this was only the beginning. Now she had told her grandparents she and Heath could finally tell everyone else the great news. Molly couldn't wait to tell Rose. She smiled as she thought of Rose saying she wished Heath could be her dad. Molly was thrilled that she had made *another* one of her little girl's wishes come true, the first being training up Buck for her. Molly closed her eyes, a feeling of complete satisfaction filling her heart. She was finally here, right where she wanted to be.

CHAPTER
21

'Knock, knock!' Heath called out at Molly's front door. Trev and Kenny stood behind him holding a large esky filled with icy cold beers. Delicious aromas wafted from the kitchen and Heath's belly rumbled in anticipation. He'd had other things than food on his mind most of the day, though. Molly had snuck into the workers' cottage at dawn that morning, still wearing her pyjamas, and had crawled into his bed to wake him. The feel of her body against his stirred a desire in him that seemed to deepen with every second they were together. Their kisses overwhelmed his senses, as though she was breathing new life into his heart and soul. They had fallen into their own reality where the world did not exist beyond Heath's bedroom door, but wanted to wait for the total privacy of their coming weekend away before fully giving in to their desires. They had eventually emerged, knowing they had to get up and start the day, and the looks on Kenny and Trev's faces had been priceless. The cat was well and truly out of the bag. Kenny and Trev had been rapt when Heath and Molly had broken the news, giving them both a friendly slap on the back, and telling them it was about time.

'Come in if you're good-looking!' Molly called out from the kitchen as Rose ran to the front door to welcome them in.

'Mum told me that you're boyfriend and girlfriend now,' she said excitedly as Heath leant down to give her a hug. 'I'm tickled pink!'

Heath grinned at her. 'Well, I'm glad you're tickled pink, Rose. I wouldn't want it any other way. I mean, being tickled purple might be a bit weird. Where did you learn that saying from anyway, sweetheart?'

Rose rolled her eyes. 'Don't be silly, Heath! You can't tickle someone purple.' She laughed. 'I heard Grandma say it to Granddad this morning when they were talking abut you and Mum being together. She looked really happy. I thought it was a great way to say that I'm happy too, especially seeing as I love pink!' Her face became more serious. 'Does this mean I can call you Dad now?'

Trev and Kenny took that as their cue to move out of earshot. They squeezed past Heath and Rose and headed for the kitchen, dropping the esky twice along the way, their playful bantering filling the hallway with laughter.

Heath smiled tenderly at Rose. 'You'll have to ask your mum first, sweetheart, but if it's okay with her, it's okay with me. Just make sure you ask her when there's no one else around, Rose. It's something you need to talk with your mum about in private, okay?'

Rose smiled. 'Okay. I'll talk to her later on.'

'We better go and help the ladies out, don't you reckon?' Heath asked, taking Rose's hand and walking down the hallway.

'That's up to you, but GG said it's a madhouse in the kitchen. It might be a little scary for you in there,' Rose said seriously.

Heath chuckled. 'I'm pretty sure I can handle it.'

'Is there anything we can do?' Heath asked as he and Rose joined the bustling group in the kitchen.

'Yeah, thanks, Heath, that'd be great. You can make the seafood sauce if you like. Rose will show you where the tomato sauce and mayo is,' Molly replied, giving him a quick peck on the cheek.

'No worries,' Heath said, blushing slightly as he grabbed the bowl Jade was holding out to him. She winked and gave him the thumbs up.

'Hi, Heath, great news about you and Molly! I'm delighted, to say the least. I think we all are.'

'Thanks, mate,' Heath replied heartily as Rose pulled him towards the pantry cupboard.

'And *I* think it's fantastic too, Heath,' Elizabeth added from her place at the sink.

'Thanks, Mrs Jones.'

'Oh love, please call me Elizabeth. I keep telling you that. I know you like to have good manners but honestly, it feels too formal calling me Mrs Jones, especially now you're dating my beautiful granddaughter.'

Heath smiled. 'Okay then, seeing as you insist. Thanks, Elizabeth.'

'What can *we* do?' Trev asked. 'Let me warn you, though, I'm about as useful as an ashtray on a motorbike when it comes to being a kitchen hand. I bloody burn toast, don't I, Kenny?'

'Tell me about it,' Kenny said, chuckling.

'You two can go out and help Granddad with the barbecue if you like,' Molly said. 'Here's the tray of meat and I'll bring the seafood out in a sec.'

Molly watched Kenny and Trev disappear out onto the back verandah and turned the CD player up, singing along to Shooter Jennings' sexy husky voice. She danced around the kitchen, grabbing Rose and Jade for a spin on the way. Elizabeth laughed at the three girls and tapped her feet to the music as she washed some dishes.

*

By sunset they were all enjoying the fantastic buffet steaks, prawns, Moreton Bay bugs and even oysters kilpatrick. Heath and Molly found themselves lightheartedly fighting over the last bug. Heath finally handed it to her, grinning mischievously.

'It's all yours. How can I deny such a beautiful woman her favourite food?'

'I'll share it with you, how's that sound?' Molly said, smiling.

'Sounds like a truce,' Heath replied, giving her a quick kiss on the lips.

Jade had made an alcoholic punch that was strong enough to run a small car. Molly had drunk two glasses of it with dinner and was now feeling blissfully relaxed. She gazed at Heath standing over in the corner of the verandah in deep conversation with Trev. She guessed it'd most probably have something to do with cattle or fishing.

'Can I join in on the conversation? It looks to be pretty interesting from the side lines,' she said with a wink as she wandered into their space.

Heath grinned back at her. 'Trev here's trying to tell me he's the best fisherman around, and I was reminding him that Kenny's been giving him a good run for his money lately.'

'I don't know. I reckon Kenny's just got lucky.' Trev chuckled and excused himself to get another drink. 'Anybody want one while I'm at it?' he called out, holding up his empty beer can and shaking it as he walked away.

'Yeah, grab us both one,' Heath called after him.

'I think I'd better slow down on the drinks. I'm feeling a little tipsy already,' Molly said, as she wrapped her arm around his waist and rested her head on his chest, enjoying his warmth and the sound of his heart beating.

Jade bounded in beside them, her feet moving in time to the music. 'Anyone here like to have a boogie with me under the stars?'

Molly raised her eyebrows. 'Oh, why not? We'll just have to dodge the cane toads.'

'Don't remind me about the cane toads! Lucky you don't have a fish pond or you might just fall into it,' Jade said, laughing.

Heath looked at Molly a little baffled.

'Don't even ask. I'll tell you the story another day,' Molly replied.

Just as the girls hit the bottom step Kenny yelled out anxiously, 'Oh shit! Fire!'

Molly felt the joyful bubble around her pop. They all looked to where Kenny was pointing and saw black smoke billowing into the moonlit sky.

'Holy shit! That's over near the stables! The poor bloody horses are all locked up in there – we were going to shoe them early in the morning. Christ, they're *never* normally in there ... Why tonight of all nights?' Heath yelled, despairing. 'I'll go and grab the tractor and fill the tank up with water.' He glanced at Molly. 'You and the other women grab some buckets and head down to the stables. Maybe you can start throwing water onto the flames. Use the water from the rainwater tank down there, okay? You men do what you can to help the women until I get down there with the tractor and the spray tank.' Heath took off in the direction of the shed, hoping the equipment they used for spraying fertiliser was already attached to the back of the tractor, to save him precious time. He could fill it with water and spray it directly onto the fire.

'Oh no! Mum! Buck is down there too!' Rose cried, her eyes wide with fear.

Molly picked her up off the ground, embracing her tightly. 'Don't worry sweetheart. We'll get him out. I'll make sure of it.'

Molly's mind raced as images of Buck and Leroy and all the other horses being caught up in the fire flashed before her, ripping her heart to pieces. She ran down the dirt road towards the stables, holding firmly onto Rose's hand. 'I wish I could leave you back at the homestead, but all the adults are needed down here and I can't leave you there on your own. Promise me you'll stay close to me, sweetheart. Stick to me like glue, okay? Fire can be very dangerous. I don't want you going anywhere near it.'

Rose nodded as tears poured down her face, visibly afraid of the awful situation unfolding. 'I love Buck, Mum. He can't die. He's my best friend.'

'I won't let him!'

Molly couldn't believe the ferocity of the fire once they reached the stables. The huge, yellow flames flickered and roared like spirits from hell, devouring the timber as windows exploded from the sheer force of the heat. Horses were kicking and neighing in terror inside the burning building. She watched on helplessly while the men ran one by one into the flames, vanishing into the thick wall of smoke. Their fears of being caught up in the fire themselves were evidently being put to the back of their minds. Jade and Elizabeth threw buckets of water over the fire while Molly attached a garden hose to the water tank. Rose stood behind them, the heat from the bellowing flames making her face turn red.

'Stand back a bit, sweetheart, over there near the round yard, where it's safe, okay?' Molly yelled, watching like a hawk as Rose obeyed. The little girl walked backwards then sat down on the grass, well away from any potential threat.

Molly screamed out over the roar of the fire. 'We need Heath here *now*!'

'I can see his headlights coming down the road,' Elizabeth shouted back.

The men were bringing out one horse after the other. Molly quickly calculated that there had been about seven horses in there to begin with. It was hard enough fighting through the thick, black smoke but once back in the fresh air they also had the difficult job of trying to calm the horses down and check them over quickly for any injuries they might have to see to immediately. Molly watched on, growing more and more anxious as time ticked by. Where were Buck and Leroy? Were they hurt, or worse, dead? She ran over to her grandfather as he stumbled out of the stables with Jade's horse, Spirit, in tow. David was choking badly from the smoke. She wanted to tell him to leave the saving of the horses to the younger men, but she knew he wouldn't hear of it. Jade took the lead rope from David's blackened hands and led Spirit away, thanking David over and over.

Molly placed her hand on David's back. 'Have you seen Buck and Leroy in there, Granddad?' she asked, panic rising in her throat.

David tried to answer her between bouts of coughing. 'There're only a few horses left in there. I gather two of them are Buck and Leroy. They're alive, love, so don't worry. The fire is worse out the front here than it is when you get through the door. So as long as I move fast I'll get them both out for you.' He ran back towards the fire and in a flash he was gone behind the smoke that was pouring out of the stable door like a raging black river.

'Be careful, Granddad!' Molly screamed after him.

Heath had arrived and was using the spray tank on the back of the tractor to douse the flames. Trev came running out of the stables with his horse, Dakota. Molly winced at the horrific burn on the horse's rump. Trev was using all his strength to keep hold of his horse that kicked and whinnied out in pain.

All of a sudden there was a loud bang and the ground shook beneath Molly as an explosion ripped through the stables. She watched in horror as the roof began to cave in and the walls crumbled to the ground. Heath slipped and fell from the back of the tractor, the impact of the explosion causing him to lose his footing. He hit the ground hard, the wind knocked out of him. Kenny and David came running out of the flames with Leroy, yelling that the horse was okay. Molly felt a surge of relief, but her fears for Buck were growing by the second. She had to get the horse out of there. God, please let him be alive! David collapsed on the ground, vomiting, the smoke finally overcoming him. Molly ran to help him.

'Buck is still in there!' Rose shrieked as she ran for the stables.

Molly screamed in horror, tears pouring down her blackened face, her voice hoarse from all the smoke as she caught a glimpse of Rose disappearing into the flames. 'Rose! No! Don't go in there! Rose!' And before anyone could stop her, Molly went tearing into the flames after her. She couldn't lose Rose; not like this, not ever.

'Molly!' Heath cried out but Molly was gone. His blood ran cold as he imagined Molly and Rose burning alive in the stables. He had to save them. They were his life, his everything.

Elizabeth and Jade tried to run into the burning building after Molly as Kenny and Trev stumbled over each other to pull the two women back. Elizabeth tried with all her strength to fight them off but they wouldn't let go of her and she finally gave in and slumped into Trev's arms, sobbing hysterically. Jade screamed out Molly and Rose's names, her helpless frustration written across her face.

'I'm going in there! You lot stay out here and look after David, you hear me?' Heath roared, running into the fire without further hesitation.

The group stood together, holding their breath. Elizabeth sobbed as she stroked David's back and Jade did her best to comfort them both, tears pouring down her face. Trev and Kenny did all they could to control the fire, but to no avail. Flames were licking around the stable door, there were only minutes before the whole building would be completely ablaze. There was a sudden crash at the side of the stables and Buck came bolting out of the flames, neighing in terror. Trev ran to the horse, trying to soothe Buck. The horse reared up in panic and landed with a ground-rattling thump but Trev skillfully threw a lead rope over Buck's neck and led the animals towards the other horses. Trev was relieved to see that, amazingly, the horse had escaped almost unscathed, aside from a few minor burns on his face.

*

Heath felt the flames burning through his clothes and painfully licking his skin. He pushed forward as smoke engulfed him like a suffocating blanket and his lungs began screaming for oxygen. But he wasn't going back outside until he had found Molly and Rose. He would rather die in here than give up searching just to save himself.

The intense heat scalded his face, as though someone had pushed him into an oven. He had to fight back the urge to vomit, the stench of the smoke making him feel violently ill.

He stumbled over the burning timber beams that had fallen from the roof, yelling out over and over to Molly and Rose. He strained his ears for a response, the roar of the fire deafening. He couldn't see a metre in front of himself as he shuffled along the ground, trying his best not to fall over.

His boot hit something and he heard a muffled murmur. Heath quickly knelt down as a tiny hand fumbled for his. He grabbed it, his heart breaking.

'Help me,' Rose choked out. 'My leg; it's stuck under something. Please, please get me out of here.'

Heath's eyes were burning and he instinctively closed them. Tears ran freely down his face. Knowing that Rose was lying here hurt and Molly was still in here somewhere was killing him. 'I'm here, Rose. I'm going to help you, darling, okay? I'm not going anywhere till we get you out,' he replied as he heaved a heavy timber beam off her leg. He slid his hands underneath her and gently lifted her up and Rose let out a blood curdling scream. 'Oh, Rose, I'm so sorry. I know it hurts. Just hang in there; I'm going to get you outside, okay?'

Kenny yelled out from the position he had taken on the tractor when he spotted Heath stumbling out of the smoke with Rose in his arms. 'I'll call an ambulance!' he yelled, jumping down from the tractor. Everybody else ran to help Heath as he gently carried Rose into fresh air and carefully laid her down on the ground. His lungs heaved as he breathed in fresh air. It felt as though they were about to collapse and he was afraid of passing out. He pushed through the pain and ran back towards the flames, knowing every second mattered now. Flames scorched his skin, but he was running on adrenaline, barely acknowledging the pain. He picked up burning bits of timber and threw them out of his way while he called out for Molly, his desperate voice not even sounding like his own. He let out a primal scream as the smoke cleared a little and he spotted Molly's body lying deathly still, her head beneath a lump of timber bigger than him. He fell to the ground, crying out her name. Carefully lifting the heavy timber from Molly's head, he groaned as he felt her hair strangely wet. Was that blood he could feel?

He tenderly lifted her limp body from the floor, unsure of whether she was alive, or, God forbid, dead. His body shuddered with sobs. I can't lose her, please God, no, don't let her die, he screamed in his head as he stumbled back in the direction he had come, holding Molly close to him to shield her from the fire. Images of the day he lost Jenny and his baby came flooding back to him, taunting him, filling him with urgency. He was not going to go through that again. *Ever!* Flames were licking his body and his legs wanted to buckle beneath him, but he fought on, his only objective to get Molly to safety. He finally emerged from the smoke and the flames with Molly cradled in his arms, the fresh air worth more than gold as he took deep gasping breaths, then yelled as loudly as his dry, burnt throat would allow for someone to come and help them. He couldn't see, everything was blurry, but he felt a man's strong arms taking Molly from him as he collapsed to the ground coughing and wheezing, utterly exhausted. And then everything went black.

CHAPTER
22

The doctor systematically checked Heath's vital signs, scribbled on his clipboard, then vanished out the door, his white coat flapping behind him. Heath was abruptly awoken by the loud thump of the door closing. His eyelids felt like lead weights as he tried to force them open, and for a second he struggled to figure out where he was. Then the pungent smell of disinfectant hit his sense of smell and he heard the methodic beeping of a machine beside him. Memories of the fire came flooding back and his heart beat frantically as he remembered someone taking Molly's lifeless body from his arms and then everything going black. Heath felt terror rise up in his throat as he wondered whether Molly was alive, whether Rose was okay. He attempted to sit up, his eyes intensely trying to focus; everything in the room spun around him. He tore at the leads attached to his chest, wincing as the strong tape ripped at his skin. He could feel something pulling in his arm as he tried with all his might to climb out of the bed and he slipped over the railings, hitting the cold hospital floor painfully, the drip that was attached to his arm toppling over with its stand on top of him.

The door flew open and a nurse came running to his aid. She held his arms and tried to help him up. 'What on earth are you doing out of bed, Mr Miller? Come on, let's get you back in there,' she said in a gentle but firm voice.

'Molly Jones, where is she? Is she all right? And Rose, how's Rose?' Heath pleaded, his throat hoarse and sore as he sat in a crumpled heap on the floor.

'Rose is doing fine. Her broken leg will have to be in a cast for about six weeks, but it will heal. Her grandparents are with her.' Heath let out a relieved sigh. Rose was okay. But what about Molly? Why wasn't Molly with Rose? Panic rose up in his throat. What weren't they telling him?

The nurse bent down and took Heath's arm, groaning as she helped him to stand. 'Now, I'll have to go and get the doctor to come and have a talk with you about the lady that was admitted with you.'

Heath noticed her avoiding eye contact with him. How could she not tell him what was happening? Didn't she know that Molly meant everything to him? He felt his anger bubble up as he shook her hand from his arm. 'No, please, you have to tell me. I need to know right now if she's okay. Don't leave me here wondering, I'm begging you. You have to tell me something, anything.'

'I *can* tell you she's alive but I can't tell you any more than that. I promise I'll get the doctor as soon as I'm finished here with you. So the quicker you let me get you back into bed, the quicker I can go and find him. You're suffering from extreme smoke inhalation, minor burns to your arms, legs and neck, and are very dehydrated so I must *insist* that I get you back into bed.'

Heath felt a torrent of relief, as though he could breathe again. 'Thank God,' was all he managed to say as he let the nurse lead him on unsteady legs back to bed. And she was as good as her word. A few minutes later the doctor appeared beside him, a somber look on his face.

'Hi there, Heath. It's nice to see you awake. We've been keeping a close eye on you over the last sixteen hours. You have a few nasty burns on your legs, but they will heal, given time. Now, I hear you tried to get out of bed to see Miss Molly Jones.' The doctor cleared his throat. Heath held his breath. 'I am sorry to be the bearer of grave news, but she's in an induced coma and it's a waiting game now to see how she goes. She had a heavy knock to the head and we had to operate to relieve the pressure on her brain. I can't really tell you any more at this time. We all just have to be patient and wait to see what happens over the next couple of days.'

Heath felt like someone had just punched him hard in the chest and he began to gasp for air. He grabbed the doctor's hand and held it fast. 'I need to see her now, Doc, and if you don't help me I swear I'll rip all these tubes and cords right out and crawl there if I have to!'

The doctor nodded, a look of sympathy flashing across his face. 'I'll get a nurse to bring a wheelchair and she'll take you to see your Molly. Her daughter and grandparents are with her, so she's not alone. The nurse will be back in a few minutes, so please be patient. We're short-staffed at the moment and everyone is working as fast as they can.'

As Heath lay waiting for the nurse to return, the seconds crawled by like hours. He couldn't lose Molly; he wouldn't! And poor little darling Rose, she must be absolutely distraught. He had to be there for Rose *and* for Molly, when she woke up. He prayed with everything in him that she would.

Trev, Kenny, Jade and Melinda were huddled in the waiting area as the nurse wheeled Heath down the corridor towards Molly's room. They all ran for him when they spotted him, their weary faces revealing their helplessness, fear and sorrow.

'Heath, mate, how are you doing?' said Trev as he placed his hand on Heath's shoulder.

'Not too good, Trev. Not good at all.'

'I'm so sorry about Molly. They won't even let us in to see her.' Trev turned his attention to the nurse. 'Apparently we aren't family and only family can go in. But, I tell you what; we aren't leaving until you let us in.'

'I'm sorry, sir, they're the rules and I don't make them,' the nurse replied sternly as she turned to wheel Heath away. 'I'm only agreeing to take Mr Miller in because he's her boyfriend. Now please, we must be on our way. I have plenty to do.'

Jade lightly grabbed the nurse's arm to stop her. 'No, wait, please. Heath, can you tell Molly that we all love her and that we're here for her? I know she's in a coma, but trust me, she'll hear you.'

Heath reached out and took hold of Jade's hand, tears stinging his eyes once again. 'I promise I will. I'll tell her over and over again.'

CHAPTER
23

The afternoon sun poured its golden rays into Molly's hospital room, hitting the crystal sun catcher Rose had bought for her and sending rainbows of colour across the walls and furniture. Heath admired the beauty of it for a few seconds before his gaze fell back upon Molly, her face pale, motionless. It had been six gruelling days since the fire, and Molly had still not come out of her coma. Heath knew she could hear him when he spoke to her. Her eyelids would flicker softly, and that tiny sign of life lifted his spirits to no end. He had never been a religious man, but now he prayed all day long for Molly to wake up so he could tell her repeatedly just how much he loved her.

David and Elizabeth sat on the opposite side of the bed, their faces solemn. Rose wriggled around on David's lap, her heavy cast clearly cumbersome to move, so she could look at David's face. 'When's Mum going to wake up, GG? I miss her and it hurts so much not being able to talk to her.'

'Hopefully soon, love. We'll make it through this, little one, it will all be okay,' David replied softly as he ran his hand over Rose's cheek, wiping her tears away while he recalled the day he had said those very words to Molly, by her parents' graves. His heart quivered at the thought, and his face showed the ravages of the past six days.

'Well, I think she's had enough sleep now, GG.' Rose said. 'I have to tell her how well Buck is going. Not that I can ride him for another five weeks, seeing as I have this stupid cast on.'

Elizabeth pulled a tissue from the half-empty box beside the bed and blew her nose loudly, her eyes red-rimmed. 'I think I might nip downstairs and get us all some afternoon tea. Do you want to come with me, Rose?'

Rose nodded and David gently helped her onto the floor, passing her the crutches she was now using to walk with. She manoeuvred them under her arms, stumbling as she tried to follow Elizabeth. David reached out to catch her. 'Whoopsy daisy.'

Rose shook her head in frustration. 'Thanks, GG. I hope I get the hang of these things soon. I feel like I'm going to have this cast on forever!'

Heath smiled as she limped over to him. He leant over and kissed her on the cheek.

'Keep your chin up, darling. Mum will be all right. You'll see.'

'I hope so,' Rose replied as she hobbled out the door with Elizabeth.

David stood wearily, his chair scraping along the floor. 'I might head down too, Heath. I could do with the fresh air. How about we grab you some food? You really should eat something.'

'Yeah, maybe just a coffee and a toasted sandwich, thanks, David.'

David patted Heath on the shoulder. 'Make sure you try to get some sleep tonight, buddy? You look like hell. I can sit here with Molly and give you a break if you like.'

Heath shook his head. 'Rose needs you at home, David, and I want to be here when Molly wakes up. I can sleep just fine in this chair.'

'She's one lucky girl having you in her life. I know how much you love her, Heath. I can see it every time you look at her,' David said as he pushed his way out the door and into the hospital corridor.

Heath ran his fingers over the worn, yellow pages of the book he was holding and opened it to the place where the bookmark was resting. At the end of the day, when everyone had retired home, he would spend hours reading Molly her favourite novel. It was about a young English girl in the 1800s who longed to escape from her underprivileged life. She had finally discovered freedom when she found herself convicted of stealing a loaf of bread for her starving family and was shipped off to the shores of Australia, to join the new colony. It was here that she met the love of her life.

Molly had lent the book to him a few months back and he had read it from start to finish in less than a week, finding himself enthralled. He continued on from where he had left off.

'The young girl held onto the ragged leather reins with shivering hands. Squeezing her eyes closed tightly, she encouraged the stallion into a gallop with a soft squeeze of her thighs. She let images of another world fill her mind as she allowed herself to believe, if only for a second, that when she opened them she would be in that place where there was never-ending happiness. Warmth flooded through her like a mother's embrace as the wind rustled her long golden locks. The freedom she felt with a powerful horse beneath her was indescribable.

She wanted to keep going, into the thick, dark forest that surrounded her family's shabby cottage, never to return. The endless days of scrubbing floors and slaving over hot coals had worn her spirit down, making her feel as though she was a thin sheet of glass that could shatter with one tiny bump. She let out a scream, her emotions coming to the surface and escaping into the cold winter's morning as warm tears rolled down her rosy cheeks and trickled onto the crisp white snow beneath her.'

Heath went to turn the page and briefly looked up at Molly. His breath stopped in his throat when he saw a tear roll down Molly's cheek. The book hit the floor with a thump as he reached out and grabbed her hand.

'Molly, can you hear me? If you can, squeeze my hand. Molly?'

Heath waited, silently begging for Molly to show some sign of life. And then he felt it. Molly moved her fingers ever so slightly. Heath jumped from his chair and it skidded out behind him, landing with a loud crash against the door. He kissed Molly's cheek, tasting the saltiness of her tears on his lips, whispering over and over how much he loved her and reminding her that she had to be here for Rose. Reaching out, he grabbed the buzzer and pumped it until a flustered nurse stormed into the room scowling.

'What on earth is going on in h—' The nurse stopped dead in her tracks as Molly slowly opened her eyes. She ran swiftly to Molly's side, talking to her gently while lifting her eyelids and shining a tiny torch into her pupils.

Molly tried to speak but her mouth was so dry that it was almost impossible to move her tongue. Voices echoed around her, as though she was in a tunnel. She tried to focus but the light above her was excruciatingly bright, her mind racing as memories of being trapped in the fire gripped her, flooding her senses with terror and panic. Where was she? What was happening? Where was Rose? Was she alive? Was her little girl alive? She could feel someone tenderly touching her face and she heard a voice. It was one she was very familiar with, and it was instantly comforting. Her eyes began to focus and a sensation of deep love enveloped her when she saw Heath's intense blue eyes staring deeply into her own.

'I love you, Molly, I love you so much,' he whispered as he stroked her hair. 'Don't try to talk yet, just save your energy. You're in hospital. You've been asleep for a few days. I'm here with you and I'm not going anywhere. Rose is alive, she has a broken leg but she'll be fine. Just take it easy now ...'

I love you too, Molly thought as relief flooded through her. Rose was alive! She was okay. Molly's head was throbbing and her thoughts were vague and scattered. But Rose was alive and Heath was with her. This was all she needed to know right now. She tried to keep her eyes open, but she didn't even have the energy. Molly drifted off to sleep, the warmth of Heath's hand in hers making her feel safe and secure and loved.

CHAPTER
24

As soon as the Land Cruiser left the smoothness of the bitumen behind and hit bumpy dirt roads, Molly felt like she was home. She gently squeezed Rose's hand, excited to finally be out of the hospital. If she had to spend another day in the cold, disinfectant-smelling, stark-white room she was sure they would have had to put her in a straitjacket, send her to the top floor and throw away the key. Rose squeezed her hand back and gave her a loving kiss on the cheek. Molly smiled as she looked affectionately at her, then towards Heath. He'd been beside her every day of these past seven weeks she had been in the hospital. She was sure she would not have made such a quick recovery without his constant support. And he had saved her darling Rose from the fire. For that alone, she could never thank him enough.

It had been a painful recovery, with loads of physiotherapy to help heal the injuries Molly had sustained in her neck and back, and too many knock-your-socks-off painkillers. Molly hated even taking paracetamol when she had a headache, so she had not enjoyed having to use morphine every day to alleviate the pain in her head. Even worse, when the doctors had decided to slowly wean her off the morphine, she'd endured the agony of withdrawal symptoms – not being able to sleep, painful headaches and excruciating stomach cramps that almost outweighed contraction pains. She had learnt the hard way where the term 'cold turkey' came from. She would constantly get cold flushes and goosebumps all over her skin, resembling a cold turkey.

Molly instinctively rubbed her head where the stitches had been, running her fingers over the raised red skin of the big, horrible scar. She was glad her hair would eventually grow back around it so that no one could ever see it. She didn't want to relive the horror of that night every time someone asked her about the scar.

Heath turned into Jacaranda Farm and Molly felt a flurry of butterflies in her belly. She was flooded with emotions ranging from elation and exhilaration to apprehension and nervousness about how she would feel when she saw the stables again. Kenny and Trev had rebuilt them, refusing any payment, telling David they felt it was the least they could do to help. Molly saw the shimmering dam come into view, beautiful dragonflies dancing over the water. Around the edges of the dam stood palm trees laden with plump coconuts, making her crave the sweet juice inside them. A flock of honeyeaters were singing in the jackfruit tree, the remnants of their fruit fest scattered on the ground beneath the tree. Oh, she had missed seeing Jacaranda Farm every day, and it cheered her up immeasurably being back.

The house came into view and Skip bounded off the front verandah to greet her, clearing the bottom three steps in one in his haste. It felt like a lifetime ago since she had been here and she couldn't wait to see everyone. Even though they all constantly visited her in hospital it wasn't the same as sitting around at home having a few laughs over a barbecue and a couple of beers. She half expected her grandparents to appear through the front door with welcome-home smiles on their faces, but they were nowhere to be seen. They would've heard Skip barking, so they most certainly knew she was back. Where was everyone? *Aren't they excited to have me home?* Heath turned off the ignition and all went quiet, except for Skip's insistent barking and a few noisy galahs perched in her grandma's prized lemon trees out the front.

'You make your way in with Rose and I'll grab your bags out of the back, beautiful,' Heath said, snapping her out of her thoughts.

'Oh right, yep, thanks.' She slid out of the passenger-side door, helping Rose down, and was met by Skip leaping up and placing his paws on her chest, almost bowling her over. She chuckled as he licked her face enthusiastically and gently pushed him away before he somehow managed to lick her eyeballs clean out of their sockets.

'Nice to see you too, buddy! It's been way too long, hey,' she exclaimed as she leant down and gave him an affectionate cuddle.

Rose gave Skip a quick pat once he had calmed down. 'He's been howling for you every night since you've been at the hospital, driving everyone nuts. Grandma reckoned it was worse than listening to GG snore all night. Nothing we did would shut him up.'

Molly giggled. 'Gosh, it must have been bad, if it was worse than GG's snoring!'

Rose nodded vigorously. 'Uh-huh. I had to sleep with a pillow over my head and even then I could still hear him.'

Heath came up beside them with Molly's bag tossed over his shoulder. Molly looked up at him and her knees went weak. His shirt was pulled askew thanks to the weight of her bag and she could see his powerfully built chest through the top few buttons of his shirt, practically begging her to run her fingertips over his smooth skin.

Heath caught Molly gazing at him, and glanced down to where she was staring. When he realised, he leant over and kissed her on the lips, brushing past her ear on the way and briefly stopping to whisper, 'I'm going to kiss you all over when I get the chance.' Then he stood back up and smiled devilishly at her.

Molly was afraid she would pass out on the spot. She desired Heath with every part of her being. Her aching for him was driving her insane.

'Come on then. Let's get inside and say g'day to David and Elizabeth,' he said casually as he grabbed Molly's outstretched hand and helped her up.

Rose giggled a little too excitedly and hobbled up the stairs. Her cast was off now, but her leg muscles were still weak after not being used for six weeks. Molly couldn't help but wonder what she was up to; it was as though she had frogs in her socks. They all took off their shoes and Heath motioned to the front door. 'You go in first, gorgeous.'

Molly shrugged, finding the increasing eagerness in Rose's jiggling feet a little strange. She pushed open the big timber door, enjoying the familiar sound of the hinges creaking loudly as though they were pleading for a good spray of WD40. She just about died from shock as she stepped into the lounge and was greeted with a massive roar of 'Surprise! Welcome home, Molly!'

Happy tears stung her eyes as friends and family jumped up from behind the furniture, their faces beaming in delight at having her home again. The room was filled with bright balloons and streamers and a huge welcome home sign was hung above the kitchen doorway, obviously painted by Rose. The childish writing melted Molly's heart.

Molly glanced around the room, trying to take it all in, clutching her chest as if trying to keep her thumping heart in her rib cage. Jade, Melinda, Kenny and Trev all had shiny party hats on, her neighbours Kathy and Fred had streamers wrapped around their shoulders while Rob and Cheryl noisily blew party blowers. In the middle of the happy chaos stood her granddad and grandma, loving looks on their tired faces.

Heath slid his arm around Molly's waist and kissed her tenderly on the cheek. 'Welcome home, Molly. We missed you.'

Molly felt a rush of happiness wash over her and she silently thanked the angels above for leaving her here on earth to enjoy such a wonderful life with such amazing people.

CHAPTER

25

The sixty-seven-year-old yoga teacher lifted her leg as though it was attached to someone else and tucked it behind her neck, smiling the whole time, continuing to talk effortlessly to the class as though there was nothing out of the ordinary about the way she was sitting.

Molly cringed, feeling her groin twinge in fright as she visualised doing the pose herself. She glanced over at Jade, who was also moving her body like a contortionist. Molly shook her head. What had she been thinking, letting Jade drag her here? There was no way she was *ever* going to be able to bend her body like that. Well, not without breaking every bone in it. Jade had hauled her to the class, saying yoga was good for the soul, and reminding Molly that she had been through a lot lately and that her body needed some TLC. Molly had gone along, feeling like a fish out of water the instant she sat down amongst the group.

The cheerful teacher continued to call out harmoniously, reminding the class not to push past their individual thresholds in case of injury. Molly scoffed under her breath as she struggled with her own leg – her tongue hooking around the corner of her lips in her effort – barely getting her leg level with her chest before an involuntary gush of wind escaped her.

Jade muffled her laughter as she turned to Molly. 'Did you just fart, Miss Jones?'

Molly felt her face flush bright red and she covered her mouth in a bid to stifle her laughter. 'Shit, Jade! It was a fanny fart! All these weird positions have sucked air into places it should never be. I'm so *embarrassed*.'

'I reckon the whole class must've heard that one. What a beauty,' Jade whispered, turning back to face the teacher, her body moving with the grace of a slinky cat.

Molly looked timidly around her to see if anyone was glaring in her direction with a disgusted look on their face, but everyone seemed too engrossed in participating in the downward-facing dog pose. Molly grinned inwardly as she thought how they all resembled Skip when he got up from a doggy nap and had a good old stretch. She felt a bubble of infectious laughter rising up within her and, try as she might, she was unable to contain it, and burst into a fit of uncontrollable giggles. Jade gave her a sideways look, her eyes pleading with her to quiet down. Molly took a deep breath and covered her mouth, a smirk still visible in her sparkling eyes.

The teacher looked in Molly's direction and frowned, in a spiritual, meditative kind of way, and Molly instantly felt like a naughty schoolgirl, seeing she was the only one not in a back-breaking position. She tried to look serious as she once again fought with her leg like it was a separate entity, feeling muscles in her thighs that she didn't even know existed as she attempted the revolved-triangle pose while taking deep breaths.

The rest of the hour-long class was no better. At one stage, whilst doing the monkey pose – or was it the lotus position? – Molly lost her balance and collapsed like a wildebeest into the elderly man beside her. Apologising profusely she helped him up, feeling her cheeks again burning a fiery red. Then Molly got back into position and attempted the pose again.

She loved the last bit of the class, though. They all got to put on socks and lie down under a blanket on the soft, rubbery yoga mats. The teacher turned off all the lights, lit scented candles and played relaxation music. Molly had never heard anything so beautiful. It felt like the music had wings and was lifting her spirit up to a place where everything was blissful and enchanted.

The teacher's voice was soft, sensual and soothing as she talked them through a meditation sequence. She asked them to picture themselves walking along a white sandy beach, feeling the warm sand between their toes as the waves lapped lazily onto the shore. 'Find a place to sit on that beautiful pristine beach,' the teacher whispered to the class. Molly could have sworn she smelled the ocean as she sat herself down in her mind.

'Now feel the earth beneath you,' the teacher continued. 'Feel the power of it. Imagine that with each breath you take you are drawing the earth's energies up through your feet. Feel the energy travelling through you, like a white light, all through your body and into your mind. The white light is releasing all negative emotions and making you feel at peace with yourself. Painful emotions are dissolving in you like a block of melting ice, seeping down into the sand beneath you.'

It was at this point that Molly must have dozed off, because she woke to Jade poking her in the ribs and asking her if she was sleeping.

She yawned sheepishly. 'Sorry, Jade, I'm just so relaxed. This is wonderful.'

The teacher spoke again. 'Now, I would like you all to take your time. When you're ready, roll into the recovery position on your right side, and then come to sitting please.'

Molly slowly pushed herself up, wishing she could stay under her blanket instead and drift back into an enchanted sleep. She had not felt so tranquil in ages. Jade reached over and grabbed her hand, the man on the opposite side of her doing the same, causing her to jump slightly. Molly followed suit and folded her legs. The class began a series of drawn-out oms, filling her body with captivating vibrations when the sound travelled through her. Just as she felt she was really beginning to get the hang of it, they stopped, leaving her voice the only one audible in the echoing classroom as she released a passionate 'Ommm'. She blushed slightly as the class smiled dreamily towards her.

The teacher bowed her head to them all. 'Thank you, class. Look forward to the future with a smile in your heart and love on your lips. Om, Shanti, Shanti, Shanti, peace, peace, peace.'

The alluring mantra made Molly feel as though she would never encounter drama in her life again. Now, wouldn't that be wonderful? She felt amazing. Everyone replied to the teacher sleepily, then the reality of the world came rolling back as the fluorescent lights above them were turned on so they could gather their things, the Dimbulah community hall instantly losing the hippy atmosphere of a place where peace and love prevailed.

The girls stumbled out into the darkness, the bright lights from the hall creating long shadows all around them.

Jade inquisitively looked at Molly as they walked over to the car. 'So, how did you like the class?'

Molly stretched her arms and pleasurably rolled her neck from side to side. 'That was bloody awesome! I think I'd like to come with you again. That is, once my body gets over the torture of this class!'

'Oh, come on, Molly. It isn't that bad. It's just that tonight was your first time and yoga always seems a bit daunting to begin with.

I'd *love* for you to come along with me each week. It would give us another excuse to hang out. Rose could come too, if she likes. Although, you might have to curb the fanny farts.'

'Rubbish, that was the highlight of the class!' Molly replied cheekily as she opened the passenger-side door and slid in.

Jade started the car and headed in the direction of Jacaranda Farm. 'Sooo, tell me, what has been happening with you and Heath since you've been home from the hospital? Have you done the wild thing yet? I'm dying to know!' Molly's whole body tingled just thinking about it as she smiled demurely at Jade. 'No, we haven't done the wild thing yet! Bloody hell, Jade! You're so to the point, but that's one of the things I love about you.'

Jade glanced fleetingly at Molly. 'Well, why in the hell not? You've been home almost two weeks now.'

'Heath wants it to be special, and so do I, so he's taking me away for the weekend, down to Pretty Beach. I can't wait! I'm glad, though, really. The thought of making sweet, sweet lurve with Granddad and Grandma in the room next door and with Rose just down the hall kind of makes me feel nauseous.'

'Well, go and ravish each other at his place then!' Jade said, her eyebrows rising so high they were nearly at one with her hairline.

'That would be even worse! Knowing that Trev could hear us ... he's like a father to me.'

'Aha, so you're a noisy one then,' Jade teased.

Molly threw her hands up in the air and laughed. 'Cut it out, Jade, you spinner!'

*

A loud thud startled Molly from her deep sleep. She sat up, clutching the sheet for dear life, wondering for a few split seconds what in the hell was going on, until she realised that it was someone knocking on her bedroom window. She instantly thought of Heath and her belly fluttered with excitement. She stumbled out of bed and quickly tried to flatten down her bed hair, glancing at her night clock to see the luminous red numbers stating it was 2.14 a.m.

She tiptoed over to her window, straightening her skimpy pyjamas and peering out through her curtains. It was so dark she couldn't see a thing so she pushed her face right up against the flyscreen. Abruptly, she saw a face materialise at the window and got the shock of her life. It was Mark staring back at her. Why isn't Skip barking? she thought confusedly. Am I still asleep?

Her mouth involuntarily dropped open and she found herself breathless with anxiety. Remembering she didn't have much on, she quickly wrestled the sheet from her bed and wrapped it around herself. Her brows furrowed as she finally discovered her voice.

'What are you doing here, Mark? It's bloody two o'clock in the morning,' she hissed through clenched teeth.

Mark shrugged. 'Um, I'm sorry it's so late, but can we talk, Molly? Please?'

'Goddamn it! You had a go at me for turning up at your place at ten in the morning, basically telling me to leave, and now you want to have a conversation at this hour?' She was finding it terribly hard not to yell and wake up the entire household.

'Please. I really have to talk to you.'

Molly could smell alcohol on his breath. 'You're drunk, Mark. Go home and come back at a decent hour.'

'Oh, come on, Molly, I'm begging you. I have to talk to you. Now!'

Molly stood and pondered for close to a minute, glaring at him.

'Oh, for fuck's sake! *Okay.* I'll be out the front in a minute.' Mark was sitting in the couch on the front verandah with Skip at his feet when Molly came outside. She sat down opposite him and motioned for Skip to sit with her.

'So, to what do I owe the pleasure of this visit?' she asked sarcastically as she jiggled her legs up and down.

Mark slumped in front of her as tears streamed down his face. She could tell he had been crying for a while – his eyes were puffy and red. A small part of her felt a strange satisfaction to see that he was actually a human being with emotions. She momentarily felt sorry for him.

'I've been such a prick, Molly. I'm so deeply sorry for acting like I didn't care about anyone else but myself.'

Molly's compassionate instincts made her want to go over and put her arm around Mark, but she made herself stay put in her chair. He had caused her so much grief. He hadn't even bothered to visit her in the hospital or check in with her to see how Rose was. News travelled fast in the small community, and it was common knowledge that she and Rose had been in the horrific fire. Mark played with the band at the local pub every weekend, so he had no excuse for not knowing *or* for not checking in to see how she was, or – even more importantly – how Rose was. What type of father would do that? She wasn't sure how she would have responded if he had turned up at the hospital, but she certainly wouldn't have told him to bugger off. She would most probably have been grateful that he cared.

'Go on,' she said gently, swallowing down hard on the lump in her throat as she began twisting the bracelet Heath had given her. It somehow made her feel like Heath was sitting there with her, lending her strength.

'Molly, before I start, I want you to know something very important. I came to the hospital to visit you. I truly did. But when I walked in Heath was asleep in the chair by your bed and I just panicked, I didn't feel like I should be there. Then I couldn't bring myself to go back there, in case your family knew how much of a bastard I'd been to you. I didn't know how much you'd told them and I was ashamed. I checked in at the pub, though, every few days, to see how you were and to ask about Rose. I think he was beginning to wonder why I was so interested.'

Molly felt a wave of remorse wash over her for thinking that Mark was such a bad person. She dropped her head. 'Thank you for caring about us, Mark. I thought you didn't.'

'Of course I care, Molly!' Mark rubbed his face and took a deep breath. 'I'm really sorry about how I spoke to Jade at the rodeo, too. I had no right. She seems like a really nice lady and I'm a bastard for judging her so quickly. I really want to apologise to her and Mel but I haven't seen either of them to be able to. Mel's never behind the bar any more.'

Molly fiddled with her bracelet. 'Melinda's got a new job now, down at the bowls club. She does all the cooking. You can call in there and see her if you like, if you're really serious about apologising.'

'Well, I'll make sure I head in there this week, and I'll give Jade a call, if you don't mind giving me her mobile number.' Mark leant back in his chair, resting his head so that he was staring at the ceiling. 'But that's not why I came here, Molly. I saw you and Rose in town yesterday, checking your postbox. I was coming out of the bank when I spotted you both, and I just froze. I stood there, staring, shaken by seeing my daughter for the very first time. It made her so real, Molly, that I couldn't go on pretending that she wasn't any more. She's so beautiful. But I knew I didn't have the right to go anywhere near her after reacting the way I did. I knew then and there that I had to be a part of her life, and come hell or high water I was going to make myself a better man so I could be a father to her. I was just so worried about not being a good dad. You know, not living up to people's expectations. I was willing myself to believe that Rose wasn't my child.' He took a slow deep breath. 'You see, Molly, I never knew what it was like to have a proper dad. My father used to beat me and my mother, well, she was too afraid to do anything about it. Not that she could, she was usually too out of it on whatever drug she could get her hands on.'

Molly leant forward and placed her hand on his knee. 'I'm so sorry to hear that, Mark. I really am.'

He looked up at her and smiled weakly, then went on, his words spilling from him like a dam that had broken its walls. 'I ran away from home when I was fifteen and I've never seen either of them again. They could be dead for all I know. I've always had to look out for myself – no one else was going to. And I discovered alcohol was pretty good at taking the pain away ... Then I found my love for music. When I became a singer, I found I could get any woman I wanted – well, nearly.' He gave Molly a knowing look. He breathed in deeply, exhaled slowly. 'I began to feel invincible, as long as I was in control of my own destiny. And then, well, you came along and told me I was a father. I freaked, Molly. It terrified me to think there was someone out there who might depend on me. Me! I can't even take proper care of *myself* half the time! But now that I've had some time to come to grips with it, I'm hoping you'll let me be a part of your life with Rose. I want you and Rose to be a part of my future; it's all I've been able to think about.' He hung his head in his hands and Molly could almost hear his heart breaking, and her own.

His voice was almost a whisper and he looked crushed. 'Please, please let me at least meet Rose. You don't have to tell her I'm her father, if you don't want to. But I have to at least meet her.'

Molly didn't know how to feel. It was what she had wanted all along, for Rose to get to know her dad, to be a family. She leant back into her chair, tucking her feet up underneath her. She sat there, silently, and finally gave a huge sigh. 'Thank you for coming to tell me all this. It makes me happy to know that you *want* to be a part of our lives. I can totally understand why you're worried and I'm so terribly sad to hear what you went through as a child. But, Mark, you have to understand my concerns, with your drinking and all the women coming in and out of your life. That's not the type of world I want Rose to be a part of. Surely you must understand this? What are you going to do about it?'

Mark slowly lifted his head up, looking directly into Molly's eyes. 'I've decided to get help. I found a really good psychologist in Mareeba and I'm starting counseling next week. I promise you, I *will* change. It's time to grow up, Molly. I have someone other than myself to think about now.'

Molly wanted to believe him as his intensely solemn eyes held hers, not faltering for a second.

'I think that it's great you're man enough to go and get help. Not a lot of blokes have the guts to do it. But is this really you talking, or is it the drink? I can tell you've been drinking tonight, Mark. I can smell it on your breath.'

'Before I headed over here, I sculled a glass of whisky to calm my nerves. I know it was the wrong thing to do, but I was terrified that you'd tell me to piss off and never come back. God knows I would have deserved it if you did, after the way I treated you.'

Molly clapped her hands on her legs. 'I reckon it'd be great for you to get to know Rose. On two conditions, though: that you visit her here and that you haven't been drinking. You have to act responsibly, Mark. But as for us all being a family, I'm sorry – the chance of that ever happening is gone. I have a man in my life now, so you'll have to accept that Rose will also have a second dad. I hope that isn't going to be a problem for you?' They both knew it was a rhetorical question.

Mark looked at her miserably then jumped out of his chair, surprising Molly, and ran over to hug her. 'Thank you, thank you! I'll be a good dad, you just wait and see. And maybe in the future, she can come and stay over sometimes and I can teach her how to play a guitar.' He stood back to look at Molly. 'I've really stuffed up and it'll be a long time before I can ever forgive myself for the pain I caused you. You deserve to be treated with respect and to be loved for the wonderful woman you are. I just wasn't the guy to give that to you.'

Molly watched him inquisitively as he scratched his head, clearly deep in thought.

'The curiosity's killing me, though; can I ask who the lucky bloke is?'

Molly went to reply but he put his hand up to shush her.

'No, hang on, let me guess. Would it by any chance be, um, let me see, Heath Miller?'

Molly couldn't hide the look of shock on her face. 'How did you know?'

'You could tell by the way he looked at you, Molly. That man is madly in love with you.'

CHAPTER
26

The cherry-red Harley-Davidson grunted and rumbled like a primitive beast beneath Molly as she gazed out over the mountains at the aqua-blue ocean before her. From here, the water looked smooth as glass. She could just make out a large boat as it sped towards the Great Barrier Reef, leaving a spray of white foamy water in its wake. She pictured all the tourists on board trying to capture the beauty of their ocean holiday with clicks of their cameras, and envied them being able to spend weeks in this amazing wonderland. She could only ever spare a few days to enjoy it, but on the flip side, most of the travellers would only see this once in their lifetimes, whereas she could visit whenever she liked.

As the bike roared along the long scenic highway, passing through the small village of Julatten, Molly's thoughts drifted back to yesterday, when Rose had met Mark for the first time. She had hidden behind Molly's legs at first before gathering the strength to emerge from her safe spot and give Mark a shy cuddle and a kiss on his cheek. Mark had wiped joyous tears from his face as he told Rose again and again just how beautiful she was. Rose had smiled timidly when she took Mark's hand. Then she had led him to the puppies' kennel, explaining how she wanted him to meet Mack and Sasha.

Molly had sat and watched them play with the puppies from the verandah. It had been amazing to observe their similarities in features and also in mannerisms, even though Mark had had nothing to do with Rose until now. Within an hour they were both laughing and rolling around on the grass, having a whale of a time together. Mark kept glancing in Molly's direction, smiling with pride. She was so pleased the meeting had turned out so well. When it was time for Mark to go, Rose had hugged him tightly, telling him that he had to promise to come back. Molly had believed Mark completely when he had said he would love to.

David and Elizabeth were initially stunned when Molly had told them about Mark. It was the first time that she had seen her grandfather at a complete loss for words. He kept going to speak but would instead shake his head, running his fingers through his imaginary hair, muttering 'holy moley' time after time. After the news had sunk in though, they were extremely happy for Rose and they had all sat down with her to explain that Molly had found her dad.

With honesty high on the list for Molly, she had gone to great lengths over the years to make it clear to Rose that her dad had left before he even knew about her. But now, they were finally able to tell her the great news – her dad was back. At first Rose had been ecstatic, but then she had become increasingly insistent that she wanted Heath to be her dad. Molly had gently clarified that she could have *two* dads. Rose had thought about it for a few minutes before pronouncing that she felt very lucky to have two dads. Molly had almost wept with relief at her innocent declaration.

Sapphire skies stretched out above them with only the odd fluffy white cloud floating about. Molly wrapped her arms more

tightly around Heath's waist as they began their descent down the
Rex Range. She could smell his aftershave as the breeze blew back
towards her, mixed in with the scent of his leather jacket. It was
divine. The dust and heat of the outback was long behind them
and now they were surrounded by lush, green rainforest. It was
hard to believe they were only an hour and a half down the road
from Jacaranda Farm. Here massive tree ferns hugged the mountain
slopes. Hundreds of multicoloured butterflies flitted among the
tropical bush and shrubs, enhancing the enchanted beauty of the
rainforest. Molly loved the way the landscape could change so
dramatically so quickly. It made her feel blessed to live in such a
diverse part of Australia.

Heath slowed the Harley down, indicating to the four-wheel
drive behind them that he was pulling into the lookout. A group
of young guys honked and waved as they drove past them, the
old four-wheel drive obviously straining as it lugged a massive
fishing boat behind it. A thick black cloud of sooty smog billowed
from the exhaust when they accelerated and vanished around a
sharp bend.

Once the bike had stopped Molly slid off the seat, taking off
her helmet so that she could feel the sea breeze in her hair. Heath
grinned mischievously as he did the same, the look in his eyes filled
with the promise of the night they were about to share together.
The sexual tension between them was so powerful it made Molly
quiver. He pulled her in close to him, gently caressing her lips with
his tongue before kissing her passionately, longingly. Molly felt her
legs buckle beneath her as shivers ran up her spine from his touch.

'Are you looking forward to sleeping with the sounds of the
ocean at our front door?' Heath asked huskily.

Molly smiled. 'I'm looking forward to sleeping with more than
the sounds of the ocean.'

Heath playfully poked her in the ribs. 'Now, now, Molly, we have some romancing to do before that. I have a few little things planned for you.'

Molly rested her head on his chest. 'Ah, that sounds wonderful.'

They stood in silence for a few minutes, drinking in the panoramic view before them.

'So, how are you feeling about Mark spending time with Rose?' Molly finally asked as she tenderly stroked Heath's back. He had been very quiet on the subject.

'I'll be honest – I was a bit jealous when you first told me. I'm delighted with the fact that Rose still calls me dad, though. And really, I think it's great that Mark's decided to pull himself together so he can be a father to Rose, as long as it doesn't affect us, Molly. I mean, now I have you I'd hate to lose you, or Rose. It'd kill me.'

Molly cupped his face in her hands and pulled him close. 'I'm not interested in Mark, Heath. At all. I only have eyes for you.'

Heath smiled broadly. 'That's all I needed to hear.'

*

It was late afternoon by the time they arrived at Pretty Beach. They had stopped in Port Douglas for a leisurely lunch on the waterfront and had spent an hour or so browsing the quirky shops afterwards. Molly had loved walking hand in hand with Heath around the village; she felt so relaxed and secure in his company. She also couldn't help liking the fact that so many women almost broke their necks to have a second look at Heath. He *was* gorgeous, and he was all hers.

Molly felt the motorbike slow down as Heath turned onto a cobblestone driveway, which seemed to go on forever. She could tell from the perfectly manicured gardens on either side of the long drive that the house was going to be mighty impressive. Once it eventually came into view, her jaw dropped. The interior matched the extravagance of the exterior with luxuriant furnishings, exquisite bath products and a fridge full of decadent goodies, and she had not even made it to the bedroom yet! There was also a massive marble-tiled patio that had incredible unobstructed views of the ocean.

Heath slid open the folding timber doors and Molly flopped down on a red suede couch, rubbing her hands over the plush material as she grinned from ear to ear. From where she sat she could almost feel the salty spray from the waves as they crashed on the golden, sandy shore close by. She closed her eyes and took a deep breath, savouring the smell of the ocean. She felt like she was on a tropical holiday somewhere in the Bahamas.

Heath wandered over from the kitchen and joined her on the couch, his feet now bare and his shirt unbuttoned, revealing his sexy abs. Molly had to fight the urge to run her tongue down them right then and there.

'How about a stroll along the beach? We could find a nice spot to drink this bottle of wine and watch the sunset, hey?'

'Wow! That'd be wonderful, just let me go and get changed out of my jeans,' Molly replied as she jumped up and looked eagerly around her. 'Um, which way is the bedroom? This place is so big I'm afraid I'll get lost!'

'How about you change in the bathroom?' Heath said. 'I have a surprise in the bedroom that I want to save for later on.'

Molly cocked her head to one side and smiled. 'What are you up to, Heath Miller?'

'Ah, never you mind, Molly Jones. The bathroom's that a way.'

The warm sand trickled between Molly's toes as she walked along the beach with Heath, reminding her of the yoga teacher telling them to envisage a beautiful beach. Now, here she was, walking in her meditation. How magnificent! It brought back all the feelings of peace and serenity she had felt in the class.

They had been walking for almost an hour and not seen another soul, making Molly feel as though they were on a deserted island. Noisy seagulls were swooping into the ocean to catch their dinner, then rising back high into the azure-blue skies and out of sight. All along the beach were little balls of sand where tiny sand crabs had buried themselves. Molly marvelled at how perfectly formed the balls of sand were as she touched them with the tip of her big toe.

'This looks as good a spot as any. Would you like to sit down?' Heath said, pointing to a large piece of driftwood.

Molly took a sip of her wine. The day had been more than she had hoped for already – and there was still the night to come.

Heath pulled her in close to him as the sun began to set over the water. He leant in and kissed her softly, tilting her head back and sliding his warm tongue down her neck, stopping in the nape of her throat to caress the sensitive hollow with his lips. Molly shuddered with desire as he slid his hand under her thin cotton top, running it along her waist and up over her breasts. She felt breathless as he stroked her nipples gently at first, then began to roll their firmness between his fingers, sending her spiralling out of control.

She dropped her glass and felt the wine splash her bare legs as she slid her hands into his open shirt, scratching her nails down his back. Heath moaned as she kissed his chest, biting him gently along the way. She ran her fingertips over the tuft of hair at the top of his jeans and undid the button with ease, sliding her hand down into the warmth and over the tip of his erection.

'Let's go back to the house, beautiful,' Heath whispered, his voice rasping with desire.

'You must have read my mind,' Molly replied huskily.

*

They just made it into the house before a sudden tropical down-pour. The raindrops hammered on the roof as Heath lifted Molly up off the ground and she wrapped her legs around his waist, her skirt sliding up around her hips. They slammed into a wall, knocking a pile of books from a table as they grabbed at one another. Molly cried out Heath's name as he pushed her against the wall, their lips devouring each other as their passion soared. She could feel Heath's arousal through his jeans, pushing into the silkiness of her underwear, making her ache for him even more. Heath slid his hand up her thigh and to the warm sweetness between her legs, circling her, slowly, teasingly, making her pulse beneath his fingertips.

'I need to feel you inside me! Now!' Molly beseeched as she dropped her legs to the floor, her eyes displaying the ferociousness she was feeling inside.

Heath smiled sexily, daringly, before pushing her hands to the wall and sliding himself down to the ground. Little by little he pulled her pants down her legs, kissing her softly as he went, breathing warmth all over her. Once they were off he slid his tongue back up her legs and tasted her, licking around her swollen lips, then thrusting his tongue deep inside. Molly moaned in satisfaction, reaching heights she had never reached before. He stood up to face her, his eyes full of desire, and Molly tore at his shirt, letting it fall to the ground. Heath placed his hands against the wall, above Molly's head, his chest bared, tattoos adorning all the right places.

They fumbled their way to the bedroom, kissing all the way. Molly took in the beauty of the room as she was led in by Heath. The whole bed was sprinkled with red rose petals and there were candles lit everywhere. She seized the moment and slowly, seductively stripped off the rest of her clothes while Heath positioned himself on the bed to watch her. He wore the most devilish grin she had ever seen. She moved to the end of the bed and helped Heath pull off his jeans, leaving him as naked as she was. Slowly she slid herself on top of him, licking his stomach, scratching her nails down his chest, until she felt her lips touch his shaft. She gently licked the tip and then breathed out a long, warm, slow breath, making him groan in pleasure. She gradually slipped him into her mouth, sliding her tongue around his manhood, feeling it throb in pleasure. Heath ran his fingers through her hair and pulled it, teetering her on the edge of ecstasy and pain. It was a glorious feeling. Heath flipped Molly over onto her back and pinned her arms down, taking in the exquisiteness of her face as he unhurriedly slid inside her, enjoying watching her cry out in fulfillment beneath him.

Molly thrust her hips in union with his as they got closer and closer to climaxing. Heath licked around her firm, pink nipples, biting down hard on them as he began to come. Molly came with him, her sweet heaven pulsing around him, sending them both to heights of pure pleasure that neither had ever experienced before.

*

A doorbell chimed noisily, waking Molly from her blissful slumber. She fumbled beside the bed, trying to see what time it was on her mobile, surprised when she flipped it open and noticed it was only nine o'clock. She felt Heath jump out of bed and she rolled over to catch another glimpse of him naked.

'That'll be dinner, my princess,' he said, pulling up his jeans. 'You take your time and have a nice, long, hot shower if you like. I have a bit of preparing to do before you join me out on the patio.'

'Gee whiz, you *have* thought of everything. I'm impressed,' Molly said as she stretched her arms high above her head, yawning contentedly.

Heath grinned as he vanished out the door, still pulling on his shirt.

Under the shower, Molly enjoyed the warm water trickling over her body as she took delight in the images still fresh in her mind: Heath touching her, teasing her, tasting her, loving her. He was absolutely gorgeous, had a huge heart *and* he was great in bed. She smiled as she turned off the taps, drying herself off with an Egyptian-cotton bath towel. She felt glorious. She slipped on her black silk robe, the material sensual against her still tingling skin, and wandered out in search of Heath.

The house was pitch black except for a trail of lit candles. Soft country love songs played in the background, giving Molly goosebumps all over. She tiptoed along the cool tiled floors, butterflies in her belly in anticipation of what Heath was up to. She found him out on the patio, a mouthwatering platter of hot and cold seafood taking centre stage on the dining table, along with a bottle of red wine.

'Oh, Heath, this looks amazing! I feel like a queen being treated to all this luxury!' Molly gasped as she sat down at the table, facing Heath. 'How did you organise all this?'

'Well, it wasn't easy, but the look on your face makes it all worth it. I organised for a fantastic restaurant in Port Douglas to make all this up for us and have it delivered. I know you love seafood. Dig in, gorgeous.'

'What a sweet thing to do! I didn't realise until now how bloody hungry I was. I think I might have an oyster first. They look divine.' Molly peeled the oyster out of its shell like a pro and slid it into her mouth, taking pleasure in the creamy centre when its flavour burst in her mouth.

Heath screwed up his face. 'You might have to eat all those yourself, Molly. I still can't get my head around the fact that they suck up all the rubbish out of the sea.'

'No worries there,' Molly said, giggling.

It was close to midnight when they stripped off and sank their bodies into the warm, bubbly spa, the moon blazing bright above them. First the kisses were lingering and tender, then became more and more passionate as the heat between them intensified. Molly straddled Heath, throwing her head back in ecstasy as she felt him slide deep inside her again. She moved her hips slowly, seductively, every inch of her body craving the ultimate in euphoria. She could feel herself on the brink of an orgasm as Heath placed his hands on her hips and directed her to move faster, his fingers clutching her hungrily as they both cried out in rapture.

Afterwards, still floating weightlessly in the spa, Molly lay in Heath's arms, resting her head on his shoulder, and looked up at the millions of stars above them. 'This is the most romantic thing anyone has ever done for me. I've had the most amazing day of my life. Thank you so much.'

Heath rolled her over and kissed her tenderly. 'You deserve all of this, Molly, especially after what you've been through lately. You're the most amazing woman I've ever met. I have one more surprise for you, though.'

Heath leant over the side of the spa, pulling something from his jeans' pocket and turning to Molly. He was holding a small velvet box, and with a little flourish he opened it to reveal a gorgeous diamond ring that glistened in the moonlight.

'Molly Jones, I love you. I'd like to spend the rest of my life with you and Rose. Will you marry me?'

EPILOGUE

Heath gave himself the once-over in his hallway mirror before heading outside to take his place under the arch that Jade and Melinda had made from freshly picked velvet-red roses on lattice. He pushed his hands into his suit pockets, finding himself unable to stand still, the eagerness to see Molly almost overwhelming him. He straightened up his brand-new akubra and gave a quick nod and proud smile to Trev, Kenny and his brother, Gary, who were standing beside him, looking smart in their black suits. 'You got the rings, Gary?'

Gary tapped his trousers pocket with conviction. 'Sure do. I haven't let them out of my sight all morning.'

Heath glanced over to where friends and family were sitting in chairs that had been covered with white silk and big red bows. His parents smiled proudly back at him from the front row. Beside them sat David, Elizabeth, Cheryl and Rob, with another seventy guests behind, waiting restlessly for the bride to arrive. Rose petals of many colours were scattered around the grounds and a red carpet had been rolled out down the centre of the chairs, adding the final magical touch to the scene. Heath thought it was a grand achievement to get the place looking so beautiful. From where he stood under the jacaranda tree he could see out to where the cattle grazed on lush green grass from the recent monsoon season. He smiled; it was hard to believe it was nearly a year ago that he had asked Molly to marry him. Since then, they had built a house of their own on Jacaranda Farm and David had passed most of the responsibilities of running the farm down to him. It was an honour Heath took very seriously.

The celebrant called everyone's attention as the wedding song Molly had chosen started to play. It was the same one they had made love to in the spa: 'I Need You', by Steel Magnolia. For a second Heath thought he might pass out from the rapid rush of nerves, but he snapped himself out of it and stood nervously, waiting for Molly to join him. He watched admiringly as Rose and Jade began to walk down the aisle, looking beautiful in their ruby-red bridesmaid dresses with tiny flowers in their hair. Rose held a basket of rose petals and was sprinkling them as she walked, smiling at everyone as she passed. Molly finally appeared from the house, and her beauty took his breath away. She made her way down the steps, her ivory silk dress flowing out softly behind her. She looked so gorgeous, so softly radiant. David stood beside her, their arms entwined. Molly's lace veil covered her face but he knew she would be smiling behind it. She slowly walked towards him, stepping in time to the music. They finally reached the arch of roses and David gave Molly a kiss on the cheek before passing her hands to Heath. Heath lightly squeezed them three times, his way of saying 'I love you' before lifting the veil from her face.

The celebrant cleared his throat, smiling at Molly and Heath. 'We are gathered here today to witness the joining of two people deeply in love, Molly Elizabeth Jones and Heath Richard Miller. We are all delighted that they decided to share their special day with all of us, here in the beautiful surrounds of Jacaranda Farm. Now let me begin.'

The time soon came for Molly and Heath's vows, which they had written themselves. Molly looked into Heath's eyes, feeling his hand tremble beneath hers.

'Heath, I love you. You are my best friend, my lover and the one I turn to for strength. I want to grow old with you and reminisce about the life we've shared. Day by day I promise to love and honour you, to treasure and respect you, to walk with you side by side in sorrow and in joy. Day by day I promise as your wife to hold you in my arms, to grow with you in truth, to laugh with you, to cry with you, to be with you and to love you with all that I am and all that I shall become. This I promise you from the depth of my heart and soul for as long as we both shall live.'

Heath held Molly's eyes as he spoke his words. 'I, Heath, take you, Molly, to be my lawful wedded wife in equal love; to be the mother of our children and to be the companion of my heart. I promise always to be there to catch you when you fall, to love you deeply, to share your happiness, to wipe your tears and to hold your hand on this journey we have chosen to walk together. I give to you my aspirations, my trust, my future. You are my soul mate and I will love you with every part of my being, until I take my final breath.'

Friends and family wept openly at the beauty and passion of their words as the celebrant approached. 'Heath, you may now kiss your bride.'

Heath tenderly took Molly in his arms for a loving embrace just as two Ulysses butterflies landed on Molly's dress. She knew at that moment that her mother and father were with her and her heart swelled with elation. The crowd cried and cheered and clapped as the celebrations began.

Tables were lavishly laid out with trays of succulent roast pig and crackling fresh off the spit. Roast vegetables and salads were piled high on crystal serving platters and there were big baskets of freshly baked bread rolls. Eskies were evenly spread about, filled with ice and beers, and small round tables were draped in red cloth with arrangements of red and white roses standing as centerpieces amongst bottles of wine and sparkling-clean glasses.

The blissful, newly married couple floated around the sea of smiling faces, accepting congratulations. There were no formal seating arrangements, as Molly and Heath had wanted their friends and family to sit wherever they pleased once they had filled their plates and glasses.

Molly and Heath moved off to the side, hidden by a cluster of brightly coloured bougainvilleas, to share a private kiss. The night sky above them was filled with stars for as far as the eye could see. Hundreds of candles had been lit and were flickering in the warm breeze, lighting the faces of the guests with a gentle glow as they ate and talked and laughed. It was a captivating scene, like something out of a fairytale, Molly thought. She wrapped her arms around Heath's waist, resting her head on his chest.

'What a perfect day. It's been everything I ever wanted, and more.'

Heath sighed. 'And to top it all off, I've married the most beautiful woman in the world.'

They took to the dance floor for their first dance as husband and wife to the Big and Rich song 'Lost in This Moment'. Molly pointed as she spotted a shooting star falling from the sky and Heath smiled and followed her gaze, making sure he made a wish: a happy lifetime with Molly and Rose forever by his side.

After the first dance the crowd joined in and boogied joyously alongside them. Heath picked Rose up, spinning her around, both of them laughing. Molly wrapped her arms around them, smiling over at Mark, who was dancing with his girlfriend of six months. He had followed through on his promise to be a good father, getting himself straightened out, and had chosen to move to Dimbulah permanently so he could live close to Rose.

The party went on into the wee hours of the morning and the crowd dwindled down until the only ones left standing were those who were determined to see the sun rise. Molly and Heath were among them, not wanting the magical night to end. Trev, Kenny, Jade and Melinda lay on the ground chuckling like a group of schoolkids, looking up into the dawn sky with their sunglasses on. They watched the sun rise into a morning haze, filling the sky with its golden rays, giving them all the gift of a brand-new day.

Finally Molly and Heath said goodbye to their friends and wandered back to their home. Weary and yet reluctant to sleep and break the spell, they took a shower together, making love under the warm stream of water, their bodies tingling with pleasure as they lingered on the brink, teasing each other, wanting the moment to last, finally succumbing and reaching ecstasy together. Afterwards, Heath knelt down and tenderly soaped up Molly's firm round belly, talking to their baby through her belly button like it was a microphone. Molly giggled at his antics, basking in the warmth of his love. They dried each other off and slipped into bed, both utterly exhausted.

Molly smiled contentedly when Heath wrapped his arms around her. They were a family now, just as she had always dreamed, and soon there would be another little addition, a brother or sister for Rose to play with. She nestled into Heath's broad chest, lulled by the sound of his rhythmic heartbeat as she blissfully drifted off into the land of dreams.

ACKNOWLEDGEMENTS

To Chloe Rose, my darling little girl, for bringing a smile to my face whenever you're around, and filling my life with joy. *And* for always yelling excitedly in the middle of a store when you spot my book on the shelf – even when I am sometimes trying to remain incognito. You are beautiful, inside and out.

To my inspirational mum, Gaye, for forever being my sounding board, my friend and the best mother in the world. Your endless belief in me drives me forward and gives me the confidence to step into the unknown.

To my wonderful dad, John, I am honoured that you spent an entire day reading my first book, *Rosalee Station*, relishing each and every word. Considering you never read, that's a huge feat!

To Aunty Kulsoom, my proofreader; what a wonderful woman you are. Hurry up and move up north so I can have you around all the time.

To my stepdad, Trevor, for teaching me to always look on the positive side of life, and instilling in me the confidence to follow my dreams.

To my sister-in-law, Hayley, and my brother, Kain; thank you for baby-sitting on the many occasions where I needed peace and quiet to write. You are both stars!

To my mates, my partners in crime and the ones who are always there for me, no matter what – thank you for being the bestest friends any gal could ask for.

To my sisters, I love you all so very much. I'm so blessed to have each and every one of you in my life.

A big thank you to a very special lady, Fiona Stanford, for your unconditional support in so many various ways; you're one in a million.

And finally, but most essentially, thanks to you, the reader. It is *you* who keeps my dream alive by reading my novels. I am eternally grateful for your support. I hope my country storytelling intensifies your passion for this captivating land down under, Australia.

Turn over for a sneak peek.

Secrets of Silvergum

by

MANDY MAGRO

AVAILABLE JUNE 2019

With Emma Kensington cradled in his arms, Zane Wolfe stared in shock and horror at the blood pooling by his bare feet. He'd been sleeping soundly until he'd heard Emma's screams, and now there was a dead man on the kitchen floor. He just thanked God she'd been able to defend herself – he couldn't stand to think of anything terrible happening to her. Ever.

He looked to where Peter and Michael were huddled, whispering between themselves. *What in the hell was going on?* 'What are you two doing? We have to call the police,' he growled, as he snatched the phone off the kitchen bench. 'Right now!'

'No, Zane, you don't want to go and do that,' Peter boomed, waving his hands about, trying to stop him from dialling 000.

Incredulously, Zane shook his head. 'Why?' Emma was shaking like a leaf, and he pulled her in tighter, wishing he could ease her anguish.

'Because, if you do …' Peter rubbed his face, huffed, stepped over the crumpled body, and came to rest his hands on Zane's shoulder and Emma's back. 'Emma might find herself on the Mafia's hit list.'

Zane dropped the phone as if it were fiery hot. It crashed to the floor. 'What in the hell are you on about?'

Emma stood back from him and lifted her cheek from his chest, her face ghostly pale. 'I only came out to get a drink of water. I didn't mean to hurt him, it's just, he came for me and I reacted to save myself.' She shuddered and her sobs rose harder.

Michael stepped in beside her, and after flashing Zane a stern look, took his girlfriend into his arms. 'It'll be okay, Em, we just have to do this right or, like Dad said, you might get hurt.' He tucked wayward strands of hair behind her ears. 'I'd never forgive myself if something happened to you, baby.'

Peter nodded as he heaved a sigh. 'Yes, you were undoubtedly defending yourself, Emma, I believe you, but Mario Zaffaro isn't going to give a shit about that. All he'll want is revenge for whoever took his cousin's life.'

'Why the fuck would the Mafia want to break into our home?' His instincts telling him it would have something to do with Peter's work, Zane looked down at the tattooed thug. He'd never seen a dead body before, and nausea swirled in his stomach at the gruesome sight.

Strangely unperturbed, Peter followed his gaze. 'I'm building a case against one of Mario's boys at the moment, and I suppose he thought he might find something in the house to discredit me, or … maybe, God forbid, he sent this thug to threaten me, or possibly even to kill me.' He cleared his throat and seemed to ponder this for a few moments. 'Whatever the case, thank goodness Emma stopped him.'

Zane found himself lost for words. Emma, too distraught to take anything more in, huddled against Michael. Zane felt a pang of jealousy that he wasn't the one soothing her, but he swallowed it down. Now wasn't the time for his hidden feelings to come into play. Hands laced behind his head, he paced, and finally found his voice. 'So what do you suggest we do, Peter?'

'I don't want you and Emma to do, anything. The less you know now, the better. I'll take care of it. Okay?'

Wide eyed, Zane turned to him. 'How do you intend to do that?'

'Like I said, the less you know, the better.' He gestured to Emma. 'Take her and calm her down, will you? Michael and I will clean up this mess. And then tomorrow, for the sake of Emma's life, and ours, I want us all to get on with our routine like this never happened. You're not to speak of it, to anyone. Ever. Do you understand?' His face was a picture of caution.

Zane was reluctant but because he cared more about Emma than some thug he didn't know, he did as Peter had demanded. If only this were a nightmare they'd all wake up from tomorrow. But it was terrifyingly real, and something told him, as horrifying as it was, there was a hell of a lot more to the story.

CHAPTER

1

Silvergum, North Queensland

Shattered after two weeks with virtually no sleep, Zane dared a glance in Emma's direction and then heaved a weary sigh. Although the classic Cold Chisel tune playing from the radio was a welcome distraction, what remained silent between them was resounding off every inch of the sun-speckled windscreen. He and Emma had talked about it all until they were blue in the face, and there was nothing to be gained from going over it with her for the hundredth time. As much as they both wanted to go to the cops, risking her safety just wasn't an option. There was no way in hell he was going to endanger her life, or Michael and Peter's, all because of his yearning to do the right thing.

Staring out the passenger window, he tried to pretend it had never happened, tried not to imagine the dead man, who he'd last seen slumped on the kitchen floor, now at the bottom of

Campfire River, with bricks tied to his feet, or buried somewhere deep in the middle of Silvergum's national park. Not that he knew what had transpired once he'd dragged a very distraught Emma back to his bedroom and locked the door. Nor did he know what it had to do with the Mafia, and he didn't want to know. All that mattered was that Emma was alive, and unharmed. He wouldn't put it past Peter to do whatever it took to cover up the evidence – the lengths his adoptive father would go to preserve his reputation as a cutthroat criminal defence lawyer were beyond Zane's comprehension. It came with the territory of representing the bad guys, the delinquents who deserved to be locked away for life that the state felt deserved a fair trial, that's where Peter came in to save the day. In Zane's opinion, Peter wrought the justice system so criminals could walk free while their victims and their families suffered. The under-the-table payoffs and the who-knew-who in the land of the Law was a goddamn joke.

A smashing headache behind his eyes, he closed them and squeezed the bridge of his nose. No matter how hard he tried, and regardless of whether the thug was a part of a cartel that harmed and hurt for money, the dead man's face continued to haunt him. He just hoped that by leaving Aussie shores, he could put it all behind him. He craved a distraction from his relentless thoughts, wanting to think of anything but that shocking night. If only it were that easy.

After an hour of driving in virtual silence, thankfully, they were almost at Cairns International Airport. Other than the odd comment here and there as they'd wound down the Kuranda Range at a snail's pace, the evasiveness between them was killing him. But what was he meant to say to fill the agonizing gaps?

Don't worry about killing a man, she'll be right? Or, *I'm sorry about making such sweet love to you when you're already dating Michael?* There was nothing he could say that would make their situation any better or less painful.

Grabbing his wide-brimmed hat from the dash, he did his best to keep his turbulent emotions at bay. A true-blue cowboy never broke down. He'd never done it to this day, and he wasn't about to do it now, even though he felt as if his entire world was crumbling around him. The most frustrating thing was that he was helpless to stop it. Catching her eye, the exquisite brunette behind the wheel offered him a brusque smile before focussing again on the long line of traffic in front of them. The tremble in her soft, sweet, kissable lips was ever so slight and the quickened pulse in her chest was obvious to him only because he knew her so well. Angry for giving into the desires he'd kept under lock and key for years, he wanted to give himself a good slap around the ears. Emma Kensington deserved so much better, better than him, better than Michael, better than *this*.

Michael had wooed her from the get-go, pulled the wool over her eyes in his most charming of ways, but soon enough, he'd go and hurt her. It wasn't in Michael's nature to remain committed, to anyone. But try as Zane might to warn Emma of this, she refused to see it. Her dream of the whole white picket fence lifestyle; to be happily married with three kids by the time she was twenty-five, seemed to overshadow her voice of reason. It was an idea that terrified Zane, but it was the life Emma was looking for.

Worried out of his mind and nervous as all hell about what lay in front of him with the American professional bull-riding circuit, and also the dark past that incessantly shadowed him,

and Emma, his stomach twisted into an even tighter knot.
He hated leaving her to deal with all this on her own, but not
wanting to make a scene at the airport, he had to pull himself
together. Squeezing the bridge of his nose again, he heaved
another weary sigh, adjusted his sunnies and then gave a few
short, sharp tugs on his seatbelt to loosen it, wishing he could
unbuckle the damn thing altogether. He hated feeling confined,
constricted, loathed anything to do with rules and regulations.
Telling him he couldn't do something was like waving a red cape
at a charging bull.

He was a self-confessed wild child; although his wayward
acts had all been quite harmless. He'd lived seventeen long years
without getting into too much trouble with the law. Having a
renowned defence lawyer for an adoptive father might have had
something to do with that. But this, being a witness to homicide,
as accidental as it was, was immeasurably worse than the times
he'd driven a car unlicensed, dashed down the main street of
Silvergum butt naked for a dare, and failed to pay a couple of
speeding fines. No amount of prayer would ever get them out
of this mess – not that he'd ever drop to his knees to try. Even
though he'd been raised by his God-fearing adoptive mother,
Kay, since he was three months old, he was no longer a religious
man. He had all but turned his back on the Church the day she'd
died of cancer almost a year ago. What kind of god took such a
kind and loving soul in such a horrendous way, especially after
all the years of verbal and emotional abuse she'd endured from
Peter's acid tongue?

Looking out the window at the rows of seemingly identical
houses becoming claustrophobically closer together – a country-
blooded man through and through, suburban living wasn't for

him – he tried to rid himself of his disturbing thoughts. They had kept him pacing the darkened hallway of the Kensingtons' old workers' cottage these past two weeks. Staying at Wattle Acres just hadn't been an option after what had happened. Peter and Michael's increasing animosity towards him, combined with the eeriness of the kitchen had him packing his bags and taking up Emma's offer to stay at her family's property, Serendipity, until he left for America. And it let him keep an eye out for her, just in case she had a mark on her back. How Peter and Michael could keep going as if nothing had happened, how they could go to sleep at night and wake refreshed and ready for the day ahead at their prestigious law firm was beyond him. He'd told them so, and they hadn't liked it, reminding him to keep his mouth shut or Emma might end up dead. Their words were as harsh and as blunt as that.

Branded as the black sheep of the family by many Silvergum locals, unlike Michael – who was his father's blood and bone – Zane had proved time and time again he wasn't Peter's progeny. Professional bull riding was a far cry from the world of Law Peter and Michael immersed themselves in. But Zane was proud that his passion lay in something so completely different. He didn't care that he was a disappointment to Peter; he'd never wanted to be anything like the arrogant, ruthless, selfish bastard. Growing up feeling as if he were nothing but a thorn in their sides, and even more so now Kay was gone, he was relieved to be leaving this life behind, and hopefully, for good. Apart from this captivatingly spirited woman beside him, who he'd known since kindergarten, there was no one he'd miss. Fighting to divert his thoughts from the heartache he was going to feel saying goodbye to her, he watched a flock of seagulls soar through the sky; the seemingly endless blue a sharp contrast to the darkness he was feeling deep down in his soul.

Nearing the airport, he stole another glance at the only woman he'd ever truly made love to, not just slept with for the fun of it. The tension in her glossy lips and the whites of her knuckles as she gripped the steering wheel unnecessarily tight told him her mind was tormented by the same images and thoughts as his. While his pounding concern for her safety was almost too much to cope with, he knew for sure that she was carrying so much on her petite shoulders. He couldn't even begin to imagine how she was feeling, knowing she'd been the cause of the intruder's death, despite the fact she was only defending herself. Zane knew that Emma desperately wanted to go to the police, but she feared for her life if she did. It was almost too much for one person to handle, he thought, glancing at her. He ached to reach out and soothe her worries away, but that wasn't his place. He'd tried to do just that last night, to comfort her when she'd come to him in tears, and look where that had led them … even deeper into unbearable secrecy. If only Michael was there more for her, it might never have happened.

Slowing, Emma indicated and pulled into the drop-off zone out the front of International Departures. Without allowing himself time for any hesitation, Zane jumped out and shut the ute's door behind him. Grabbing his suitcase from the back while avoiding slobbery licks from her Great Dane, Bo, he paused to drink Emma in one more time. He knew not to let her innocent appearance fool him – she was like him, as wild as they came.

Resting his forearm on the open passenger window, he feigned a nonchalance he was far from feeling. 'You sure you're going to be okay, Em?' Man, his heart was aching.

Tucking wisps of wind-tousled hair from her lightly freckled cheeks, she offered a sad smile and shrugged. 'If I say no, are you going to stay?'

Wishing he could say yes, he found himself at a loss for words.

'Thought as much.' She blinked her dazzling, gold-speckled green eyes, wet with tears. 'Then I suppose I'm just going to have to be, aren't I, Casanova?'

He flinched at hearing his nickname. 'Yeah, I suppose, I'm so sorry, Em, about everything.' He didn't feel the need to elaborate.

She laughed softly as she picked at the grease beneath her short fingernails – she'd been under the bonnet when he'd found her this morning. 'Even though I should be, I'm not sorry about what happened last night, Zane. It felt so right, and sooo good.' She looked at him. 'I know you felt whatever it was, too. I could see it in your eyes.'

So many emotion-fuelled words tumbled to his lips, but he fought them back. Now wasn't the time to tell her how he really felt about her – not when he was leaving for good. Unable to hold her intense gaze any longer, for fear of jumping back into the ute and throwing his dreams away, he looked down at boots. Drawing in a breath, he shook his head. 'I don't know what to say, Em, but if I don't go now—'

She cut him off. 'I know, Zane, it's okay. If I were in your shoes, after everything that's happened, I'd be running like a bat out of hell and never looking back.' She sighed. 'I'm so happy for you, finally getting the break you deserve.'

He dared a glance back at her and his heart tumbled. 'I wish you could come with me.'

'Me too … but then I'd probably cramp your style, Casanova.' She tried to flash her knee-buckling smile, but failed, miserably.

Once he could cop it, but not twice in a matter of minutes. 'Please, Em, don't call me that, not after last night ...' He shook his head, his heart feeling like a lead weight.

She unbuckled her seatbelt and slid across the seat, her fierce gaze daring the mean-looking parking inspector heading towards them to try to tell her to move on. 'I'm going to miss you, Zane Wolfe.' She brushed a kiss over his lips, igniting the blazing fire in his heart all over again. 'Take care, won't you?'

'I will, you too.' He cleared his throat. Damn this was even harder than he'd expected.

Ever so gently, she placed a trembling hand against his cheek. 'Please don't ever forget me.'

'How could I ever forget you?' Desperate to lighten the mood, he tried to laugh it off. 'I'm not going away forever, you know. I'll be back sometime.'

She offered him a smile that showed how much she doubted that. She knew him all too well. 'Remember to keep our secrets under lock and key, okay?' She eyed him carefully.

He shrugged and forced a smile he was far from feeling. 'What are these secrets you speak off, Miss Kensington?'

'That's the way.' Nodding, she sniffled and wiped at her eyes. 'Bye, Zane.'

'Yup, catch ya round like a rissole, Em.'

'Gravy and all,' she said. Then buckling herself back in, she revved the Holden V8 to life and pulled out and away, taking a huge piece of Zane's heart with her.

It was a fight not to look back when he stepped through the sliding doors, the coolness of the air-conditioning like a sharp slap to the face. Finally taking his sunnies off, he groaned and cursed beneath his breath. The airport was jam-packed with travellers, the line to the check-in counter a mile long. He joined the queue, and the nerves and doubts multiplied. Checking his phone almost every five seconds, just in case Emma texted or rang him, he had to fight the urge to look over his shoulder, as he had done for the past two weeks. Having witnessed the unthinkable, and knowing it had something to do with the Mafia, he found it incredibly hard to stand still. He wanted to stay and play Emma's bodyguard, to make sure no harm came to her, but they had to get on with their lives. Besides, she had Michael there to do that for her.

Finally, he was standing at the check-in counter. The impeccably dressed woman with lips painted bright red offered a smile, revealing lipstick-smudged teeth, as she handed back his passport. Zane shoved it in his top pocket, wished her a good day, and then made his way down the corridor leading to airport security. Emptying his pockets, cursing when he pulled out his favourite pocketknife that would be confiscated for sure, he tried to shake the unease from the pit of his stomach. The terror of that night had a grip on him so damn tight he was powerless to be free of it. It had all happened so fast – Emma's panicked cries, him running from his bedroom still half asleep, the thug tumbling backwards and smashing his head on the granite bench, the pool of blood beneath his motionless body spreading further by the second. He'd never forget the strange expression shared between Peter and Michael as they raced into the kitchen to find the intruder on the floor. Peter's explanation of exactly who the dead man was believable, but it hadn't excused the way he and Michael had reacted.

Through the metal detector, and with his pocketknife frustratingly taken from him, Zane slung his backpack over his shoulder. Every step he took towards the waiting plane was a step away from the life he loathed, and the family he despised. A head above the rest, and with shoulders as wide as a professional footy player, gazes followed him down the aisle of the Boeing 747 – some subtle, some not so much. His country get-up of cowboy boots, faded jeans and his trusty Akubra (there was no way he was risking it getting squashed in his luggage), and the tattoos that were visible, drew all sorts of attention. A few passengers looked cautious, others were curious. Zane took it all in his stride, offering a courteous smile whenever his eyes met those of a gushing woman. In his line of work, female admiration came with the territory, and like his mum had always said – God rest her soul – it cost nothing to be a gentleman. Opening a door for a woman, young or old, was a given in his world, as too was standing whenever a lady walked into a room.

Hopeful the seat beside him was going to remain unoccupied, so he could unravel his six-foot-three frame, he sat down and latched his damn seatbelt. He couldn't get away from constraints today. The only place he truly felt free was on the back of a one-tonne bucking bull – at least then he could get off whenever he wanted. At last, right where he needed to be, and with the dreaded goodbye with Emma done and dusted, he released a pent-up breath. This journey was going to bring a whole new meaning to a long-haul flight – an entire eighteen, or so, hours, to think about the horror of the last two weeks, and the mind-blowing pleasures of last night. Damn his lack of willpower. And even though he'd gone and stuffed everything up, just as he always did when it came to women, not that Emma was just *any* woman, she'd still insisted on dropping him off as planned. In the throes of passion, she'd also promised not to hold it against him, because it took two to tango. Her determination to shoulder her share of the blame made him fall for her even harder. The tears that had been building in her hazel eyes, and the quiver in her lips as she'd unravelled from his arms and crawled from his bed at some ungodly hour, so she could sneak home before her parents got up, had almost broken him.

While the plane taxied and lifted off, his eyes darted around as he familiarised his surroundings. Staring at the seatbelt sign, keen for it to be switched off, he clenched his clammy hands together and cursed himself for the hundredth time that day. He wasn't afraid of flying, but having never passed over the oceans, this was all new to him. He trusted in the pilot to get him to Dallas safe and sound, but if it were possible, he'd prefer the feel of a well-worn saddle beneath him, and the sound of pounding hooves as he voyaged to his new home.

He fought to focus on the here and now. This was meant to be a momentous moment – leaving Australia to chase his bull-riding dreams. It was one he'd counted down to for what felt like forever and worked damn hard to achieve. He should be elated he'd made the cut, but he was finding it near impossible to be anything but anxious. As the plane rose higher and higher, the sun shone from behind the cottony clouds and sparkled on the turquoise water far below – it was a sight to behold. After years of his mother encouraging him to become a world-champion bull rider, as fearful as she was for his safety, he'd finally taken the first step in making his lifelong dream a reality. It broke his heart she wasn't around any longer to witness it.

His face pressed up against the window, he watched the scenic coastline of Far North Queensland fade away. His heart ached as it reached back for Emma's. Memories of last night came thick and fast – the fresh scent of her hair, the silkiness of her skin, the sharp intake of her breath as he'd become one with her, the feeling of her fingernails scraping down his back, and the look in her eyes as she'd tumbled over the edge with him. When her lips had first touched his, while they'd ripped at each other's clothes, as if trying to tear away the layers that were stopping their hearts caressing one another's, something deep inside his soul had slipped into place. In that lust-filled moment, they'd been stripped of pretence, and all their worries had faded away in an instant. It was as if they'd been skin on skin a thousand times over, a thousand years ago. Emma was spot on when she'd said it had felt so right, so damn good, even though it had been so very wrong of them. As difficult as it had been in the heat of the moment, he'd made sure to not make promises to her he couldn't keep – he didn't have the nickname of 'Casanova' around Silvergum for no good reason. Commitment terrified him, and Emma knew that so well.

The *what ifs* slogged him – what if he stayed instead of chasing his dreams. What if he gave into how he really felt about her, what if they ran away together, what if she wasn't so tied to her family property, with a dream to make it her own one day, what if she wasn't in a relationship with Michael? Trust his luck, he'd gone and found the girl of his dreams, but only realised it when it was way too late. But if given the freedom, would he have jumped at the chance to make her his? If he thought about it rationally, Emma's dreams of picket fences and having an army of children had never been his thing, and if he were being honest with himself, he wasn't sure it ever would be.

Shaken from his deep thoughts by a wave of bone-shuttering turbulence, his hands clenched the armrests. If this giant tin can dived and crashed, he'd have no hope of survival. It was completely out of his control – and he didn't like that. One. Little. Bit. He squeezed his eyes shut, desperately trying to block out images of Emma as the sounds of rattling bags and nervous passengers heightened his panic. His mind tumbled and twisted, filled with thoughts of surviving a plane crash and not seeing her again. Flashes of them skin on skin came into his head – the desperate crash of their lips, the scent of rum on her breath, and her whispers, her sweet rasping voice telling him how she wished he wasn't so scared of commitment, squeezed his already pain-filled heart tighter. Goddamn it, this was hardest thing he'd ever had to do, other than watching his mum wasting away from cancer.

Knowing he needed to get a grip, Zane fought off the memories. Even though he worshiped the ground Emma Kensington walked on in her sexy cowgirl boots, in his soul he knew he could never have her without the big possibility of letting her down, of somehow breaking her beautiful heart because he was so scared of tying himself down, of laying roots. That meant they were never possible. They could never be. Would never be. He had to keep telling himself that, and he needed to let the thought go of there ever being a *them*. He just had to. He wasn't good for her. He wasn't the one for her. He was doing her a favour, leaving her behind. And one day, she would thank him for it.

As the turbulence cleared and the nervous excitement of the crowded plane settled, he allowed his heart to calm too. When he stepped from this plane and strode into Dallas International Airport, there was going to be no looking back, no longing for what could never be with her. Ever.

BESTSELLING AUSTRALIAN AUTHOR

MANDY MAGRO

Novels to take you to the country...

Available in ebook

LET'S TALK
ABOUT BOOKS!

JOIN THE CONVERSATION

HARLEQUIN
AUSTRALIA

@HARLEQUINAUS

@HARLEQUINAUS